Bound: Where Truths Lie

A Message from the Author

Thank you to my readers, I genuinely appreciate your support. I look forward to sharing my next book with you. I just want to remind you, no one can ever tell you what you can't or can do. If you take the time to do what you love, you can accomplish anything. I wish you well in this challenging time. Please take care of yourself. And remember, you don't know what tomorrow brings.

This Book Is dedicated to my soul mate, Tyler Cole,
and brother Solo Wallace.
Thank you for your unconditional love and continuous
support.

TO: Drew,

I hope you enjoy reading My book, As Much as I've enjoyed Writing it. Please feel free to reach out, and let me know what you think!

- Your fan

Chapter One

It is now a quarter to midnight. The summer breeze welcomed the moonlight into the window. The soft hum of crickets is no comfort to Kinzie now. Shelie wide awake, yet her eyes are closed. In her mind she is breathing in and out slowly. This is one of many attempts to recover a memory. Knowing it's there, not wanting to see the ones she desires to forget. Buried deep into her

subconscious. *"Kinzie! Kin, hold on." A voice echoed. She was being carried, her vision fading in and out. The pain in her body intensifies.* Confusion crowding her mind. The vigorous vibration was shattering her thoughts. Dreading the incoming call, she rolled over and reached for the device on her nightstand.

"This is McCoy," she answered, clearing her voice. Doing her best not to sound weary.

The hope of her having a case grows stronger. Anything to get her mind off of the recent events, "Alright thank you. Yes, absolutely. I'm on my way."

With great eagerness she hastened to get dressed, and fix her appearance. Her boisterous movement woke her sister, who was resting in the room next door. She lingered in the hallway, " Kinzie, what th-".

"I have a *case!*," she replied, her voice rising an octave higher than usual.

"Ah, at last. A one way ticket to your sanity," her sister yawned.

"Yeah, no kidding. Where is it?" Kinzie said pacing back and forth examining the room

"Your purse is downstairs. There's also a couple of canisters of your favorite nutrition combination," She stretched and shuffled down the hallway.

"Thanks. I'll be back before sunrise!" Kinzie called while running down the hall. At the end of the staircase her heels clicked on the marble floor. She adjusted her navy blue blouse, and black slacks in the hall before moving on. Passing her office and at last entered the kitchen, noticing her purse and two containers. Scooping them up she hurried out the door. Her car was waiting patiently in the driveway. Feeling as though it was opening its arms to welcome her, she got in the driver's seat. *Oh my God. It's been far too long.*

Quickly removing the keys from her bag she turned the engine and reversed. Watching her house slowly fade as she rolled down the hill. She rolled her windows down. Every sense in her body grew with excitement. Breathing in the summer night air she continued forward to her one way ticket to sanity. The moonlight showing her the way. After what seemed like twenty minutes, the police lights appeared. Cameras flashing, forensic specialists flooding the scene, hungry for some answers. Though her hunger was greater than all of them.

As soon as she stepped out of the car her partner approached, "What have we got, Tim?" The familiar scent of Tim's cigarettes provide her a warm welcome back. He was wearing a black suit with a white shirt and a crooked red tie.

"A Jane Doe, mid to late twenties. Cause of death is unknown."

"Why is the cause of death unkn-" Her voice cut off while approaching the body. Taking every effort she had to keep a straight face.

"Hey, are you alright?" His voice filled with concern.

"Yes, I'm fine. Just isn't something we see too often," She replied with a false smile. Knowing full well Tim would know it's fake. But she wanted to try it out anyway.

"Okay," He replied, giving her a gentle squeeze on the shoulder, "I'll leave you to it."

Hearing his footsteps distancing themselves further away, *Come on Kinzie. You've got this.*
Her voice rang through her clear mind, as she continued examining the body. Making every attempt to rid the discomfort that lingered in her stomach.

There are two sides to being a detective. One, you see victims who didn't deserve to pass on to another life. Speaking with the parents or family members of the deceased. But promising them with every ounce of your being, that you will put the bastard away, who dared harm your loved one. They caused you suffering, and traumatic memories for the rest of your life. Then there's the side of saving a life. Seeing someone cry out after being either tortured, beaten, stabbed, shot, buried alive, or anything else this big cruel world can offer up as a method of murder. They don't shed the tears of suffering. They shed the tears of being alive. There's something about that side that drives a detective. That's the main reason why anyone on this team does what they do. Knowing what reward may lie ahead.

Kin continued examining the body. *This is too clean. There should be more blood with this much damage.* The car that Jane Doe is lying next to, also is too clean. The great detective cocked her head in thought. *Doesn't a woman usually carry a purse?*
"Tim!"

She heard his footsteps approach. He too was calm, but deep in thought, "Yeah?"

"Look at the body. It's much too neat.There should be more blood. And did you notice there's no purse in the car?"

"Yeah, what about it?" He asked, shrugging.

"When you were dating… What was her name?" Kinzie's voice faded and she snapped her fingers.

"I don't even want to remember. But I know who you're talking about," He shook his head.

"My point is. A woman never goes anywhere without a handbag of some kind. There's no purse in the car," Kinzie gestured to her hand to the car.

"Yes? And…?" Tim's voice trailing off lost in thought.

"Oh my…" Kinzie groaned in frustration, "Bryte, there's no ID. No, nothing. No traces of this woman at all! I find it odd that there's no purse, very little blood on the ground. And most importantly no blood at all in the car."

"Oh! Kinzie… I'm sorry. I'm just," He growled quietly, cursing under his breath. " The body was dumped here for what reason exactly?"

"I'm not sure… But what I do know is the killer either had an accomplice driving another car or he walked a few miles and hitchhiked home," Kinzie replied deep in thought.

"Good point Mac. Do me a favor-"

" Tag and bag, go over forensic samples needed for results, and take extra camera shots for backup. I know. Thank you for the reminder though," she said, nodding her head.

"There she is. Welcome back Mac," He smiled and went back to fill out his notes.

"Thanks, Tim," she smiled. This time it was a true smile.

What was the purpose of taking the ID, perhaps a trophy? Her voice echoed in a moment of curiosity.

Kinzie did as Tim asked. Taking pictures of every angle of the car. Even the tires. Noticing footprints she took photos of those also. She followed the trail of footprints to another set of tire tracks. Which she took photos of. *Why go through the effort?* Her stomach pain grew as time wandered on. The coroner took the camera and she made her way to her car. The airy feeling in her head had yet to cease. Her eyelids are drooping heavily. Her body is not allowing her control. Yet her stomach continued to churn.

Where could the killer have gone? Why make so much effort to dump a body out in the middle of nowhere? How long has she been laying on the road like this? She sat in the driver seat. *Maybe we could try and catch the bastard that did this. But there's no point. He's way too methodical to make a mistake, such as leaving himself out in the open.*

Kinzie remains limp in unfamiliar arms. She wondered if she was going to die. Her body ached all over. Michelle… What happened to Michelle? Every effort she took to control her body failed. She couldn't even cry like she wanted to.

"Open the gates!" A man's voice shouted.

Gates? Where am I going? The pace of her being carried quickened. It felt as though time dragged on before she was gently placed onto padding.

"What's this lady's name?"

"Kinzie McCoy. Quinn sent her here, Master," The voice who carried her in
    `such a way, spoke softly and with concern.

"Shhh. Say no more. Despite her limp state, she can still hear her surroundings. Leave us for a moment please. I wish to examine Kinzie alone," The master spoke once again.

The footsteps exited the room.

"Ms. McCoy, I'm sure you're in shock and fear at the moment. Please don't be afraid. We are a safe haven for those in need. You have been brought here due to your medical state. In two weeks you will rise. But now I'm going to examine you for any further injury. Then you shall be in our hospice unit until you rise. I'm going to walk you through every step of the way," Headmaster said. He sounded old, and wise, but kind. So kind....

The knock on Kinzie's window made her jump. It was Tim. She opened the driver door, thankful that she didn't turn the car on. With a groggy reply, " Hey, Tim."

"I'm going to ask one more time. Are you alright?" He said firmly. His arms crossed and eyebrows hardened.

"Yes, I'm fine. I just didn't get much sleep last night. That's all," Kinzie smiled in every attempt to sound innocent. But it was clear Tim didn't believe her.

"Do you want me to take you home?" He replied, giving her a stern look.

"No, *really* Tim. That's not necessary,"Trying to protest didn't do any good.

"That's not necessary, my ass. Get in the passenger seat…"Sighing he waited.

Kinzie sat in stubbornness. Hating the fact that she showed him her weak side. She doesn't want anyone to know she's struggling.

"*Now* detective," His voice rising slightly higher. Not intimidating her in the slightest.

She stood up cursing under her breath. Wishing she didn't have to explain to Tim what the heck was going on. But it has to happen some time or another. She sank into the passenger seat. Timothy called out to one of the forensic specialists and let them know he was taking Kinzie home. They nodded and Tim grunted as he turned the key. Seeming to forget Kinzie's car is a manual, she put her left hand on the shifter. Now they're both walking down memory lane. Timothy Andrew Bryte will never forget the day Kinzie saved his life. As he drove and McCoy shifted gears. He stared at his left arm or at least what would have been his left arm. Now there's nothing but a nub slightly below the elbow. He sighed and continued looking at the road.

The silence was deafening most of the way. All these years working together and she still hates when he sees right through her.

"How's the department running without me?" Tim's anxiety faded at the sound of Kinzie's voice.

"We're doing what we can. Honestly it doesn't feel right not having you there," *Because I miss you.* Those words wanted to exit his lips so badly. Instead he bit his lip. She sat next to him staring out the window as she always does on car rides.

"Are *you* alright?" It's as if she could hear his muscles tensing up. Trying to hold back things happening that can possibly stress her out.

"Yeah, just a lot going on," Tim tapped his hand on the wheel. She shifted again as they made a right turn.

"Don't pull that bullshit with me Bryte. I know you. Please don't hold anything back because you think it'll stress me out. You just called me out on my flaws…talk to me. I want to know," Her isolation had driven her to madness. She wants to know every single moment that goes on in that office. Who has a crush on whom. Did this couple who broke up time and time again gotten back together? Any detail at all, she would consider juicy and sweet.

"Well Susan is on me about 'not finishing my work on time' even though she knows my condition. As well as my accommodations, but the woman has yet to see that I'm trying. Even though I put in a request for a mini keyboard, it has yet to go through. And with my crappy pay I can't exactly afford the one that I truly need," He sighed feeling lighter.

"Well that's dumb. And don't worry about the keyboard. I'll get you one. How much is it?" Kinzie asked, her voice filled with concern. Tim was an excellent Lead detective, and has earned every level of respect there is.

"Two hundred and fifty five dollars," He forced a sarcastic laugh..

" That sounds about right. It's custom made, and the quality. Then you have to consider shipping. electronics," Her voice trailed off. She began feeling light headed again. *Damn it! Oh no...*Kinzie looked to the east and began to panic, light barely appeared on the horizon. Tim looked and remembered her telling him, *"I always have to get home before sunrise. Regardless of what day it is. I can't tell you why, yet. It's just... not good.."*

The house looks to be a mile or so away. Tim gestured his head for Kinzie to shift. Doing so, he slammed on the gas. As they get closer to the house, the more overwhelming the day break is becoming. Kinzie's body went limp suddenly. Thankfully Kinzie's driveway is covered in shade Tim pulled in. He hurried to get out of the driver's side, and ran over to the passenger side, rushing to get her out of the car. Fortunately she was light and petite. He shut the door with his foot and hurried up the stairs and barely managed to get the front door open. He shut the door with his foot, hollering, "Michelle!"

Appearing around the corner, "Tim what happened?" she gasped, and ran over to the foyer.

"She fell asleep at the scene, so I drove her home. I didn't realize that the sun was coming up. I'm sorry," He panted, rushing inside the house.

The foyer was large and there was a hall closet to the right of the front door. To the right was a Hallway With pictures along the walls. The Hallway wasn't so narrow. Straight across from the door was a beautiful staircase going up then to the right, behind a wall and a dark gray rug ran up the center of the staircase.

"No apology is needed. I'm glad you were driving. Poor thing. We need to get her in the office. That's the only place in the house that doesn't have windows," she replied, hurrying down the hallway. Tim followed right behind her. Michelle stood in the doorway and gestured for him to set her on the couch. He did so, feeling guilty as ever. Michelle walked over and rubbed his arm, "Come. Let's go get some coffee."

Tim shook his head and sighed, " I would enjoy some coffee, but I would rather stay here with her…"

"Tim, we need to leave her to rest. Please, trust me like you always have," her voice pleading loudly. She rubbed his back, "She'll be alright. You can come back a bit later, alright."

"Well you are her sister… Fine. Let's go get some coffee," he didn't know how to feel. Numbly he rose to leave the room.

"Plus I would like to update you on some things that have been happening while she's been home. Do you need a cigarette while I make breakfast?" She stepped aside so he could exit the door. Which he did. His eyes glossed over.

"I only have a few left," He replied, rubbing the back of his head in anxiety.

"Why don't you go out on the deck and relax?" She replied, shutting the door gently behind them. Then turned and winked her right eye.

"Aright," He nodded and walked through the other side to the Kitchen. Which was neat and well put together. Dark wooden cabinets linger on each side of him. There was an island in the middle, which had a sink in the middle of it and a dishwasher next to it. The countertops were marble with black veins. On the other end of the kitchen was a larger dining room table that could seat a party of eight. It too was dark. The flooring was hardwood that looked to be the color gray. And past the table is a set of double doors that had a white trim. And silver door knobs. The back door swung out in case they wanted to let in any night air.

To his delight two packs of his brand of cigarettes and a lighter were waiting in a silver ashtray. He smiled. *Always knows what's best.* He sat down on the white painted rocking chairs. The table matches the texture. He remembered these chairs well. He spent over six months in recovery here. Kinzie even made up a spare bedroom while he was in the hospital. He painted these chairs as practice for balancing only using one full arm. Kinzie being fond of design he also painted patterns in the middle of the table around the ashtray, and matching ones on the back of the chairs. He also worked in her office. This place is known as a second home. For two women so small. They had a huge house. Always well kept, and always a resting place. He smiled, rocking back and forth. Admiring the pink, and orange clouds. The smell of bacon and biscuits filled the air. And coffee...

"Tim!" Michelle called.

"Coming," He tossed the cigarette bud into the ashtray. He thanked her as we walked inside. The best food he's ever tasted waited for him patiently at the table. Along with a steaming hot cup of coffee, "Catch Up time?"

"You know it," She seated herself, toward the middle of the table.

His mouth was watering from the smells, he seated himself in front of his plate. *God* he missed her cooking. Bacon, eggs, sausage gravy, and homemade biscuits. He couldn't help but dig in. Breakfast melted in Tim's mouth. At last they both were finished eating. Shell had asked him about work and the department. He remained honest, and told the same thing as he did Kinzie. She nodded and stated the circumstance with his boss is stupid. Tim had enough. He didn't want to wait any longer to know what was going on with Kinzie. Michelle sighed. She admitted that Kinzie isn't as good as she makes herself to be. Most of the time she doesn't want to show weakness. Tim of course asked why. He had never seen a vulnerable side to Kinzie before. He didn't think it was possible. Shell said it was because of their father. Kinzie was the second oldest. So things were pressed more so on her, than Shell. Tim didn't know what exactly to say. The feeling of loss and desperation grew in his chest and in his throat. His voice pleaded more than he intended, when asking if there's a way to help. Anything he can do. Michelle nodded.

"I need your help with staying here with her. I have to go out and run errands from time to time. I need someone I can trust to care for her. I too need to rest at night. But Most times I can't. I'm just too worried," She looked down at her coffee cup.

Tim got up and gave her a hug, "I'll be happy to stay. I just want to let the department know and get some extra clothes."

"Already taken care of," She embraced him and after letting go took a sip from her coffee mug.

"Michelle, how much did you spend on me?" He asked, leaning down, giving Michelle a worried look.

"Isn't it the thought that counts? Not the price you pay?" She gave him a look in return, squinting her right eye.

"Oh alright, alright. I'm sorry," He smiled and kissed the top of her head. Then walked over to her seat and kissed her on the top of the head.

"Thank you," She Smiled. She turned to check the time on the stove, "Hey, how about you check out your room? I've gotta go give kinzie a snack. She's cranky when she feeds." She smiled, standing up and getting the plates. She put them in the sink. And grabbed a cup from the refrigerator and hurried into the office.

Always a busy bee. He tried to smile. '*Feeds'?*

He decided to wander around. The McCoy house was huge. Four floors, which includes a full basement. And It took a minute to get from one side to the other. He entered his bedroom, putting his hand on the doorframe. His bed directly across the entryway. The walls are soothing gray, not dark. But something you would see in a beach magazine. Window sills were white, and hung on either side of the bed. The blinds aso white. He felt his eyes water. There was a good three feet of room on all sides of the bed. Next to the loveseat is the bathroom. He went over and turned on the light. Finding it the same way, as if he never left. Towels were neatly hanging on a rack. Same pattern as always. Grey and white. On the white tile floor rested grey mats, even around the toilet. There was a soaker bathtub and a stand up shower. He began to sob. He didn't want to lose her. He always loved her. Even when they first caught each other's eye. The woman who sat here every night to make sure he had everything he needed. The one who cuddled up with him when he was running a fever, because she's always cold. He'd do anything so she can continue living. Even if he sacrificed himself. His tears began to subside. He rose to his feet and washed his face. *Don't fall apart Tim. You have to stay strong for her.* Maybe now is the time to tell her how he really feels. After she wakes up. He wandered numbly to his king size bed, took off his shoes, curled up and faded into his own mind, until his body allowed him to go to sleep.

......*

Michelle heard Tim enter his room. *Finally,* she entered the office doing everything in her power not to shed any sunlight on Kinzie. She succeeded in shutting the door. Dim fluorescent lights from the ceiling helped her see. Only a little bit, but just enough. She put the straw to her lips. Kinzie pulled away.

"No, no. Kin, you need to drink. Please. It's okay," Michelle stroked her sister's hair. She made another attempt, this time she got Kin to drink. It took a while until the straw made a noise of protest.

*Good girl. S*he kissed the top of her head. Seating herself on the floor, and began telling Kinzie of a memory of childhood. Shell wasn't sure if she remembered or not, but she didn't care. Anything to keep her from screaming in her sleep. It was now eight o'clock in the morning. The sun shined bright.

"I remember when we were kids. It feels like forever ago. Dad was away and it was just us and the boys. Mom was in the Kitchen and you asked her if you could go and play with the boys. And she said no. Boy were you mad. You've always been strong and temperamental. You matched dad to a T. And I matched Mom. And I think that's why we get along so well. I also remember the time you asked Zachary to teach you how to fight? And he said yes? You were so excited," Michelle continued to smile and tell her stories.

While everyone was resting Michelle found herself dialing a number and speaking with them about looking Kinzie over. Hoping in the pit of her stomach that they can help. Just because of their constant traveling and tight schedule. But this is family.

Somehow she knew they would drop everything to care for Kin. She's important to a lot of people. And Most can't imagine a life without her. Years in the detective industry and has worked her way up to the point where she's a public figure. She almost works too much. But she loves her job. And oftentimes Kinzie can't imagine any other job.

When the answer was yes, Michelle did her best to contain her excitement, and asked when they were coming. As soon as possible is the answer given. In other words it could be anywhere between a few hours to a few days. Just to wrap things up and make sure they're in a good place to put things on hold. But another person to help is all Michelle needed. A wave of relief swept over and she exhaled a sigh.

"Shelly, who was that?" Kinzie mumbled. Clearly half asleep.

"It's Quinn, he'll be on his way in a little while," Michelle replied, still smiling.

"Oh mkay," she rolled over, and remained silent.

Michelle exited the room, and went to the living room and allowed herself to rest. Relief overwhelmed her knowing that she'll be able to get some help. She didn't expect Tim to stay. But she was hoping. At this moment she couldn't help but smile knowing the support she and her sister have.

Tim's phone chimed with a new message. Groggily, he looked at.

Body Number One: Jane Doe
Height: 5'4"
Age:25-29
Condition: Severe burns over 100% of the body. Estimated time of death 2 days ago.
Cause of Death: Asphyxiation, inhaling too much smoke into the lungs.
Condition of the Body: Several Broken bones, and sleeping drugs in her system.

Chapter Two

Tim rose from his deep sleep. He stretched and got up to take a shower. He found his bath products on a shelf. *How did she know I would say yes?* Somehow he felt as though today is going to be as long as ever. He kept his head down allowing the hot water to run down his back. The steam filling the room. He barely saw his black t-shirt and tan cargo shorts. For some reason he couldn't believe Michelle remembered the bath products he likes. After changing he met with Michelle in the living room, to discuss Kinzie's condition.

"Do you know why she changed?" Tim fidgeted his fingers.

"No. That's what bothers me. She's been sleeping a lot. She hardly eats," Shells voice tailed off.

"That's not like her at all. She fell asleep at the crime scene. It took me knocking on the window five times to wake her up. And she was so withdrawn. I was wondering if I was doing something wrong," he choked down the tears that begged to be in his eyes. He didn't know whether to be angry or understanding. But he took a deep breath to keep his composure.

"No, it wasn't you. She doesn't want to show weakness. Which got so bad I had to put a baby monitor in her room," She began to rub her temples.

"How did you accomplish that?" he replied surprised.

"I told her to go take a bath," Shell sighed. She too looked as though she was about to cry.

"Seriously?" *I didn't think that would ever be possible. She's so alert...*

"Yes. While you two were asleep, I called Quinn, and explained her symptoms. He said he'd be stopping by as soon as he could. I'm hoping he can stop by this evening," Michelle rarely looked distressed. Her right eye had a dark circle. While her left eye was covered with an eye patch. Tim never asked why. He felt it would be too rude.

Tim pulled out his cell phone and dialed a familiar set of numbers Michelle knew well. He was calling his department. Michelle gave him a look of relief and surprise. He fought like hell with Susan, knowing his stubbornness. There's not much she could do. She can't fire him, because he's taking his own time off and sacrificing his check, and she can't punish him. He's still on the case. She asked how long he'll be staying at the McCoy house. *As long as need be.* The voice in his head sighed. His c response was six months. Michelle beamed. After he got off the phone she hugged him. For a woman so small she did have a ton of strength. Like Kinzie. Anytime he needed he had a place to go. When he needed help. He got it. Now it's time to take care of them. His family. Granted, he has a family of his own. But they aren't as close to him as Kinzie, Michelle, and Quinn are. This house is the island of misfit toys. Kinzie is the Queen. The only one he considers perfect, because he loved her.

The day went on Michelle fixed some sandwiches for lunch, and continued to feed Kinzie her "nutrition." On a few occasions you'll find her lingering in a window, looking at a world she could barely see. The sun shines on her left side. Revealing all the details of the night she'd gotten burned in a house fire. Despite her deformities she is still optimistic. She's still beautiful. Her long red hair ran straight down the middle of her back. Her one eye is green, with honey olive skin. Her being a neat freak is a habit. Partly because she needs to have a clear walkway. And the other part is as she says "better". Tim couldn't help but want to be next to Kinzie. He asked Michelle if it would be a good idea to be in the office while Kinzie rested. She said she didn't think Kinzie would mind. She also reminded him not to shed light on Kinzie at all. He nodded in understanding. He walked over to the dark wooden door which opened outwards. He assumed it's to get in easily without shedding light on Kin.

The office was very dim. After Tim's eyes adjusted, he drew in a breath. He looked up to see nothing but books. The shelves were in a circumference. The ceiling is fifteen feet above his head with dim lighting that looked to be implanted into it. Providing the light. Two curved couches sat on either side of the room. In the center of everything she had a massive oak desk. It looked to be about five feet long, and four feet wide. Beautifully dangerous. A monitor on the far right corner. Tim approached the desk. Careful not to wake Kinzie. She must have come in here every day. The keyboard looked overused. Some of the letters faded. Scattered notes lay on the desk. Then he noticed a picture which looked older than the current generation. It was painted. Slightly larger than the average photo.

There was a woman with long red hair. She had a cloak on a light green. She looked to be very thin but healthy. Her eyes were green. Her red hair looked to be at the length of her hips. *Just like Michelle's*. Next to the woman a tall man stood to the right of her. He too was wearing a cloak, had jet black hair, slightly past his shoulders. His eyes a bright blue, he looked to have a navy blue cloak. *Kinzie looks just like her dad.* Michelle stood in the middle of their parents. She was wearing a lighter green cloak than her mother. Kinzie stood to the right next to her father wearing a black and dark blue cloak. To the Left of their mother stood a younger looking version of their father. Older looking than Kinzie and slightly shorter than their father. He too had black hair which rested at his shoulders. Bright blue eyes.

Then on either side of Michelle stood identical looking boys.
Same colored hair as Michelle and

their mother. They too had green eyes. They looked to be about
nine years old. They wore dark green cloaks. They all stood in
front of a fireplace.

Below it a note with Kinzie's beautiful handwriting:
*Not all know the pain of loss. Let this pain help me walk. No one
knows true love when it's gone. Good night light. Good night sun.
I shall find you in the stars.*
Kinzie's voice came from behind him, "Proof that heaven is not
afar. Goodbye loved ones. Sing the songs of the angels from
above," She stood next to him.

"Kin, I'm sorry. I didn't mean to invade your privacy..." Tim
stumbled over his words.

"Please don't be. Now you truly know that I knew how it felt
when your mother passed away," her eyes began to glisten.

"What do you mean?" Tim's breath grew heavy.

"Read the note to the right. Out loud," She stood frozen.

He nodded, "Rest In Peace: Elizabeth Ann McCoy, Phillip John
McCoy, the parents whom I love. Zachary James McCoy, the
brother who gave me wisdom. Jonathan Andrew McCoy, and

Drew Mark McCoy, the twins who couldn't say goodbye." Tim felt his heart ping. He stood speechless.

"Tim…," Kinzie stumbled in and leaned into him. He caught her.

"Kinzie you need to stop pushing yourself so much," He whispered. He carried her gently to the couch, "I'm going to stay right Here, and keep you company."

She nodded. He stroked her long hair. Kinzie felt her spirit soar. The gentle touch of his hand. He couldn't be angry at her stubbornness. Nothing is worse than being forced out of work because of a terrible sickness or injury to the body. Tim couldn't stand to hold still. Kinzie's company helped his sanity. He knows well that doing the same may help her remain still. Seating himself on the floor next to her. He lay his head down next to hers and slowly fell asleep.

The doorbell gave a soft ring. Michelle shook her head, attempting to bring herself back to reality. Her swift movements to the door are as quiet as ever. She opened the door to Greet Quinn who was standing on the other side. Michelle half bowed her head, "Please come in."

He replied with a slight nod, "Thank you Shelly." He made his way to the living room. Michelle not too far behind, "Is anyone else here?"

"Timothy and Kinzie. But they're both in the office," she seated herself on the couch. He remains standing.

"Excellent. He's on the current case I assume." Quinn replied walking into the living room.

"Correct," Michelle did her best not to show any fear or anxiety, "Did you want me to go let Timothy know you're here?" She followed close behind.

"No, not necessary. I would rather speak with you first." He gestured a pointer finger in her direction.

"Alright," She crossed her legs and sank to the back of the couch.

"When did her illness start?" He took a seat in a chair across from her.

"I want to say a few months ago. Maybe more." She closed her right eye.

"What was the first sign?" He pulled out a pen and paper.

The first sign Kinzie ever had was sleeping a lot. Michelle had assumed it was dehydration. But it wasn't. She fed normally. Then weeks later she began screaming in her sleep, and a few more weeks later she complained of having a stomachache. Michelle had waited for her to vomit. But that time never came. For someone as special as Kinzie. This topic is extremely delicate. Quinn's and

continue to scribble down the notes. He continued to ask questions like, "has her mood changed," and "How often does she eat on her own." It hurt Michelle to tell him the truth. The relationship the McCoy sisters had with Quinn Roberts is that of daughters. In Michelle's mind, Quinn is very similar to her own biological father. Same mentality. Similar values. Nearly identical beliefs. This is the man that saved her life. And of course Kinzie's. It felt as though time faded into another world. Once Quinn was through asking questions. He asked how Michelle was doing. Her response was, "Alright I suppose."

Quinn shook his head. How can anyone explain their heart ache? How can anyone express their anger and frustration to the universe for having a sick sister who is normally stronger than a rock. She doesn't want to lose the only blood relative she has left in this world. The only one aside from Quinn who keeps her safe on a daily basis.

"Shelly, please don't silence the ache inside of you. Please speak aloud. You can tell me," He gave her the look she adored. The sparkle in his eye shows he cares.

"It's just…" She sighed. Feeling all her defenses fall, "I've come to a halt in my thoughts. I feel helpless. I don't want to be immortal anymore. I feel as though I'm going to lose Kinzie. Then I will wander the world alone… Forever…"

Quinn inhaled a deep thoughtful breath, "Oh my dear girl. No one wanders the world alone. Even those who remain immortal. Everyone always needs someone. Whether it's family or a friend. A confidant is the strongest bond. Your bond with Kinzie is very strong. She's not going to give into this illness. Knowing her, it's because she can't bear the thought of you wandering this world alone."

The words pulled on her heartstrings. She teared up a little. Quinns wisdom always put her at ease.

"Now my dear. I would like to talk to Timothy," He gave her a smile.

"Yes, father " She gave a gentle nod to his request. She rose slowly and made her way to the office. There she found Tim and Kinzie asleep. He had his knees curled underneath him and his head next to Kinzie's on the cushion of the couch. His left arm was on his lap, and was holding her hand. She had her body towards him, her head close to his. Her long hair sprawled across her shoulders. Her left leg stretched out while her right leg curled up. Looking as though she was hugging a pillow. Michelle gave a soft *awe*. She walked over quietly. She reached down to rub his back, "Tim," She whispered.

"Hmm?" He half opened his eyes.

"Quinn is here and he wants to talk to you," She kept rubbing his shoulders.
"Okay," He stretched, "I… I need coffee…"

"I've already got you covered," She smiled.

Tim nodded, and turned to Kinzie, "I'll be back." He rose and exited the room, Quinn not too far behind. He gave a slight nod to Quinn, who gave one back. They heard Michelle say she's going to make coffee and left the gentlemen alone to talk.they walked into the living room. The first thing Tim noticed was all the lights were on, and the second it's dark outside. "What time is it?"

"Almost ten," Quinn replied thoughtfully.

" Oh wow… Anyway, that doesn't matter. What can I help you with Quinn?" He asked while seating himself across from him.

"Well first I would like to know some small details. Pertaining to the case that is," Quinn replied, pen and paper in hand ready to write.

Tim rubbed his eye and sighed, "Please don't share this with anyone unless you have to."

"What would you consider it needed to know?" He asked, raising an eyebrow.

"If it has a tie to Kinzie's well being, or if you know someone who could help with the case," Tim replied groggily.

"Well I find that very agreeable," Quinn nodded, "You have my word."

Tim nodded while rubbing the back of his neck, " Very well. When I first arrived at the crime scene I was a little confused as to why that specific location. Long story short; there was a woman mid to late twenties. She was burnt beyond recognition, and there was no form of ID. Which is unusual. I needed a second pair of eyes… So I called Kinzie out to the scene. I wanted an extra pair of eyes for this one in particular. When she arrived at the scene and saw the body, she froze up. I'm assuming it's because of what happened to Michelle," Tim Sighed.

Just a moment later Michelle appeared with a steaming hot cup of coffee and announced she'll be in the office, helping Kinzie change clothes. . Tim thanked her with a smile. Waiting for Kinzie to wake. The gentlemen nodded. Once she left the room, Quinn spoke up, "Timothy, I must ask something of you."

"What's that?" He took a sip of his coffee. A small taste of sugar with half and half. Just the way he liked it.

"I wish for you to stay here with Kinzie and Michelle for a while," He looked tired. The man had long shoulder length salt and pepper hair. Dark circles under his eyes.

"Michelle actually made the same request. And I told her I'll stay," Tim replied with a smile. *They even think alike.*

"Good, I'm so glad to hear," A wave of relief washed over him.

"Father! Tim!" Michelle called from the office.

There was no hesitation. Quinn rose first, and Tim followed. Once Quinn entered through the office door he froze in his tracks. Tim Bumped into him, "This is far more serious than we thought," Quinn exhaled softly.

There they found Michelle leaning over Kinzie, her skin turned from pale to a light gray. She wasn't waking up. The dark circles under her eyes make her look lethargic. Quinn stepped closer to Kinzie. He began touching her forehead, and feeling the temperature of her shoulders and arms. Her temperature was dangerously hot. Quinn excused himself and noted he'll be back in a few hours. Michelle announced that they needed to put her in the bathtub of cold water. Michelle looked distressed. Tim gave her a stern look, "Michelle I've got her. Please… I want you to go rest. I don't need both of you collapsing or getting sick."

"But T-"
"But nothing. I've got her. Please let me do the honor of taking care of her. If I need anything I'll let you know in the meantime. Do what you must to replenish your energy," Tim knew Michelle's stubbornness.

"Alright. I'll be down here in your spare bedroom. It would probably be best if you took her upstairs," Michelle suggested before exiting the office.

Tim looked down at Kinzie, "Hey, Kin. Can you hear me?"

She barely moved her head, with a nod.

"Alright. I'm going to carry you upstairs. I'm going to put your arm around my neck and I need you to grip as best as you can. Here we go," He whispered. And she did exactly as he said.

With what little strength Kinzie had she did a good job at holding onto Tim the way she did. In the moment he silently gave thanks to her lightweight. When they got up the stairs He gave a soft sigh. He had never seen her bedroom. The bedroom looked to be bigger than average. A Perfect square. Once one enters the threshold, if they turn their head to the Right, They'll see Kinzie's bed which has four posts. It also had two nightstands resting on either side. There was a dim lingering light coming from the Bookshelf which rested straight across the doorway. And the bathroom was to the left. He entered the bathroom. Placed Kinzie into the tub and ran some cold water over her. After she cooled down, Tim did his best to dry her off.

After doing so he carried her over to her bed, noticing the right side was more wrinkled than the left, and looked to have a slight pivot. He lay Kinzie down, she curled up into a ball. He covered her up With the fuzzy nightmare before the Christmas blanket which was folded at the end of the bed. He hadn't noticed before but There was a large welcoming leather chair behind him. A place where Michelle most likely sat, monitoring Kin. Feeding her, and doing whatever else in the two months being away from the workforce. He knew her being away for that long drove her beyond sanity. Everyone knows Kinzie McCoy is a workaholic. Tim took a seat in the chair and examined her bedroom. Above the bookshelf she had two framed newspaper articles, "Kinzie McCoy Catches a Serial Killer of 10 years," and "Kinzie McCoy Hero to Her Fellow Partner Timothy Bryte." They had two pictures in the article. He gave a silent thanks that no one took one of him Specifically.

I didn't realize this meant a lot to her too…

Next to the Bookshelf had two windows on either side, with pitch black curtains to keep the sun out. He found it odd that she Seemed to have everything in twos. But it didn't matter much to him either way. He still loves her.

It seemed as though time dragged on. He honestly didn't take her for the organized type. Probably because most of the time she shows signs of being very scatterbrained. He looked at the clock. It's almost midnight now. "Tim?"

He jumped a little, not noticing that Kinzie was sitting up. The blanket was pushed down to her feet and she had her arms around her knees.

"Did I wake you?" He asked a little below a whisper.

"No, I just find it odd," She shook her head, "It's been so long since I've had nightmares…"

"How long has it been?"

"One Hundred and forty eight years," She forced a sigh. As if trying to get the images out of her mind.

"I'm sorry to hear about your dreams Kin, but that seems to be a little. What's the word? Drastic." Tim tried to say as kindly as possible. *There's just no way.*

"It's not an exaggeration at all," she replied looking deeply into his eyes, "I've been wanting to tell you a story. I'm just not really ready to tell it just yet."

"Well, my ears are open whenever you're ready," He half smiled. *I'm so glad she trusts me as much as she does.*

Kin let out a rather loud Yawn, "Back to sleep." She pulled up her blanket and Rolled over facing Tim.

"Can you tell me a story?"

"What kind of story?"

"Any kind really. Just please no fires."

"Alright. Well, when I was a kid. My mom and I were really close. I don't think you've ever met her Kin, but she was one beautiful person. She always told me I can do anything I can put my mind to. And I remember one year for my birthday, she got me a whole doctor's kit. We were in an apartment at the time. And Our storage was on the ground floor. But one night a really bad rainstorm hit and the neighborhood flooded. It went from an adult's knees to one's hip. And we went back to check on our storage. I was Kinda bummed out, but hey. I became a pretty fantastic cop, if I do say so myself," He sighed, "I miss her even though she passed so long ago" He paused as he faded out of his memories… He looked at Kinzie, "Are you alright?"

It seems like a stupid question. But this question is the only way to get the truth out of Kinzie McCoy. If you ask a direct question, she can't lie. If you make a comment she can make a false remark about being fine. It took time to come over to her house for the first time to discover that. Michelle gave him that tip.

"No, I'm rather weak and miserable," her voice cracked.

"Go to sleep, Kin," Tim said softly and began to hum a lullaby she hummed to him while he was in recovery.

He would have guessed three minutes went by before Kinzie actually went back to sleep. Questions began to build up burning sanity out of his mind. *How old Is Kin? How long ago did her family pass? Why is this happening now? What's the story she wanted to tell me?*

Tim closed his eyes, and he too fell asleep.

It felt as though minutes went by when he heard the sound of Kinzie vomiting. His body moved so fast he couldn't count how many steps it took to get to the bathroom. He saw red before Kinzie flushed the toilet

"Oh my God. Kinzie we're going to the hospital," His voice sounded more desperate than he wanted.

"No," She shook her head, "Tim please-"

"No nothing! Kinzie you're going to the hosp-"

"Timothy Bryte, I am *not* going to the hospital. They can't help me," She looked up into his eyes. He froze. *Her eyes...*

The moon blue irises are no more. Instead, she had gray irises and the eye itself was red. She looked more sickly. Her face is light gray. He sighed. He hated enabling her stubbornness, "Alright… As long as you promise me you will tell me why."

Kinzie nodded her head.

"Can you walk?" He asked softly.

She shook her head. He didn't know how grateful she was for him. He'd put up with all of her secrets. All the white lies she told to protect him from what she really was and always will be. He lay her on the bed once more. His pleading eyes made her heart break, "Do you have the energy to tell me?"

She shook her head, "No, but I can show you."

He raised an eyebrow, "How?"

"Close your eyes, and clear your mind," She tried to speak louder but her body did as it wanted.

He did as she asked. She closed her eyes. She searched for the aura in him and once she found it she was able to enter it. Almost like a door. Then, she showed him where it began:

◇...◇...◇

The house ahead was high in flame. The snow glowed along with the flames. The dead bodies in the living room of her mother and her three brothers. Her body felt weightless as she ran. Full force to her shoulder the door flew forward. "Michelle!" She continued down the hall. And Hurried up the stairs that were on the right side. The flames already began to crawl up the wall. "KINZIE!"

"I'm here Michelle. Get back from the door!"

Kinzie once again drove her shoulder into the door. Michelle was barely even visible. Kinzie grabbed a sheet that was laying on the mattress. Then she opened the window.

"Michelle come here," she reached her arms out for her sister.

"No! Kinzie, please. There must be another way," She sobbed.

"There isn't. Come Michelle. You need to trust me. I'm not going to let you fall," She looked Michelle in her eyes.

She limped over to her sister. Kinzie cradled her as if she was a child. She was only 19 at the time. Kinzie had tied the sheet to the dresser, which rested next to the window sill. She climbed out of the window, and slowly down the ground. Once they reached the snow. Kin tugged the sheets as hard as she could, tearing the rest. And bandaging her sisters deeply burnt wounds. The smell stuck to her nasal cavities.

"Lay here. I'm going to get Caesar," she said and ran into the barn. She whistled halfway to the barn. Caesar came to her call. His face was spotted with black and white, while the rest of his body remained gray. Except for close to his hooves, which were black. He had the most beautiful eyes. His eyes looked to be a light blue, "Come old friend." She spoke softly while stroking his mane. She instructed Caesar to kneel. And he did so. She Lifted her sister onto him. And instructed him to take her to Quinn.

"I knew her wounds were too severe. She had no time to wait. I tried to walk the remainder of the way."

The snow crunched beneath her feet. She didn't feel an ounce of cold. The moonlight is more than enough to light her way through the forest. She paused, eyeing a stranger. She couldn't see his face. She tried to show her calm despite her heart racing.

◇...◇...◇

The image faded. Tim instantly opened his eyes to find Kinzie unconscious. He ran downstairs. And almost ran into Michelle, who let out a small cry, "Oh my *god* Tim! Please don't ever do that again!"

"I'm sorry. But this is urgent. You need to examine Kinzie," His voice sounded beyond urgent. Which caused Michelle to run down the hallway. She entered Kinzie's room. She inhaled her cries. Tim came up behind her, "It's her eyes."

Her sister approached slowly, once she got close enough, she spoke softly, "Kin, it's me Michelle. I need to see your eyes. Can you open your eyes for me? Please. Even if it's for a second," she pleaded.

They both waited patiently. It felt as though it took three minutes or more. But Kinzie opened her eyes long enough for Shell to see her irises, then her eyes rolled into the back of her head. Michelle covered her mouth then backed up into the chair. Once she slumped down, Tim was on his knees below her. They were both at eye level. "Shell, Kinzie was vomiting earlier while I was asleep. As I was approaching the toilet she flushed it. All I saw was red. Before she went back to sleep she was showing me how she 'came to be'. Or something like that. But it didn't get very far."

"What did you see?" Michelle replied, sadly. Her head was down, and her voice filled with sadness and defeat.

"Well I saw her coming up to the house and saving you from the fire. By the time it got to her walking in the forest and meeting a stranger she was passed out," Tim spoke gently. He rubbed Michelle's left arm.

"Timothy, what I'm about to tell you is serious, and may change your view of Kinzie. You might want to take a seat," Michelle's voice sounded unsteady, but serious. A side Tim has never seen before.

"No, I'm fine. Please tell me what it was she was trying to show me," His eyes dove into hers.

"She's a vampire," she replied softly.

Chapter Three

Kinzie's room began to spin. In all these years. He would have never suspected his partner to be a, "Vampire…"The word escaped his lips.

"She would've told you sooner. But I don't think she would want to have your perception of her change," Michelle pulled him closer. He didn't expect her to be so strong he didn't expect any events that happened today. But Michelle's warm embrace was more than reassuring. He thanked her, and unexpected tears came to him. He still loved her the same. This news changes nothing. It just surprised him a lot. To see someone you love in this much agony would cripple any true man.

"Now it's *your* turn to sleep," She gave a slight smile. He tried to smile back. His attempts inevitably shattered. There was no way he could sleep now. But he left the room out of respect and slowly made his way back downstairs.

……*

Michelle sat quietly in the dimly lit room, watching her sister rest as peacefully as she could.She had changed her clothes once again, into a red tank top and some black leggings; she even changed her underwear since it was wet. She sat up suddenly l at the sound of knocking on the bedroom door.

"Come in," she replied.

"I'm sorry to disturb you Shelly, but I came to check on Kinzie," Quinn entered the room.

"Should I wake her?" Michelle inquired, with a sad look.

"No, she must rest. Her condition is highly delicate," A soft sigh escaped his mouth, " She appears to be getting worse."

"She is. As Tim was watching her, her eye color changed. And she couldn't hold down anything that suits her nutritional diet," Michelle's voice fills with concern.

Quinn's eyes winded, "Show me her eyes…"

They both approached Kinzie's resting body. Michelle spoke softly, asking her once again to open her eyes. She did so a few seconds later. Quinn gasped, no words could describe the fear in his eyes. Michelle's heart pinged, it had been a long time since she's seen her father figure out hesitation on how to help someone, or even who to go to. He looked at her with thoughtful eyes, " I sense there's more you want to share."

"Yes. Tim recently has come to discover what Kinzie truly is," she looked down at her fidgety fingers.

"Well I suppose that's one angle of optimism," His voice rang with less concern. He walked slowly to the bed and sank into the mattress at Kinzie's feet. Michelle had a sudden thought. *What about the archives?* She sat up.

"Shelly, what are your thoughts?" Quinn asked.

"What about in the archives? Hopefully we can find a clue of some sort," Michelle replied, her voice trailing off.

"A good idea, shall we alert Tim?" Quinn inquired.

"No, let him rest. Finding out Kinzie's true identity is hard enough, discovering we have archives may overwhelm him much," Michelle chuckled a little.

Quinn let out a laugh, as he rose to his feet, "I will begin the process and pull all the books from the shelves."

......*

Kinzie's body resisted her every attempt to move. *"Why is this happening?"* Her voice echoed in the darkness of her mind. Her body began to warm and her feet began to rise, and it moved up her body. Her veins constricted. A horrible combination of hot and cold. A vampire's torture. She began to scream. She couldn't open her eyes but she heard everything around her. Michelle's light footsteps rushed over to her. "Kinzie?" Kinzie tried to find her hand. She felt someone's palm , *"I'm getting too hot. Cold water... Col.."* her voice echoed once more.

"Kinzie's getting too hot, she needs cold water," She heard Michelle's voice announce to Quinn.

The door flew open, "What's happening?" Tim's voice rang in her ears.
"Tim, we need to get her to the bathroom, *now!*"

His heavy boots approached closer, "It's going to be okay Kinzie... It's going to be okay. I've got you," His arms were so gentle as he lifted her to his chest. Every footstep grew louder, Kinzie's head spun. She tried to speak. Anything so she could stay awake. A cool feeling washed over her. Literally, Tim had submerged her in the bathtub.

Kinzie opened her eyes to find a blurred vision of Tim sitting on the toilet, "Tim," her voice.

"Kin," His voice sounded strained. He sniffled.

"Tim... Come closer please," She felt weak, but cooler than before.

He brought himself to his knees, and leaned himself over the edge of the bathtub.

"Why are you crying?" She could see his face, his eyes were swollen red, as well as his nose.

 "Because I don't want to lose you," He looked into her eyes.

"You're not going to lose me," Her voice croaked.

"How can you know for sure?" His eyes began to gloss again.

"Because, I'm strong. I may not look at it. Please, Tim. Have faith in me," She reached out to touch him.

"I do. I just can't bear the thou-" Tim attempted to reply, reaching for her.

"Shhh. If that's what occupies your mind, then join me," Kinzie's voice sounded terrible.

"What?" Tim asked, giving a puzzled look.

"Join me. The tub is more than big enough for the both of us, and I'd feel safer if you were in here with me," her voice pleading more than she intended.

He nodded, and dug through his pockets, placing all valuables on the counter. In addition to taking off his belt and shirt. Leaving only an undershirt and pair of shorts, " Am I going to have to move you?"

"Yes, I can't bear my own body weight," Her voice began to crack.

He impressed himself by lifting her body forward with his only and stepped into the cold water with her. The bathtub was only partially filled. He sat in and spread his legs so Kinzie could lie in between them. Once he adjusted fully, he pulled her to his chest. Her body dead-weighted into his.

"I can hear your heartbeat.." Her voice trailed off.

"Is that bad?" Holding her closer.

"No," she reached for his hand. He took it. His hand was much bigger than hers. Everything about him was bigger. His height, his weight. But his heartbeat was soft, gentle and steady. Just like his personality. He pulled his hand away slowly and began to stroke her hair. They Heard a knock on the door.

Tim spoke, "Come in."

She didn't know whether he answered to save her voice or if he answered just because. Either way She was thankful. She didn't want to give Michelle anything else to worry about.

Michelle peeked in, " Oh, poor thing. Is she asleep?"

Please say yes,Tim.

He nodded, " Is everything alright?"

"I suppose so. Quinn and I are looking through some archives, but we haven't found anything yet. That being said, He and I are going to have to travel to one of his contacts, and see if they can help," she sighed.

"Alright that's fine. Both of you can go, and I'll stay here," his breath warmed her neck. He still was stroking her hair.

"Are you sure?" Michelle asked, raising an eyebrow.

"Michelle, after all these years you still ask me if I'm sure. If I weren't positive about something I wouldn't have said anything in the first place," He chuckled.

"I'm sorry. It's a habit I guess. But thank you Tim. I'll prepare a few things before I go. Do me a favor," She tapped on the door

"Sure," Tim looked up.

"Don't stay in there too long. Here are some towels," She reached for the towels which rested on the rack nearest to her, and left the bathroom door ajar while looking for a change of clothes for Tim.

Oh Michelle. Always a busy bee. Thinking ahead, that's what I love about her.

"Once she leaves, I'll carry you to the bed," Tim whispered.

"Here you go," she announced before she placed the pile of clothes on the toilet seat, and hurried out the door, "See you, phone numbers are on the counter."

"See you!" Tim called.

She could hear Michelle call Quinn to come along. The front door closed and locked, "They're out the door," she hated the sound of her voice. It was raspy.

"Alright, let's get you changed. Will you be alright if I Step out first?" His heart tugged further into his stomach.

"I'll be fine as long as I'm leaning against something," If she had working lungs, she would've sighed.

"Alright," His voice rang gently in her ears. The feeling of him touching her gently, and treating her as though she was a glass doll. It's something she could appreciate. Even though she was soaking in the tenderness of his touch, the longing for her own mobility grew.

It had taken a little longer to dry them both off, but it was successful. Before taking Kinzie to the bed, Tim dried himself off. She envied his quickness. He bent down to carry her. She shook her head and asked if she could just lean on him instead. He was hesitant at first, but then thought about how he felt, not moving for long periods of time. He just nodded in agreement and made certain his grip stayed steady. Her shortness didn't help with that. Kinzie felt somewhat human again. Or, rather normal again. Deep down she really did wish she was human. She had long forgotten how breathing rhythms worked. What's a normal breathing pace? What's a normal cardiogram? What pace does the heart have to be to be considered life threatening? How do doctors take pulses? How long can a friendship last before that person dies? Then Tim would ask what's wrong, and she'd say, 'I feel weak.'

"Stop it Kin. What happened, is just that. It's simple. Stop thinking about it!" And that's when she realized, *"Do I love him? God it's been so long, I can't even remember the last time I've been in 'love'."* She shook it off. There's absolutely no way. He's her boss. She pushed the thoughts out of her mind so she could concentrate on walking without passing out, or plowing Tim into a wall. She felt the strong itch to sit behind her desk and attempt

to help Quinn and Michelle find clues, and possibly get clues on the case. Tim would never allow it though, it would be an alien if he did. Maybe he would sit with her and keep her company. Deep down she appreciated the precious time he was spending away from work to take care of her. *What time is it?* She opened her eyes. She was resting upright, pillows behind her and her nightmare before the Christmas fuzz blanket over her legs and chest, "Tim?"

"Hey Kin, I've been meaning to ask, where's your closet?" Tim asked with a concerned tone in his voice.

My closet… That's right, we were going to change clothes and. Oh my god! The last thing I remember was taking a step at the bathtub. How long have I been out? "Erm, it's across the hall. Tim, how long have I been out?"

"About ten minutes or so. I figured you could rest while I grabbed a change of clothes for you," Tim sat in the chair, "Wait, are you alright?"

"No… I'm not. The last thing I remember was taking that first step while leaving the tub. That's it. How did I fade so quickly?" Her voice trailed off.

"It's probably because you haven't eaten anything," Tim tapped his chin in thought with his first finger.

"Yes that's a possibility, but it wouldn't have that kind of effect on me normally," Kin nawed on her thumb.

"This isn't exactly a normal situation though. At least as far as I've understood in the short time of me being here," His voice rang a calmness in her mind.

"True," Kinzie looked down and noticed most of her clothes were off.

"How about this, I'll go get you some nutrition, but before I do you can go to the closet and get changed," He suggested as he stood up.

"Sounds good. I want to try and walk on my own," Kinzie threw off her blanket and moved her legs to the edge of the bed.

"You did a great job walking to the bed. I didn't really have to help you at all," He stood by her.

I can't remember that either? What kind of craft is this? "Alrighty then," She stood up. It felt great to be mobile again. And have control of her own body. Tim followed her closely. Not enough to breathe down her neck, but to catch her in case she falls. Once she got across the hall to the closet, she heard Tim smack himself lightly on the forehead. She could imagine him saying, "Well I feel stupid." But He didn't. He just wandered down the hallway.

The closet could be a smaller bedroom. There looked to be shelves evenly across each wall. That's where she placed her shoes and a couple of boxes. Underneath the equally leveled shelves were racks. Where she hung her cocktail dresses, buttoned up shirts, and coats. There was a dresser across from the entryway, and the wall to the right. On the left side there was a hamper of dirty clothes and above them three shelves where she lay undershirts and other folded things. A circular black and whit checkered rug lay in the middle of the floor, and right above that a simple chandelier. Kinzie rummaged through her dressers and found herself some black leggings, and a black spaghetti strap top. Her long wavy hair hung over her shoulders, down the center of her back. She wandered back to her bedroom, and sat in her usual place on the bed. Her hair brush rested on the blurred nightstand, she tried to cry out. But all she could do was reach out into the darkness.

Tim's heart pounded as he ran up the stairs. Once he entered the bedroom he tried not to cry out in fear. A woman was sitting in the chair staring at Kinzie.

"Hello, Detective Bryte," Her voice sounded classy, almost flirty.

"Hello, how did you get in here?" Tim hardened his eyebrows.

"Oh come now, that's irrelevant. You should be asking, 'Why', not 'how'," She tapped her fingers on the arm rest.

"Alright, I apologize. Why may I ask, are you here?" He changed his face and tone of voice to sound romantic, despite the crippled fear he felt.

"That's better. I am here to deliver a message. From someone hidden in the shadows," She continued to tap on the arm of the chair.

"What may I ask, is the message dear lady?" He successfully made it sound as though he wasn't afraid. He never thought being around Quinn for long periods of time could help at a time like this. He gave a silent thanks for small favors.

She rose from the chair, and walked toward him. She was wearing a long black cloak with a lacy black dress underneath, and began to speak softly, "I am the one of a different time. Try to find me, future or past. The present is nay born to last. I thirst for pain. I seek for lady thy Kinzie to join the game," she was face to face with him. She lifted her cloak enough so he could see her face. He held in a shout as he saw her eyes. Her irises are purple, and the rest of the eye red. Her face was beautifully scarred, and pale. A long blond curl appeared below her jaw. She walked past him, "Goodbye Mr. Bryte." And exited the room. He stood frozen in fear. In the time he took to try to get his body to move, he couldn't help but stare at Kinzie's helpless body. She looked weaker than before. The stainless steel water bottle grew heavy in his hand. He almost forgot that he even brought it up the stairs. *I hope Michelle and Quinn are safe.*

Tim's phone chimed, and he reluctantly took a look at it.

Medical Examiner Report: Jane Doe #1

Cause of death, asphyxiation caused by inhaling smoke. Has several broken bones. And a sleeping agent unseen before. She's been deceased for well over a week. In conclusion she was tortured before her death.

Medical Examiner Report: Jane Doe #2

Cause of death, asphyxiation caused by inhaling smoke. Has several broken bones. And a sleeping agent unseen before. She's been deceased for well over two days. In conclusion she was tortured before her death.

They found another body but didn't tell me? He thought to Himself. At this point it's safe to assume he's off the case. Otherwise he would've been notified that they found another Jane doe.

"You're heart racing tells me you're upset. What's wrong Tim?" Kinzie asked Her eyes still closed.

"They Found another Jane Doe, but didn't tell me anything. So I'm guessing I'm off the case. I just got the ME report and everything is almost identical. The only difference is when the victims died," Tim sighed.

"Don't worry about them. I know it's a stab in the back, But Michelle needs you, and I need you too," Her voice pleaded more than she meant to.

Tim's heart fell into the pit of his stomach, he was touched by her words and honesty, all he could do was nod and say, "Alright."

......*

Quinn had been driving for what felt like forever. In all that was real it had only been maybe an hour and a half maybe more. Michelle did everything she could to ease her anxiety. It had been so long since she last went out of the house, on a long road trip. Most of the time she goes to a local grocery store, or orders her groceries and has them delivered to the house. But she makes an attempt to avoid road trips. Period. This time she made an exception. Quinn had made several attempts to make Shelly comfortable. But in this instance it was almost impossible. He didn't blame her in the least. With her loss of vision she couldn't enjoy the travel like she used to so long ago. Michelle asked where they were going more than once. Quinn simply said,

"You'll see." With the little sight Michelle had she'd see colors and some shapes. Nothing but mostly tunnel vision in her right eye.

His soft voice broke the silence, "Shelly, we're almost there. I hesitated to reply to your inquiries. But I feel foolish for even attempting to remain silent. We're going to Madame's house. I'm highly certain she or her son, James, can help us." He sounded drained. Once he spoke of James her heart pinged.

" I had a familiar feeling as you were driving. I can't explain how. And now I know why." She mostly remembers the time she spent there. Before going there all she remembers Kinzie calling her name and saving her life. Then a few weeks later, she woke up with bandages and darkness, "To be honest I didn't even know he was alive." *Or is he?*

"Shell, what's the matter?" His voice ringing with concern and curiosity.

"I'm trying to remember their house and what happened. My memory is fooling my conscience," She sighed sharply.

"Alright. Well, we're almost there," Quinn's voice sounded highly optimistic despite the tension that held in the air, and the tiredness in his breathing.

She herself was tired. Probably more so than she would've liked to admit. But Kinzie needed her, just as much as Michelle needed Kin. Her stomach began to churn. The thought just struck her. What if Madame and James were dead? That's the curse of being immortal. You live on and the world continues on with it's own time. While you stay as you are. You never grow old, and the effort you put to change your physical appearance is exhausting. Dying hair, wearing different style clothes each generation, and keeping up with every era. Who knew being immortal would be so damn expensive. She amused herself by thinking of the vampire books and how any immortal being is wealthy beyond any mortal's imagination. It's because they have to be. Kinzie is the opposite. She doesn't invest nearly as much in physical appearance and covering her tracks as her sister does. The only thing she changes is the clothing style and makeup. She never really did care since she lives in the night time. The feeling of the car slowing down cracked her thoughts. Once he parked, she heard him take the keys out of the ignition, "May I help you out?"

"Yes please,"she nodded nervously. Quinn's movement wasn't too slow. However her heart went faster and faster as she took a breath. If they are alive and well, that would be a shock. James helped her through everything. Believed in her when she couldn't believe in herself. He helped her make the progress she's had for more than many decades. The thought of having someone to spend the rest of her immortal life with while society changes and generations was exhilarating. She felt Quinn touch her arm, "

Lean as far forward as you can. I'd prefer you not to hit your head."

She did so. Once she stood the smell of lavender, basil, rosemary, and roses filled the air. She shifted her feet to hear and feel the gravel under the souls of her shoes. A map appeared in her head. She took the first step and counted, "One." She spread her arms out and took another step, "Two." Once the third step came she felt the wooden railing underneath her fingertips. She couldn't help but smile. After all these years she *still* remembers. Then again she did spend a little over a year in this house.

"In 15 steps the railing will veer to the left and to the front stairs. There are five low stairs and four steps away from the front door," she guided herself. It wasn't anymore than a minute later she had come to the front door and Quinn at her side, "Well done, my dear." He spoke in a tone so an average mortal wouldn't be able to hear, "Are you ready?" Michelle felt frozen, it felt as if only her head could move. Quinn knocked on the door, and took Shelly's hand. He gently placed it under his arm. Michelle inhaled as deeply as she could. Familiar footsteps echoed in her ears, and vibrated through the floor beneath her feet. The door opened, "Quinn Roberts! And Michelle McCoy. What a pleasant surprise! Please come in."

Shell felt Quinn gesture a bow, "Thank you Madame." She too gave a slight curtsy. As she entered she let go of Quinn's arm. Spreading her own to feel the spaces inbetween. The texture on

the walls were the same. After all these years this house hadn't changed in the least. Michelle was relieved. She took three steps and instantly lowered her hand, avoiding the painting that she had knocked off the walls before. Her fingers dragged on until at last she found the threshold to the living room. *One, two, three…* The arm of the couch rested before her. She walked around to the front of the couch, Madame insisted they both be seated. She offered some tea, which is something neither of them could use. Madame made the best tea known in their world in the forever of existence. A refreshing drink, to clear their minds. The sound of clocks ticking brought her back down to memory lane. That was the first sound she heard after waking up in darkness. After many healing ointments, and healing bowls of soup, she managed to get slight vision in her right eye. Only enough to see blurs and colors. But that was enough for her. With as bad as her injuries are, that was a miracle
.

"Tea's ready my darlings. Now, what's the reason for your visit, Mr.Roberts," Madame approached the living room. The smell of honey and wildberry filled Michelle's nose. The loud clinking of the tea cups on the saucers drove her insane. But she kept a straight face.

"You know me so very well. We are here on an urgent matter. Do you recall ever meeting Michelle's sister, Kinzie?" Quinn's voice soothed Michelle's eardrums, as the try stopped rattling.

"No, I do remember you both talking highly of her, in the time of your recovery Michelle. What happened?" Madame's voice was high pitched and sweet. She was a short woman with a pear figure, which Michelle envied. Her black hair was pulled into a neat bun and she wore a dress with an apron in the front.

"She's become ill. And a person such as herself isn't known to get illnesses." Quinn replied, reaching for the tray.

"How do you mean?" Her voice went into a high squeak. Even though Michelle found it Adorable, the high register rang loudly. She was curious as to how she could keep such a straight face.

"Madame, she's known in the immortal realm, such as yourself," Quinn sipped his tea.

"I'm sorry Mr. Roberts I don't follow," She too sipped her tea.

"She's a Vampire," He spewed. Michelle jerked up. There were very few times Quinn would ever simplify his sentences, and that's only when he gets frustrated. Which isn't often. Michelle gave a silent thanks for that, otherwise she would have to spend more time getting to know Quinn Roberts' voice patterns, and attitudes. The thought of it all was beyond exhausting at that moment in time.

"Oh, my. What happened?" Madame asked in shock. Her eyebrows hardened.

"That's why we've come. We're unsure of how her illness came to be, and how to cure it. I was inquiring if your son would be willing to come and assist us in finding out," Quinn sipped his tea.

"Well that does sound serious. I'd be happy to assist in any way I can. If that means sending my son to your destination, so be it," She sipped her tea.

Michelle never understood how people could drink piping hot tea. She's alway been fond of Iced tea or tea a little above room temperature, "Papa could you put some ice in my tea please?"

A deep voice entered the room, "I'll do it."

Michelle's heart jumped. *Is that really him? I thought he was dead. Why is he alive? Is there something, wait. Papa said that Madame' is an immortal being. He's a-*

"That would be greatly appreciated, thank you James," Madame spoke up.

"Yes, th- thank you," Michelle stammered, her heart starting pounding into her chest. It was hard to manage her surroundings.

He moved swiftly and quietly to the Kitchen. Michelle could hardly hear his footsteps, his scent came closer as he dropped two ice cubes in the tea cup. They clinked together as they surfaced themselves to the top of the glass, "You're welcome."

"We were just talking about you James," Madame' breathed into her teacup.

"Oh? What about me?" His voice melted in Michelle's sinus cavity.

"Assisting in discovering why Michelle's sister is ill, and how to cure the illness," Quinn spoke while reaching across Michelle's lap to hand her the now cooled tea. Michelle gave a slight nod of thanks, and took a sip. Sweet berries and a slight flavor of honey burst in her mouth.

"Ah, I'd be happy to help. As long as it's okay with you mother," James smiled, Michelle had a feeling it was sarcastic.

"Yes dear, that's fine with me," She sipped the last bit of tea.

"When do we leave?"James asked.

"We'll leave here in a few minutes. I'd like to call someone first, and make them aware we'll be on our way," Quinn sighed and rose from the couch, "Remind me where your telephone is."

"Near the front door dear," Madame' announced, as she too rose to clean up the dishes, "Are you almost done Michelle?"

"Yes ma'am," Michelle chugged the last drop of tea. And lifted the cup toward her., "Thank you Madame. As usual, it was delicious."

"Very good," She smiled and walked into the kitchen humming a soft lullaby she will never forget.

James' scent drew closer, "May I sit next to you?"

"Of course you may," Michelle smiled. Her heart raced. *It's been so long since I've heard his voice. I wish I knew he was still living...*

"It must be a bit of a shock knowing that Mama and I are alive and well," His voice trailed off.

"Yes, it is. It *is* a relief though. I've really missed you James," Her voice grew soft. She couldn't help but lower her line of sight.

"May I take off your eye patch?" He asked gently, "Only to see how it's healed."

    She said nothing. Tears grew in her only eye, and nodded. She felt his warm fingertips slowly slide off the patch. He traced it to her jaw and gently pulled her face toward him, "You're beautiful." Michelle couldn't help but lean into the warmth that rested beside her. She cried a little. Not tears of sadness. But tears of joy. Happiness in knowing that the one man she confided in and related to the best, is alive. Maybe now she can live as an Immortal, and be happy again. They heard Quinn talking to Tim. Letting him know James was coming, and they'll be on the way shortly.

Chapter Four

Tim thanked Quinn for the update and hung up the home phone. With a deep sigh he grabbed something for Kinzie to drink once more. It felt as though they'd only been gone for an hour. He was mistaken. They'd been gone for five hours. The sun started to show in the kitchen. *Good thing Kinzie's in her room.* He gave a soft thanks. He heard Kinzie's voice in his head *"Are you alright?"*

"Yeah, just zoning out. I'm coming up now," He hurried up the staircase. It was nice not to have to yell. He probably would've lost his voice. He was careful not to shed any sunlight into her room.

"Is the *sun* coming out?" Her voice sounded awful.

"Yes, and that was Quinn on the phone. He and Michelle are coming back with a 'guest'. I have no idea who it is," He handed her the cup and straw.

"Ah… Tim… I'm so sorry," Her voice trailed off as she placed the straw in the cup.

"For what?" His voice rose.

"For not telling you about what I really am…" She started sucking on the straw, then paused, "Could you turn around please? I don't want to frighten you."

"You won't frighten me. I'm staying put. I can close my eyes," Tim shook his head.

She nodded, "Please."

He did so. Kinze closed her eyes also, and began to sip the straw. Her fangs dug into her lower gums. She drank harder and her taste buds exploded. Her senses heightened. She heard Tim's heart race. She heard the straw protest and gulped the last drop of blood. She opened her eyes, she felt high. The room became a blur, and black. Tim jumped up to catch Kinze as she leaned off the bed. Why was she so light? He pushed her back on the bed. And covered her as she lay resting. His heart felt as though it was skipping beats. He, too, closed his eyes. Rest was well needed that moment. After all, he did stay up with her all night.

......*

Michelle was asleep in the back seat, on the car ride home. Quinn and James took this time to catch up on recent events. James kept looking back toward Michelle. He too had memories he'll never forget. Like the first day he saw her damaged skin peeling away at her flesh. It broke his heart to know that this kind of thing happens to beautiful people like Michelle. It was a pleasant surprise to see how well she's doing. He was glad to know all the tools he gave her helped her go through daily life. How has she been alive all these years? And he didn't even know. That moment he decided to never let her go again.

......*

Kinzie lay resting with her eyes closed. She couldn't sleep despite her desperate tiredness. Her body felt as though it was jello. Her stomach churned, she could feel something crawl up her throat. Her eyes flew open as she ran to the bathroom. *Not again...* She didn't miss being sick as a human. As she gagged she heard Tim's heavy footsteps hasten and the light in the bathroom turned on.

"Oh my God, Kin," He knelt down next to her. She didn't have the strength to sit up on her own. She leaned into him.

"God this sucks," Her voice was almost gone. She sat up once more and lost her strength again. Tim's heart broke with her voice.

"I'm so sorry Kin…" He stroked her hair, "Is there anything I can do to help?"

She shook her head. Tim felt his heart plummet into his stomach. He'd never felt this useless before. All he wants is for her to be her usual self. Knowing there was no way for him to help speed up the process took a chunk out of his sanity. Kinzie began to shiver. She curled up on the bathroom floor into his lap and welcomed his body heat.

"Actually there is one way you can help," She tried to lay still, but it was no use. She also couldn't believe the words that were about to come out of her mouth.

"And how's that?" He replied aloud, while in his head he sighed in relief. *So I'm not totally useless.*

"Hold me,"Her voice cracked. It's been over 150 years since she last desired to have someone hold her. But she trusted him. He's always been there for her, just as she has with him. The bond that they've had since the first time meeting has only grown stronger. As he pulled her closer he began to hum and continued doing so as he touched her hair. He gently rocked from side to side. She nuzzled into his shoulder. As he hummed Kinzie drifted off into another place in her mind. Slowly her body grew heavier. If she had any breath she'd probably breathe slow and steadily. To see her in this state broke his heart, he cried a little. He had no words. Deep down he hoped Quinn and Michelle would arrive soon. He started making his way toward standing up when he heard Voices downstairs. *"Holy cow! Did he speed? Or was the traffic terrific?"* He placed her in the bed, "They're back, I'm going to go downstairs. I'll be back in a few minutes." Kinzie gave a slight nod.

......*

Michelle entered the door first, "You all go ahead into the office, and I'll make some coffee. Would you like some James?" She turned to see his figure.

"Coffee does sound terrific, that would be great," He smiled.

"Alright I count three, Papa may I get you some tea?"

"Yes please Dear," Quinn's voice trailed off.

"Wait three? There's only t-"

"Tim will be joining us, would you like cream or sugar?"

" No thank you," They said simultaneously.

Michelle nodded. James was breath taken by the house. The entryway was painted gray, A staircase was directly across the white marble floor. The wood was darker than he's ever seen on a staircase. Nearly black. There was a hall closet to his right. And a chandelier above his head. Toward the right was the hallway to the Kitchen and other rooms. The kitchen was to the right and the office door was a little further but a door to the left. He entered the dimly lit room, to find bookshelves in a circumference. And a large wooden desk in the direct center. On either side were couches that followed the shape of shelves. He heard a man's voice in the hall, "He Shell, I'm guessing they're in the office?"

"You're correct. I'll be there in just a sec," He could hear her shifting around, and things clinking.

A tall man appeared in the doorway. He had dark red hair, and green eyes. His face held a strong jawline and freckles. His lips were average, and his nose slender, "Oh hey, I'm Tim," He held out his right hand.

"Hello, I'm James," He replied, shaking his hand. That moment he noticed Tim's left arm, "If you don't mind my asking, how did that happen? You know, erm." His voice trailed off.

"Oh, I was trying to catch a suspect and he tried to blow me up. Thankfully Kinzie was there," He replied, swallowing hard. "Oh Kinzie requests that we keep in mind that she can hear us. And to try and include any information with that in mind."

"Understood, my dear. How's your progress been?" Quinn said aloud. He paused for a moment, "Ah, I'll let him know."

I wonder if he's feeling alright...

Michelle entered with a tray, "Alright everyone. Let's take a seat and get started," She placed the tray on the desk and handed out everyone's beverages.

"Did you hear us speak about Kinzie's request?" Quinn asked.

"Yes, I did," Michelle took a sip from her mug, and took a seat on the couch. James grabbed his cup and seated himself next to her.

"Alright, who would like to be the one who translates what Kinzie is saying?"

"I'll volunteer," Tim spoke up.

"Okay wait a minute… What do you mean, translate?" James blurted.

"She holds many abilities due to the fact that she's a vampire. That's why she can hear us despite the fact she's a whole floor above our heads. But due to her weakened state she cannot connect with us all. There must be one who translates her words. And no she cannot be here herself because it is daylight," Quinn paused to take a sip of his tea.

"Okay, I'm sorry I'm just not used to being in situations like this. I thought I was in the middle of some cult activity or something," James sighed.

Michelle burst out in laughter.

"I'm sorry to ruin the fun here, but can we please focus," Tim spoke up.

Michelle's laughter ceased, "Yes, I'm sorry Kin. Let's continue." She wiped her right eye.

James' heart grew warmer. That was the most beautiful sound in the world. He was pleased to see her happy, and living well. He couldn't help but smile.

"Thank you," Tim nodded.

The meeting began with how long ago Kinzie's symptoms began, and how her illness was so severe she couldn't be present at work for a lengthy period of time. Her lethargy and the negative influences on her body. They began going over the who, and the why. Quinn began to pace. He announced that it would have to take someone with a strong power and ability to take a hold of Kinzie as an Elder Vampire. Michelle then chimed in and asked questions about the council, or anyone in the council. James melted every time she spoke.

......*

Michelle reviewed all the events in her mind. Deep down she didn't want to. She didn't want to know who was making Kinzie suffer, nor did she want to know the possibility of losing her sister. The one who risked her life to save hers, and made sure she remained safe, always. The hardest of truths were facts. One) Kinzie would sacrifice herself anytime, any day, and anywhere.

Two) Kinzie would witness her dead parents and brothers burning over again if it meant saving anyone. Three) The absolute certainty that Kinzie feels as though it's better for her to be ill than anyone else. *Why would anyone even attempt to hurt Kinzie? She's been a hero to all of us one way or another.* It took Michelle to put her coffee mug to her mouth to realize it's empty. She let out a sigh. She was relieved that she was not dealing with this heartache alone. Hopefully James would see what they all see. Kinzie is an amazing, strong, powerful, gentle vampire. And there weren't many like her. This meeting was draining, but everyone hoped to gain some sort of understanding or solution. Whatever needs to be done, will be. Whatever the cost may have been at the time, would be worth it. Quinn looked awful, the dark circles under his eyes made him look nearly thirty years older. He's usually the one with the plan. He always had a solution to everything. But in the gathering he stood numbly.

......*

All Quinn longed for was a clue. Even if it was the smallest. He had plenty of contacts, but no one had heard of this before. Perhaps it's magic? If it is, where did it come from? And who would have developed such power? How long have they been watching Kinzie? Perhaps it's a curse. But that's the same as magic. He sighed deeply in frustration. He took a sip of tea. Hopefully they'll find the riddle to the problem before this illness claims Kinzie's life. He asked Michelle if she's certain no one has tried to enter the house. She nodded and replied saying she hadn't seen anything suspicious. He gave a slight nodd. *"Alright, then whom else, or what else could this be?"*

... ...*

As all the talk continued, Tim took a moment to remember that one creepy looking lady who was in Kinzie's room. *God I'm an idiot!*

"Wait!" He blurted.

Ow... Please watch your voice Tim , "I'm sorry Kin... I've neglected to tell you something. Quinn... While you and Michelle were out, and I was down here getting something for Kinzie. and a woman came into the house. And she told me something. 'I am the one of a different time. Try to find me future, or past. The present nay born to last. I thirst for pain. I seek for lady thy Kinzie to join the game..'" Tim paused. He was ashamed. His eyes filled with tears. How could he forget something like that? Maybe, she made him forget. He had yet to tell Kinzie how he felt. Hopefully she wouldn't die before he got the chance.

"Timothy, What did she look like?" Quinn froze.

" She had long blonde hair. She was wearing a black cloak and a lacy dress underneath. Her eyes," he shivered, "Iris's were purple and the part around that was red. Her face was damaged with old scars. As I said before. She was creepy."

"That almost sounds like Ashely," Tim spoke suddenly.

"Why do you say that, Dear?"

"Because I saw her while I was training with General William. She was his most loyal assistant. I wouldn't be surprised if he was behind this," Tim closed his eyes, and took a breath.

"Isn't General William a son of a Council Member William Senior?" Michelle squeaked softly.

"Yes, he is. That would explain why he's able to cripple one of the strongest they've ever trained," Quinn sipped his tea, "He also has a horrible obsession with starting wars, and riding the world of good immortal beings. He also has a horrible history of becoming jealous of others."

"So he kills people? He sounds like a coward. Why doesn't he build himself into something else?" James lifted a brow.

"No one knows. He's fascinated with games and seeing people suffer," Tim spoke once more.

"Whoever this guy is. I'm sure if we could review his history, we can take him down," James rose up from his seat.

"If only it were that simple," Kinzie's voice came from the doorway. Making everyone jump out of their skin. She approached James slowly, "Hello James. I'm sorry we had to meet under these circumstances," She held out a Hand. He took it gently, and shook it. She then turned to Tim and walked slowly to the couch so she didn't overwhelm herself. Once she was seated she curled up into his shoulder.

"Kinzie, how did you get to-" Tim breathed. He had no words. Her head felt heavy..

"I teleported, I felt strong enough to do so for just a moment. But I realize now that was an awful idea," Her voice sounded worse. As if by the second.

"Ms. McCoy May I examine you?" James said softly.

Kinzie gave a slight nod, "Tim, can you lie me down please?" He scooted toward the edge of the couch and gently sprawled her out.

James approached gently, and got down on his knees.

......*

James could feel Tim's eyes staring him down. Kinzie's skin tone had been a tint of grey. Instead of pale white. Her irises were gray, and her pupils were dilated since the light was so dim.. He gently touched her fingertips to see the palms of her hands.

She was so tiny. No heartbeat, and unusually warm. He noticed she moves her chest out of habit to blend in with mortals.

"When did you start feeling poorly?" He looked her directly in the eyes

"About four months ago. I had a loss of appetite and I felt dizzy. I knew that was unusual for my con-" Her voice cracked. She tried to clear her throat.

"No, no. Stop. Tim, sit her up please. Kinzie, I need you to open your mouth, I'm going to look down your throat. Quinn, will she be bothered if I shine a flashlight down in-"

"No serious damage, just major discomfort," Quinn seated himself.

"Michelle, get-" He looked over to see a flashlight before him, "God woman you're a miracle." He turned it on and looked down. Kinzie made a noise. Tim grabbed her hand, and she squeezed. Popping every knuckle he had. "I'm sorry, I know I just need a good look. Alright I got it," He took the flashlight out. He touched her forehead. "Well I have some good news, and a bit of bad news. Which would you like to hear first?"

"Bad news, please," Tim looked at Kinzie. Came up behind her welcoming his shoulder as a pillow.

"Bad news is, your illness is far more advanced than any of us thought. The good news is I've seen this before, and I can make a few 'potions'," He gave air quotations, " that can help with any pain, fever, or discomfort. Have you been able to hold anything down?"

She shook her head.

"Well I'm going to change up your diet, a bit. What type do you usually drink?"

Kinzie Shrugged.

Michelle spoke up, "O negative. I don't know how to access any other blood types."

"Alright, you and I need to go over her health, routines, and sleep schedule. Everything. Before we continue. I need to announce that this is caused by highly skilled and highly advanced Magic. Now the question remains who would be as advanced to cast a spell such as this one. Quinn and Tim, I would like you two to make a list of people she's connected to past or present so we can maybe identify someone and we'll go from there. In the meantime Michelle and I will get her some medicine that will help. Show me where the Kitchen is again? I'll take the tray," James gathered everyone's glass and pailed it on the tray. Michelle led him out to the hallway and reminded him to watch the sunlight.

The Kitchen was beautiful. It was an off white color with marble countertops and black and grey backsplash. The sink was stainless steel, as well as the stove, dishwasher, and refrigerator. He placed the tray on the counter, "Where's the closest Clinic?"

"About a thirty Minute drive from here," Michelle moved around the Kitchen swiftly. It was nice to see her progress. And her confidence in the fact that she could travel and know she wasn't going to fall down.

"Alright. Well, your sister doesn't have any time. Michelle I'm going to need a knife, and a cup."

Michelle's eyes widened and jaw dropped, "What? No, I can't," she stammered.

"Michelle, you must. Please trust me. Your sister needs it. I don't mind," His voice rang with reassurance. She nodded. She grabbed a plastic cup and a small non serrated blade, and placed it on the counter.

"I'm going to grab some gauze pads and other medical things. I'll be right back," She left quickly. She couldn't bear witnessing him doing such a thing to himself for Kinzie. That's what she loved about him. His willingness to help people no matter what the cost may be. They're similar in that way.

While Michelle was out of the kitchen James did what was needed and covered the wound with a paper towel. Afterward he rummaged through the kitchen and found all the spices necessary to put in with his own blood. His family didn't believe in going to the store and buying medicine. Their culture says that the earth provides all herbal needs for everything. His mother taught him the basics when he was no more than nine years old. Now he's an advanced alchemist. When Michelle returned he was done. He handed her the cup, "Here give this to your sister and I'll take those," his voice was so calm. So warming. Before heading back to the office she grabbed a lid and straw.

"James," She blurted.

"Hmm?" He replied, his mouth held the gauze pad while he applied some ointment.

"Thank you. It's been so good to see you," She smiled and hurried out of the room.

......*

Careful not to shed any light, Michelle re-entered the office. Tim was seated in the same place, Kinzie lay resting on his lap. Quinn was at Kinzie's desk, scribbling on a piece of paper.

Michelle spoke gently, "Tim, can you sit her up a little for me?"

"Sure," He gave a slight nod, he wrapped his arm around her chest, and pulled her up closer to his stomach.

"Hey, Kin. I have something James made. I need you to try it," Michelle's whisper was almost audible. She pushed Kinzie's bangs out of her eyes. She put the straw to her lips. Kinzie's lips instantly wrapped around the straw. The flow of the straw was steady and calm. Until It protested.

"Thank you,' Tim translated.

"You're welcome, let me know if you need anything else," She rose slowly, hoping that the mix James made would take effect soon. She doesn't doubt him, nor has she ever. She's a living example of his good works. Hesitant to go back into the Kitchen Michelle walked slowly.

"I will," Tim spoke a little softer.

"I'll go make dinner for the rest of us. I'll let you know when it's ready," she exited and walked into the kitchen with a sigh. When she looked up she noticed that the dishes were no longer in the sink, the medical supplies she brought James were neatly placed on the counter. And all the spices were put away.

Thank God. One less thing I need to worry about. She went straight for the pots and pans, and looked through the fridge. She heard footsteps approaching.

"Thank you for cleaning up the Kitchen," She said, grabbing some steak and what seemed like green onion.

"You're welcome. Can I help you with dinner?" Jame's voice made her heart pound.

"That would be great," She smiled, her smile made his heart pound. It was nice to have a little bit of help. His thoughtfulness made her blush. And Just for a moment, made her feel human.

Chapter Five

Quinn still found himself captivated by his own thoughts. This would be a perfect opportunity to dig into Kinzie's mind and find out what she's thinking. How long has she been like this? Was she ever planning on telling anyone? At this point he didn't know whether to be angry or frightened. The love he holds in his heart for Kinzie is deep and filled with the purest intentions.

Tim's throat cleared, crumbling all thoughts, " Quinn, Kinzie's wants to connect with you through me. Since Michelle and James are making dinner," He said softly.

"Certainly, I was just having the same thoughts, " Quinn replied, clearing the agony in his chest.

"She wants to apologize for not telling you sooner. She was trying to stay strong for everyone, but she didn't realize the damage she was doing to herself. She wants you to know she appreciates all that you've done. "

"What is this preposterous death at bedside sort-of-talk? Kin you'll be fine. You *are* fine. You must rest. Let us not worry about what has been. Let us worry about what will be."

"Yes, Papa," Tim echoed, " She's getting heavier. My best guess is she's going to sleep. I genuinely wish she'd stay resting," he sighed, stroking her hair.

"That's just the person she is, you'll appreciate it later on. Trust me," Quinn smiled. Still deep in thought.

"You mean not giving up or her stubbornness?" Tim's voice dripped in a heart break.

"I'm referring to both. I too am angry with her for withholding information and acting as if nothing is wrong, " Quinn's heart pinged, "We just need to find a way to get a hold of the vampire council, and discover who would have the power to accomplish this."

"Accomplish what?" Tim asked, frustrated. He seems to know nothing about her at all.

"Kinzie is an older Vampire, therefore it is significantly harder to kill, cripple, or give illness. Someone must be *extremely* skilled and strong to get her feeling this poorly," he took a deep breath, in doing so the aroma of steak and garlic filled the room.

"How old is she?" Tim asked, while stroking Kinzie's hair.

"Five hundred- Forty six- years old," Quinn tried not to tremble. Even now he still remembers the McCoy family. Her mother called upon him to save her children, if any harm came to them. He was even present when they were born. The day he walked into their lives was the day he promised to protect them. Their mother was so wise, "Memories can either cripple us or strengthen us."

"Who's the leader of the council?" Tim's voice broke Quinn's focus.

" There lies our problem. It's not just one leader. There are six. William, Adrian, Bethany,Arron, Matthew and Tyrr. There used to be three men and two women. But it was believed that adding another woman would be a better judgement and equal opportunity."

"Ah okay. That *does* make sense. I'm assuming their location is isolated," Tim's voice rose with curiosity.

"Yes, truthfully I think it's best we send a written request," he rose and started to pace. His stomach gave a small growl.

" And how is that a possibility?" Tim can't believe Quinn. A letter would take much longer than they have. He heard another growl. Tim assumed it was Quinn's stomach again.

"Well I was considering sending it by portal, but is that legal?"

"Wait wha-?"

"Just like human society the vampires and any other beings have laws to accommodate the needs of everyone. We can't just go there and trespass carelessly. We must receive an invitation. So it's either a portal or we have to wait!" Quinn barked. His voice was louder than Tim had ever heard.

Michelle came barging into the room, " Papa you must calm down."

"No! I promised your mother I would protect you and I am failing! I don't want to lose anyone else in this life!"

"Have you taken your potion today?' Michelle remained calm and her voice steady.

"No… I ran out," Quinn's voice turned into a soft growl.

"Tim, could you do me a favor and take Kinzie upstairs? It's dark outside. I'll be up in a little while to check on her," Michelle's eye didn't move from Quinn.

Tim nodded and did so. Kinzie's body was heavy. She was really asleep. *"What about her meal?"*

"I'll bring her some blood in a few minutes. I'd just like to speak with Quinn real quick," she replied with a smile.

......*

Quinn's veins filled with fire, furey and impatience, and carelessness. Nothing of his quality nor personality. The moon must be coming up.

"Michelle please. Put me to sleep. And inject a potion if need be," Quinn's voice pleaded.

"Very well," Michelle sighed "Can you be seated?"

"Yes," Quinn sat on the couch.

Michelle rummaged through one of the desk drawers. There rested a wooden box at the bottom, below a few files. She opened the box which held three small glass bottles. There was a thick dark blue and green substance inside. Her fingertips touched one of the bottles, as she heard a deep growl. "James," Michelle called.

"Coming," he replied from the kitchen. Michelle rose slowly to find Quinn no longer himself. Crouching to the ground, his arms deformed and his fingers extended. A face is no longer a human face. No longer a man.

Entered the office and froze, "Are you alright?"

Michelle nodded, "Yes, I just need to give him this." She gestured to the bottle, " Please close the door."

James did so, "Alright,what do you need?"

"I'm going to need you to hold his mouth open while I give him the potion. Then close his mouth to get him to drink it," Michelle replied slowly and steady. Trying her best not to increase her heart rate.

Catching Quinn has never been easy out in the open. But hopefully behind closed doors, hopefully things will result a little differently.

......*

Kinzie lies on her right side away from Tim. Who was sitting in a chair near her bedside. Her movement was minimal. Tim could tell she was awake. But her rest is more important than exchanging words.

"Tim," her voice was beyond familiar. But refreshing, broke the silence.

" Yes kin?"

"Come lay with me? Please? She echoed in his mind. He heard her hand pat the place beside her. Which was on the opposite side of the room.

"Yes," he rose slowly. His heart began to pound. Taking off his boots before laying himself beside her. He lies resting on his back.

"May I lay on your shoulder?," She asked. Her voice was trembling as it echoed in his mind.

"Of course. Come here," Tim replied, patting his chest.

She pulled herself closer to him and lay on his chest, and he helped a little. The sound of his heartbeat seemed to melt away her sorrows. How can something so simple be so beautiful?

"Michelle is coming up here, please stay."

"As you wish Ms. McCoy," he whispered. Heard a soft chuckle. And knew that despite her skin color she's blushing on the inside.

Three knocks later, Michelle entered the bedroom, " is she awake?"

"Yes, just resting," Tim spoke softly

"Alright I've got to get back downstairs. Here you are," she said, handing him a plastic cup with a wide but also thick straw at the top.

"Thank you Shell," he replied, taking it.

"No problem," she hurried out of the room, she sounded a little more overwhelmed than usual.

Once the door shut, Tim brought the straw to Kinzie's lips. She took a couple of sips then shook her head. "Please don't make me drink any more. Please?" I can't right now." This time her voice wasn't in his head. It sounded much worse. Scratchy and broken.

" Kinzie I will never force you to do anything you don't want to," Tim's voice stirn. He placed the cup on the night table next to him, and pulled her close to his chest.

"Thank you, Tim, " yet again if she had working lungs she would sigh.

"You're welcome. If you'd like we can go to sleep," he suggested. Though he wasn't sure he could sleep much. He would try, for her. Anything for her. She nodded. His heartbeat lulled her to sleep. She wished she had one. So she could remember what it was like to feel it pound. The feeling of the blood pulsing harder making her light headed. Deep down she's grateful. If she did die again, at least she wouldn't be alone.

......*

Michelle exhaled a sigh. *Someone is intentionally messing with Quinn. To get everyone off track. Or so she believes. Someone wants Kinzie dead. But who? She's loved by almost everyone. And anyone who dislikes her is in prison and immortal.*

"Are you alright?" James asked, approaching the living room couch.

"No, I'm exhausted. And someone successfully corrupted Quinn. And has made Kinzie so ill she can't afford to be her stubborn self,"she replied, rubbing her temples.

 James seated himself next to her and began to rub her back, "How long has Quinn been without corruption?"

"If I remember correctly,it was well before our time," Michelle replied, arching her back. Her muscles felt a welcoming warmth.

" Alright. Are we to write the council letter?" He asked, continuing to provide comfort.

" I'm not sure I can, I don't know the language. But how are we going to get it there quickly enough?" Michelle wondered aloud. She leaned into James slowly.

"Momma showed me how to make a portal out of herbs. She always says the earth can provide everything here for us. It is bountiful and rich in many different ways," James replied, Holding her closely.

"Oh James, that's brilliant! I can't believe I forgot about our green house. Usually Kinzie is the one who takes care of it then she'll go into the office before sunrise. Which is why there's no windows," Michelle brought her hands together and tapped her first fingers together.

"That also explains the couches, I'm sure she rests occasionally," James nodded and paused.

" What herbs do you need?" Michelle asked while her finger tapping continued.

" I'll make a small list," James almost rose. Loosening his grip on her waist. Michelle grabbed his arm.

"No, I'll remember. Please, stay," her voice pleased more than she intended. She put her hand to his chest.

"Oh, alright," he seated himself back down, "If I remember correctly, it'll be rosemary, lavender, and erm. There were two or three more. I just can't think of the name," James' eyebrows hardened.

"Do you remember what they look like?" Michelle gave him a hopeful look. He never noticed how beautiful her one green eye was.

" Yes actually, I do," James nodded, "it would help if I could see them."

"Alright. Let's go to the green house. I'll see if Kinzie and Tim are awake so they can join us," Michelle replied happily, pulling away from his warmth.

"Shouldn't she rest?" James asked, remaining seated.

"Yes, she should. But she's the only one that knows where it is. And since it's dark out I can't see anything too well," she felt guilty for even thinking about asking her to join them. But the urgency is high. "I'll be back." She hastened toward the stairs. Her footsteps are as light as always. Once she approached the door she heard Tim's voice.

"Come in, Shell."

She entered, " I'm so sorry to disturb you, but James found a way to create a portal with herbs. But we need to go to the green house. Which means Kinzie would have to show us," her voice trailed off.

"Sure. I'd like that. I may need some help with stability," Kinzie croaked, for once she felt well enough to go somewhere and do something. She's grown tired of resting for so long. So often.

Her sister's voice broke Michelle's heart,"If you're sure. James can assist you since I know nothing about plants."

"I'll join you. I'm curious about this green house. And a cigarette would be lovely," Tim smiled.

"We'll be down in a bit. Thank you Shell," Kinzie Sat up slowly.

"You're welcome," Michelle nodded and exited the room.

Once the door shut, Tim asked, "Kinzie, do you think this a good idea?"

"I don't know. But what I do know is I'm sick of not being myself. And I'm sick of being stuck inside the house," Kinzie stood up.

"Okay. I can understand that. Do you need anything?" Tim asked me to get up also.

"Erm. A brush and my boots please," Tim got up and grabbed the brush off of the dresser, "where are your boots?"

"They're in the closet. I can get them," Kinzie wandered out of the room and came back. She had black leather combat looking boots, black tight jeans, and a red and black plaid shirt on.

"Oh, hello,"Tim smiled.

"Hey," she smiled back. And grabbed the brush from his hand. And brushed her hair into a hair tie, which spiraled down her back, "You ready?"

"Yeah, my tennis shoes are downstairs," Tim smiled. His eyes sparkled.

"What?" Kinzie let out a small laugh.

"You looked beautiful," Tim breathed.

"Thank you," Kinzie replied softly, she looked down and fidgeted with her shirt.

Despite the color of her eyes and her condition, Tim's heart raced.

While Michelle and James waited downstairs, she told him he'll probably be helping Kinzie, Which he shrugged his shoulders to and sat back. Once he heard Tim's footsteps he sat straight up.

"Alright. Are we ready?" Kinzie asked.

"Yep," Michelle replied excitedly.

"What about Quinn?" James asked.

"Oh I'm sure he's fine," Michelle gave a slight wave of her hand, "He could use the rest. I'll leave him a note telling him where we're going."

"Alright, then. Let's go," Kinzie replied, rushing toward the back door.

"What's the rush detective?" Tim asked

"I'm ready to get going. It feels like forever since I've last been out of the house. But you're right I'll slow down," Kinzie stopped.

"I just don't want you to overdo it. It's important we can keep you healthy," Tim replied, lighting a cigarette.

The crisp evening air felt good on Kinzie's skin. Michelle and James exited at the back door once everyone was on the back porch they departed to their journey of going to the greenhouse. The trees were thick and it was very dark. Kinzie had done this a thousand times before. For the most part it was a straight trail. She made it about half way on her own but after a while she paused and rested. Tim pulled her close and insisted that she lean on him.

She accepted his embrace. In the dark it feels like forever traveling somewhere. Kinzie heard Michelle struggling a bit, but wasn't too worried since James was with her. She wished the moon would visit her tonight. This walk reminded her of when she first turned into a vampire.

Her body felt weak and she was stumbling to get help. She knew a place she was going, someone would know Quinn. Or at least would know what to do. Her blood felt as if it were on fire. Her neck was throbbing. It felt as though her body went into paralysis, right outside of the door. Sure enough She heard a familiar voice. Not Quinn, but a woman who knew him well. And who knew her. She couldn't remember her name. But she opened the door as Kinzie's body hit the porch. She attended to her as quickly as possible. And got into a carriage to carry her off somewhere. She didn't know where she was going. But it felt like forever until she heard a voice reassuring her she's safe.

Tim held her up as they climbed over some thick roots. This is where the trees grew taller. Healthy grounds for growing planets. *"Almost there."* Her voice rang in her head.

As they continued Kenzie called "Just a heads up Shell there are a lot of roots, so please be careful. Have James carry you if he has to."

"Thank you for the heads up," Michelle replied, stumbling a bit," Now fully aware of the roots being so thick. Her little sight of the forest and it being pitch black didn't help.

"Would you like me to carry you?" James's voice was soft.

"No thank you. But Could you trade places with Tim please? I need to talk to him," she stopped.

"Sure, I'll be right back," he hastened ahead, "Tim! Tim!" his footsteps approaching quickly

"Yes?" he turned back a little, finding James jogging in his direction.

"Michelle is requesting you and I to switch, she wants a word." James stood patiently

" All right, please take care of her," Tim's voice pleaded more than he intended.

"Of course," James stepped forward

Kinzie welcomed his assistance.

"I'll see you in a few," Tim called.

"Alright!," Kinzie croaked.

......*

Michelle heard running footsteps, "Tim?"

"Yes it's me, what's wrong?" Tim replied, panting a little.

" I'd like to talk to you about my feelings for James, and perhaps maybe I could get your advice or rather your perspective,"Shell fidgeted her fingers.

"Alright, I'm carrying you. I'll give you the option of a piggyback ride or regular way," his voice was firm.

"Piggyback ride," Michelle smiled and giggled.

" All right," Tim turned around and crouched down, "Hop on, take your time."

Michelle wrapped self gently around him

Tim stood up, "So, what did you want to tell me?"

" I think I'm in love. I say 'think' because I haven't felt this way in a long time," Michelle's voice was hopeful and optimistic

"Honestly, Shell, so am I," Tim took a deep breath.

"Awe. Oh my gosh!" Michelle squealed. Tim's ears rang along with a headache.

"Ow," Tim laughed a little," I'm happy for you Shell you deserve this happiness. He seems like he's a great guy."

"He is Tim. He's kind, understanding, gentle, and just so sweet I'm happy it feels effortless you know? No no tension, just pure enjoyment of each other's company but he's so sweet," Michelle let out a soft giggle

"Yep my dear sister, you're in love," Tim smiled big and laughed.

"How do you think Kinzie will react?"Her voice sounded concerned.

"Honestly I think she would be happy for you, she would support you one-hundred-percent, no doubt. What's your connection with James, if you don't mind my asking anyway." Tim's voice was genuine.

"I don't mind you asking. He helped me with my recovery. I stayed with him and his mother for over a year. He has seen the worst of me. Physically he helped me with counting my steps and getting around. He fed me. And encouraged me to be confident despite my appearance after the accident. But I never got the chance to thank him, or tell him how much I love him," Michelle tightened her grip as Tim climbed through a gap in the trees.

"Then you should tell him now. I need to do the same," Tim grunted a little.

"How? Do I just say it?" Michelle's voice lowered. *What if he doesn't feel the same?* She thought.

"Usually I would come up with some smart remarks. But I'm trying to figure that out myself," Tim replied panting.

"Well I would just tell her. I'll do the same with James. But the timing has to be right," she replied smiling. Tim could just hear it.

......*

 "How much farther is the greenhouse?" James asked. He remained silent most of the way.

"Not too much further. Michelle and I own this property. She wanted lots of land and I wanted a green house. So it works well for both of us. I usually enjoy the walk here and taking care of the plants helps me clear my head," Kinzie's voice was raspy and broken sounding than earlier.

"Ah, that makes sense. This journey is quite enjoyable," James smiled.

"Yes, I'm glad. James I can't help but ask, but are you in love with Michelle," she looked up to see the reaction on his face.

His eyes grew brighter and a gentle smile appeared, "Yes. I've been in love with her from the moment I met her," he looked down at Kinzie. His heart swelled. Her eyes. They were sad, and looked worse from the descriptions given to him earlier. The dark circles under her eyes made her look ancient. The look of a young girl ready to be strong again. The same look Michele had.

"I'm quite certain she loves you too. She has that sparkle in her eye when she sees you," Kinzie smiled.

"Yes, I see the same when you look at Tim," he grinned.

"Oh yeah. I've liked him for a while now. I just haven't had the opportunity to tell him," Kinzie stopped, gesturing her arm," Here we are."

James looked up. The entry doors were stain-glass, purple and blue. Diamond shapes. One wall on either side. The walls spread 3 feet before connecting to the walls which expanded almost 6 feet. Those walls connect to an additional six feet . Then the remaining will begin the building, which connects to either side. There were surrounding trees, with a variety of fruits.

"It's beautiful," James spoke softly.

"Thank you," Kinzie replied, removing herself from his support and waking independently. While doing so she removed a key from her pocket. Leaning in the glass she opened the door. James not too far behind her. He noticed the key looked old fashioned. It has a four leaf clover at the end, with two teeth. And was almost three inches long.

"Is everything you have custom made?" James asked.

"Yes. I never purchase anything with poor quality. I'm also very picky about what I buy," she replied entering her safe haven. There was a set of benched one on either side of the walls. She seated herself.

James followed her inside," Seems like a lot of money," he paused," Oh! I'm so sorry this isn't any of my business."

Kinzie let out a light laugh, " I appreciate your acknowledgement, but I couldn't care less about people knowing how much money I have. I know people are curious about how I'm so young and I can afford expensive cars. And not to mention people want to know where I live," she crossed her legs.

"Thank you for your forgiveness," James' voice trailed off. He remained in awe of her green -house. She grew everything or so it seemed. Green peppers, red peppers, onions, carrots, potatoes, tomatoes, and practically any produce you can think of.

"I also have a pear tree, an apple tree, and a peach tree," Kinzie's voice wasn't getting any better.

"My my Ms. McCoy, you could run your own supermarket," Tim said as he entered.

"Indeed," Michelle breathed.

James walked through the greenhouse. The other side of the green house had herbs, and flowers. He found the five ingredients he needed, "I found them," James smiled as he picked the plants.

"Great, we should get back to the house. I don't want to run the risk of Kinzie getting hurt," Tim announced.

"And we need to check on Quinn," Michelle nodded in agreement.

"Alright, let's go," James said, ingredients in hand.

"There's a basket in that corner," Kinzie pointed, knowing the struggle of carrying ingredients and losing some along the way.

"Oh,Thank you," James hastened, "Alright, I'm ready."

Michelle went with James ,and Tim helped her up, "Let's go,"he whispered.

"Yes, let's," Kinzie nodded.

Kinzie felt a small glimmer of hope, glad James found a way to get a letter to the council. Finding out James is in love with Michelle for who she is. And listening to her still heart and telling someone she loves Tim. Now she needs to tell him. But she doesn't want to hurt him any more than he already is. But maybe it would ease his pain? Either way, now is beautiful. Things are taking place. At last. Little did Kinzie know while James grabbed the basket she added some extra ingredients so he could try and make a potion he looked up for vampires.

Chapter Six

Quinn opened his eyes to find himself in Kinzie's office. He sat up, in doing so his head began to pound. *What happened?* He thought. His veins felt as though they were fuelled with fire, "No, Good Lord. What have I done?"

The last time he felt this way he almost killed a whole town. This was before Kinzie and Michelle were born, "Oh dear," he stood and wandered to the kitchen. He set up the tea kettle and continued to drown in his guilt. The house was quiet. He assumed everyone was asleep. He hoped he didn't harm anyone. The tea kettle squealed, making him jump. He let out a small cry of surprise, and sighed.

"How could I do this? How was I triggered after so many years? Whoever it was, they're powerful. Magic like that takes years of training. That specific spell takes lots of energy. To accomplish resurfacing the beast I've spent so long putting away, is truly and undoubtedly fearing." He thought to himself while finishing his tea. Mug in hand he went back to the office as he continued to look at the archives. He paused and looked at the photo on Kinzie's desk

"I promised I would care for their well-being. And I have failed. But I swear on my life, I will mend my mistakes," his voice cracked. He took a deep breath and exhaled a sigh. The girls are like daughters. They're both strong and oh so intelligent. But how are they going to get the letters to the council in time?

The back door opened and a flood of voices came into the house, " I wonder if Papa's awake," Michelle said.

"Yes, I'm in here," he called.

"Oh goody!" She smiled, "Did you see my note?"

"No, my dear. I just opened my eyes not long ago," he replied, sipping his tea.

"Well James found a way to get the letter to the council, so we had to go to the green house and get some supplies," Michelle and the others entered the office.

"That's great news!" He smiled.

He turned to Kinzie, "It's good to see you standing."

"Thank you. I'm glad to be standing," she gave a corner smile.

"How do you feel?" He asked.

"I'm not better yet. But this is progress," she turned to Tim, "I think we should start heading upstairs. I'm a little tired from our small journey."

"Wise idea. Good night my dear," Quinn breathed in relief.

"Good night, Papa," she replied, grabbing Tim's hand and exiting the room.

Quinn waited till they got further up the stairs before speaking, "James, by chance did you get any other supplies for our friend?"

"Yes sir, I did," James nodded, "I'm going to go get started on the portal. Michelle, I could use your assistance."

"Oh, okay," she replied, surprised and walking with him out to the kitchen.

"I certainly hope this potion works for Kinzie. I'm sure she needs the relief as much as we do," Quinn thought to himself. He pulled out a pen and a piece of paper and started on the letter. The house is quite perfect for Kinzie to get some sleep.

Michelle sat at the dining room table as James stirred the potion. It had been a while since anyone had made a sound. As she heard the pot boil it reminded her of when she stayed with

James, and his mother. Back then she had lots of soup and tea. So the sound of boiling water was comforting. She couldn't count how many times she cried because her family was gone and she had no idea where Kinzie was. And James sat with her and held her close. Changed her bandages and helped her see the brighter side of things. She never thought she'd see him again. James looks over to her wondering what she's thinking about. Quinn entered the kitchen breaking the long silence, announcing he finished the letter. James nodded and told Quinn the potion is almost done. Everyone's voice sounded drained.

"Alright. Quinn I'm going to chant, which will open the portal. While I'm chanting you must name the place two times. Once you see the place appear, place the letter in the center of the portal and the portal will close," James said, putting the ingredients into a large bowl that was waiting on the counter.

Michelle knew what to do, James warned her earlier that it wouldn't kill him but it would take a good majority of his energy. She nodded in understanding.

"Get ready Quinn," James said before closing his eyes and beginning to chant.

Quinn stood ready. A cloud appeared in a spiral about the bowl," Vrykolas Kidea," he said said softly, " Vrykolas Kidea " The clouds formed into a large city. Multiple small buildings resting below a castle. Quinn places the letter in the center, which withdrew itself in the portal. The clouds dispersed into smoke.

"Fascinating, " Quinn breathed. He didn't even notice Michelle standing behind him, until she asked for help with getting James on the couch. He placed himself underneath James's underarm. They helped him to the couch. Once they got him on the couch and comfortable, Michelle told Quinn she'd stay with him. And Quinn went back to the office.

......*

James wandered through a foggy moonlit forest. Feeling as though he's seen. This place before. *What year is this? And where is this place?* He continued walking. The trees grew thick at the roots, which he claimed effortlessly through. Since he's lived in the mountains all his life, and a traveler. After a few minutes passed he ended up out of the woods to find the old McCoy house. A man stood admiring the house back toward James.

"Excuse me sir, who are you?" James's voice is smooth.

"I hope you know who I am," he turned to face him. He had long salt and pepper hair braided on either side of his shoulders. His voice sounded like home.

"*Dad?*" James breathed.

" Yes! I know you probably don't remember me," he paused, "Not well. I mean."

"I remember your voice," James exhaled.

"Ah I'm glad," he smiled, "do you know why you're here?"

"No," James shook his head.

"You're looking for answers. I noticed you opened a portal."

"Yes my good friend's sister is ill,"James cleared his throat.

"She's immortal," his father started to pace, "and she's a vampire?"

"Yes, how do you know all this?" James replied, raising a brow.

"I'm in your head James. Whatever information you retain I'm able to access from your consciousness."

"Hmm. Interesting," James blurted.

"And I know you've been wondering two things. How Kinzie is sick, and how Michelle has lived this long if she's mortal. Correct?"

"Yes," James paused," could you help us?"

"Certainly I have contacts in different places," his father nodded.

"Thank you," James sighed.

"You're welcome my son," he began to turn and walk away, "I'll return when I have more information. Until then, stay safe."

James looked down for just a moment, only to find his father gone. The house lifted and slowly started to fade away.

James Jerked forward his eyes , *"Of course it was a dream..."* he thought. He wanted nothing more in the world than to see his father again. But that's the truest hurt to reality. Just because someone is buried doesn't mean you can't miss them. But don't burden yourself with the could be, could have, and would have. Despite the throbbing pain in his heart, he was happy to see his father in a better place. Though it would be nice if it lasted a little longer.

He looked around the room to find Michelle curled up in a worn leather armchair close to him. She had a black and red checkered knit blanket over her legs. Her head lay rested on a pillow. Her eyepatch was off. There wasn't much to see. Except for burns that enclosed where her eye would be. All that was left was a small hole where her eye would be. *"It healed well,"* his voice rang. He knew she used the eye patch for comfort. Both visually and self consciously. Her breath is slow and steady. Her red hair reached past her shoulder blades. *"She's so beautiful. Always has been,"* He thought to himself while laying back down. Closing his eyes, his heart filled with hope to see his father again. And of course reality being what it is, he didn't. At least not yet.

......*

Tim's eyes snapped open. A blanket still resting over him. Kinzie still lay resting. It appears as though she hadn't moved. At all.

"Kinzie?" Tim whispered softly.

She still lay silently. Too still for comfort, *"Maybe she's still asleep? Oh God I can't check her pulse! What time is it?"* He checked his watch, *"Wait."* Taking a few deep breaths he thought it best not to wake her. Instead he turned to his side and rubbed her back or started stroking her hair.

She remained still for hours. Tim rose, *"I need to get Quinn."* Careful not to let any sunlight in the room. He went to the office and knocked on the door, "Quinn?"

"Come in Timothy," Quinn's voice called.

He entered," I'm concerned. Kinzie isn't responding. I'm not sure if she's asleep or what. I don't know how to explain it. I feel like something is wrong."

"All right. I'll look her over. I keep failing to remember that you don't know how to look over a vampire," he shuffled out of the room, Tim followed.

"Gee, thanks old man. Not like I feel useless already or anything," Tim thought to himself and sighed quietly. He has high respect for Quinn, and much appreciation for his care for Kinzie and Michelle. Tim took a deep breath and exhaled, clearing his negative thoughts. Maybe Quinn can teach him how to care for her, or Michelle.

They reached the bedroom. Quinn swift and silent, reached her side of the bed. Tim seated himself on the other side. Quinn gently picked up her arm and looked closely.

"What are you looking for?" Tim. Blurted.

"To see if any of her veins are enlarged, and puffing out of the skin, if so she needs to feed," Quinn cleared his throat. He gently lifted her eyelid, "Oh, Lord.".

"What is it?" Tim's heart skipped a beat.

" Her eye color is much more severe. We've got to get James and Michelle. They need to get started in the potion for her," Quinn breathed.

"I'll get them," Tim started to rise.

"No, allow Me. Stay her with her," Quinn replied and quickly exited the room.

Lingering in suspense while Quinn spoke with Michelle, and James. It's similar to waiting in the hospital room waiting for the doctor to return with the test results and thinking the worst. Michelle came up to the bedroom and looked at her eyes herself. She gasped, "This is bad. Very bad "

"Please tell me what's happening," Tim blurted. His voice sounded a lot more harsh than intended.

"She's getting worse, Tim," Michelle's voice barely audible.

"How much worse?" Tim breathed.

"In her case, and circumstance. She would be considered in a coma if she were human," Michelle replied quietly. "I'm going to go down and help James with the potion," Michelle excused herself and exited out of the room.

Tim's throat started to swell. He's anything but angry. The woman he loves most is sick as ever. And he can do nothing. Simply nothing. All he can do is hope the fighter in her continues fighting. And no one else gets hurt.

......*

Kinzie's headache. She couldn't reply. Or open her eyes. A mental block came between her and Tim. Maybe she can connect with her sister. Connect with *anyone*! Just so she can tell someone she's not asleep or dead. Searching for an aura while Tim was emotional was difficult. Her heart too ached. She didn't want anyone to worry. "*Come on focus,*" her thoughts rang. She felt a familiar aura. She entered through as if it were a door.

"Hello?" Kinzie whispered

"Kin?" Michelle's voice echoed back.

"*Yes, thank* God, *are you with Tim and the others?*"

"*No, but Tim and Quinn and I checked in you and I. Assisting James with your potion. Do you want me to get Tim? Maybe I can speak to him for you.*"

"*Yes, Please.* "

Michelle turned to James," Kinzie managed to contact me. She wants me to go talk to Tim."

"Alright. Thank you for your help Shelly. I'll see you when you come back," James gave a small smile.

Michelle returned the smile and made her way upstairs. So grateful for James being understanding.

She entered the bedroom, " Hey," she said softly

She found Tim in the bed resting with her. He had pulled her closely. And stroking her hair, "Hey." He replied softly.

"Kinzie contacted me. She was trying to get to you but she couldn't. But she asked me to come speak to you."

"Okay," Tim continued to stroke her hair. It's so soft.

"She's having temporary paralysis. But she's alright. She's saying for some reason her connection with you is blocked, but thank you. For bringing her comfort," Michelle paused, "she also wants me to remind you to be strong. She can do this. She just needs you to be strong too. Once you're calm. She may be able to contact you again."

Tim nodded, "Thank you, Kin."

"I'm sorry, Tim," Michelle said softly.

"No need to be sorry, K-"

"She's not saying that, I am," Michele approached and sat in the chair, "You've been. Through a lot. But so has she. She's been through hell and back. But she still pushes forward to be a better person."

"What has she been through?" Tim asked. Hoping he can put his mind at ease.

"That's up for her to tell you. She's stronger than she looks. Trust me. I'm hoping the potion will help with a lot of what's happening. I'm also going to see if she can eat. Maybe that will reverse," Michelle sighed, " You know I've been thinking. Maybe we should have you and her sleep in your room downstairs. So she can be closer to the office and the living room."

"I think that's a wonderful idea," Tim forced a smile, " I know she'd like that a lot."

" Alright. I know we have extra curtains to sun proof the windows," Michelle paused abruptly, " Kinzie says to go back to your apartment and find any clues. And when you get back, tell her about them."

"Leave? I can't just leave, I don't want to leave you like this," he replied looking down at her expecting her eyes to be open. But they still remind me. Almost lifeless.

"She knows you don't want to. But since this is going to take a while, she wanted to remind you about your cat. And she said maybe you could pack some extra clothes and just let your landlord know you're going on a trip," Michelle's tone remained calm.

"Oh crap! I almost completely forgot about him!" Tim let out a sigh," Alright. Tell you what. After the potion is finished and we move you downstairs I will go to my apartment, and do ask you to ask."

"She says thank you," Michelle rose.

" You're welcome."

"Alright. I will be back, I'm going to see if she'll eat," Michelle went to exit the room.

"Wait Michelle. Won't she choke or something?" Tim's voice sounded curious and concerned.

"No. Not that I enjoy saying this, but she's a vampire. If she's thirsty, she'll drink even though she can't control her own body. Because her body depends on that specific nutrient to survive.

And believe me, she doesn't enjoy it," she said while walking out of the room.

This is the most human Kinzie has ever felt. Since she turned. It took well over a year to adjust to behaving like a mortal. When she first turned she was brought to one of the largest covens known in the vampire community. The headmaster was kind. And so was everyone else. The only one she had a problem with was the headmaster's right hand man. General William. He would threaten someone within the coven and when the head master confronted him. He denied everything and always tried putting the blame on someone else. At some point Kinzie took his place. She still remembers the hatred that grew and one day he left. Little did she know, he would return. Kinzie's energy is fading fast. Then Michelle came in, with the cup, and straw, and handed it to Tim. He put the straw to her lips. Her lips wrapped around tightly and she started to drink.

"That's a good sign," Michelle nodded.

"It is? How so?"

"It means that she needed to 'eat'. And now there's a good chance that she'll get her strength back and be able to communicate. It'll help give her energy. Same concept with us eating the right foods," Michelle seated herself down again, " I'm really glad you're here Tim. She needs you, just as much as you need her."

"Some days it doesn't seem like it," he said, still holding the cup, Kinzie still continued drinking.

"Well it's true. Just because she acts like nothing is wrong doesn't mean that's the case. Most times she doesn't want to talk because she's just not ready," Michelle looked at Kinzie waiting. The straw provided a loud protest.

"Good call shell," Kinzie croaked.

"Kin!" Tim said smiling.

"Hey, love," Kinzie smiled," how long is that potion?".

"It's going to take a while. Since it's such a complex potion, maybe eight hours or so," Michelle replied standing, " So that being said I'm going to go see if James needs help."

"Thank you shell," Kinzie croaked again. Her voice was raspy and terrible.

"Well at least I can have a few hours with you," Tim said, playing with her hair.

"Yes, and I'm so glad," her voice was weak.

"Me too. Save your voice, hon. Please…" Tim pleaded more than he intended.

She nodded, "*Do you remember the day we met?*"

"How could I forget?" Tim said, letting out a soft chuckle.

The night they met Kinzie, was working a case. She was in the office taking notes and looking at evidence. Tim had just joined the. He had transferred from another unit. Kinzie paused and Rose from her seat. She walked over to him, "You're my new partner?" She reached out to shake his hand.

Tim nodded, " Yes, Timothy Bryte," he replied shaking her hand.

" Kinzie McCoy," she smiled. His red hair was spiked, green eyes held her gaze.

"Do you mind if I call you Mac? It's just a buddy of mine back home his name's McCoy," he let go of her hand.

"Sure. You'd be the only one who calls me that. Everyone calls me Kin. But I like it," She let out a soft chuckle. Her hair was down around her shoulders. And her smile made his heart throb.

He cleared his throat, " So what are you working on now?"

"Oh, well," she started walking over to her desk, her heels clicking on the floor, " There have been several homicides in the

local area. M.O is the same but the victims are different. No preference in male or female. It's always one gunshot wound to the head, execution style. And all of the victims have drugs in their system."

"What's your theory?" Tim crossed his arms. That was back when he had both hands. He wore a suit and tie.

"Well I was thinking all the local gangs in the area or drug dealers had some sort of argument. So they're punishing them or there's a war on our streets and we need to clean it up," she locked eyes with them.

" Alright, well done. Keep up the good work," he nodded and turned around. Impressive, she found the what, why, and who. She's incredible.

"Do you remember the first day I came to your house?" Tim smiled.

"Oh yes, how could I forget that?"

"Are you kidding me?" Kinzie said, rushing over to her car, "Dammit!" She pulled out her cellphone, " Hey, I'm probably

going to be home late. No, no, Shell I'm fine. I got two flats on the car, and I need to find a cab home and I have to find an shop a-"

"Everything okay?" Tim asked while approaching.

"No, I have two flats on the car. And I've gotta find a cab. Hold on Shelly, Mr. Bryte is here."

"Please don't ever call me by my last name again. And why don't I take you home?"

"Erm. Well it's far away. And, my sister is kinda shy about strangers. What was that? Oh okay. Sure. I'll see you in a bit," Kinzie hung up.

"She encouraged you to take the ride didn't she?"

Kinzie nodded, " Yep."

" Does she want to see how cute I am? Or does she want you home safe?"

" Probably both," Kinzie laughed.

"Alright then. This way," he gestured to his car.

They walked further down a parking lot, "how far do you live?"

" About two hours," Kinzie replied, digging through her purse.

" Two hours?" Tim replied, unlocking his truck.

"Yes. I told you I live far away," she got in the passenger seat, "Here's a hundred dollars for gas."

"Erm why?" Tim asked, turning the truck over.

"Because this is a 2002 Ford F150 and the gas mileage is garbage. And I don't want to feel guilty for having you drive two hours to my house, because of a mistake I made," she replied, removing the money from her wallet.

"And what mistake is that?" Tim asked, putting the truck in reverse.

"Ermm. Well I may or may not have been speeding to get to work on some sharp rocks knowing my tires were balding," she smiled.

"Alright well, thank you for the gas, and your honesty," Tim chuckled, "Do you mind if I smoke?"

"Do you mind me giving you a hundred dollars?"

"Hell no," Tim laughed.

"All right then. That's your answer. By the way, Michelle is going to make you something to eat so if you're hungry don't even worry," Kinzie smiled. Hoping she knew she was just playing with him.

He made many more visits and was welcomed into the family. They've worked together for more than 3 years.

"I should probably rest," Kinzie said, moving her hand up to hold his face.

"Alright," he replied, kissing her forehead. He's not not tired. Since he woke up earlier. But he doesn't mind holding Kinzie while she sleeps.

Time continued to wander. Quinn lingering in the office trying to find answers. James in the kitchen. And Michelle rummaging through the basement. It was so quiet. A great atmosphere for Michelle to set up Tim's room. Findinding the sun proof curtains she let out a victory dance and started making her way up to the room. James telling her the potions are done. The sun is so close to going down. Michelle quickly finished hanging the curtains and went to the kitchen. And started making Kinzie's drink, and giving it to James to mix in. He poured a little over a tablespoon of the mixture in the cup, and Michelle turned to make her way upstairs. When she knocked no one gave a response, she opened the door ever so slightly. What she found sent her heart into a flutter. Kinzie lay on Tim's chest and Tim's arm curling around her holding her closely. Michelle can't help it, quietly pulling her out her phone and taking a picture. Then walked over to Tim, giving him the potion.

"Oh, awesome! Thanks Shell!" He said, taking out of her hand and gently nudging Kinzie awake.

Kinzie letting out a groan opened one eye,"Hmm?"

"I need you to drink this,"Tim said, struggling to get up or move. Kinxe had him locked into place. Michelle took the potion from Tim's hand and put it to her lips. Instantly Kinzie started to drink.

"I got the room ready downstairs, so when it's dark enough we can move her," Michelle spoke softly.

Tim nodded, "I'm glad. Thank you Shell."

"What's with that sparkle in your eye Tim?" Michelle smiled.

"I'm relieved, because maybe there's a slight chance she's going to feel better. And we were talking about how we first met and the first day I came over," he said as his smile got bigger.

"I'm relieved too. She deserves peace. She's suffered long enough," Michelle replied, still holding the cup and straw. Kinzie pulled away and licked her lips.

"Can we see your eyes?" Tim asked, looking down.

She did so looking around, locking eyes with Tim. Her irises were blue once again and around her eyes looked like light pink. Then she and Michelle locked eyes.

"Much better," she said smiling, "So we'll wait till the sun goes down to switch you downstairs. In the meantime I'll pick out some clothes for you to wear." Michelle replied with a wide smile. Relief filled her heart and she exited and closed the door behind her.

" I don't want to go anywhere," Tim said, sighing.

"I know but your poor cat is lonely," Kinzie chuckled.

"What am I doing to drive to get there?" Tim asked

"My Honda, I use it for long road trips. It's in the backyard underneath some trees. The key is in the hall closet behind the coats," Kinzie closed her eyes again and lay her head on his chest.

"Ah okay. Interesting place to put them, but smart," He sighed.

"Thank you," Kinzie said, even though her voice sounded less horse-like.

Tim nodded. Though his reluctance to leave grows larger. He's relieved to know Kinzie is feeling better. Everyone knows that feeling of being sick as a dog, and not being able to function normally. He's fully aware that she'll be safe. She's in great hands. But for the first time ever. He felt good and comfortable by a woman's side. That didn't make him feel incomplete, or incompetent. Even when he was going through his physical therapy, she knew his capabilities. She pushed him in a healthy way. Stayed up late to make sure he got all the comfort he needed. And Michelle had to take over a time or two so Kinzie could rest up.

It only felt like ten minutes before Michelle came back and told Tim and Kinzie it's dark. Tim sighed, *"Do you want me to carry you, or would you like to try on your own?"*

Kinzie's voice echoed, *"I'd like to be carried if you don't mind. I don't want to push myself too hard."*

Tim smiled, *"That's my girl, I've got you."* He sat up and pulled her close. Kinzie wrapping her arms tightly around his neck. He picked her up and let his feet touch the floor. Michelle stood aside and shut the door behind them. In her head she was squealing, she found Tim and Kinzie's attraction so adorable. And the fact that he managed a way to carry her and support her. They made it down stairs once Kinzie got comfortable, Tim kissed her on the forehead and made his way toward the front door. His heart couldn't help but sink to the pit of his stomach. But he grabbed the keys to the car anyway and exited out the front door. The moonlight helped him see he made his way to the trees. He found the car underneath the tarp and pulled it off revealing the 2010 Honda Civic Hybrid. Jet black and custom leather seats on the inside. Fortunately it's an automatic engine. Which Tim sighed and thanked the Stars for. He started the engine which let out a soft pur. Despite the fact she hasn't traveled in months Kinzie kept this car in good shape. The gas gauge shows that the tank is full. Tim put the car into drive and headed toward the city not able to shake a bad feeling in his gut.

Michelle lingered in the living room, sitting on the couch. James entered and sat next to her, "Are you alright?"

"Yes, I'm just tired,"she said, nodding.

"You need to rest," He replied, locking eyes with her.

"I know, it's hard for me," She said, not taking her eye off of him. James moved closer and put his arm around her. Her heart began to pound.

"Michelle, you spend all of your time helping everyone else. Let someone help you. You deserve to be taken care of,"his voice gently.

"I haven't found anyone immortal to spend a life with," she stammers.

"You found me," he said, putting his hand on her cheek.

"I love you," she replied with a soft whisper.

"I've loved you since I saw you,"James whispered back. Michelle let down a tear. James wiped it away with his thumb, and pulled her close to his chest. She tilted her head up, and James leaned in for a kiss. Her heart beat swelling in her ears. His lips are warm and full of life. Grateful she feels the love for him freely. No more secrets. No more holding back. Just living and bringing peace and livelihood back to Kinzie. In that moment hope grew.

Chapter Seven

As Tim continued to drive. He couldn't help but hope that his cat is alright. Tim's cat is an orange tabby. Mischievous but loveable. He loved laying on his neck when he's laying on his side. The name Felix came to mind, when he looked at him. They've been inseparable ever since. Tim knew Felix was going to be pissed as hell. So he figured he'd drop by the pet store and pick up and get him his favorite treat. Sighing, Tim prepared himself for anything. After what feels like forever. He arrived outside of his apartment complex. The feeling in the pit of his stomach started growing.

His apartment complex wasn't fancy, just a brick building, five stories tall. With a few others around it. The bricks are a lighter tone with the windows and doors white. His apartment is on the first floor. It was unusually quiet this time of day. Normally people would hurry out the door and hop in their cars rushing to work. Maybe even take the kids to school. He got out and approached the security door, the bag of cat treats around his wrist. After he entered the safety door, a feeling of dread overwhelmed his stomach. He continued down the 5 small steps and turned to the left. He pulled out his keys and turned the lock slowly. Taking a deep breath he opened the door, "Felix," he called ,"here kitty."

A meow came from the kitchen. Tim exhaled a breath of relief as he shut the door behind him and went to the kitchen. He knelt down on the floor. Felix came up and started rubbing himself on Tim's leg and letting out a pur. Tim put the treats down and pet Felix, "How would you like to go on a road trip?" Felix paused looking up, and meowed.

"Yeah?" Tim smiled," okay, let me pack a few things and I'll be back." He opened the pack of treats and set 2 down on the floor. He carried the rest with him to pack. He went to the hall closet and grabbed a small bag. He packed as many clothes as he could fit into the suitcase. Grabbed Felix's bed, and emptied the litter box. He grabbed the cat litter and brought everything into the kitchen. He packed Felix's cat food and bowls. He didn't care about anything else. He just wants to get back to Kinzie, "Well I think that's everything," Tim said, pulling everything toward the door. Felix jumped up on the couch and sat down.

"Whatcha doing buddy?"Tim asked looking at Felix and noticed a folded note on the glass coffee table.

"Felix, was someone here?" Tim asked. Felix meowed and purred. He knew that meant yes.

"No wonder you're not pissed at me," he said, walking over and picking up the note.

" Dear Mr. Bryte,
What a lovely home you have. I must admit I didn't expect to see myself writing to you, or being in your home. But things change. Plans change. Since you're a detective, I will give you a hint on what's happening now. One word, it starts with a letter 'B'. I'd best be going now. Your vampire friend won't be doing so well by the time you read this. I suggest you hurry."

Tim crumpled the piece of paper in his fist and shoved it into is pocket, "Come on Felix, let's go on a road trip,"

He picked up the back and placed all the other things on top of the back. Fleix jumped off the couch and followed him closely. After locking up he hurried out the car. Felix is still close behind. Once he got everything in the back seat, he opened the door and Felix jumped in. Tim got in after him," Okay you know the rules no jumping and no scratching."

Felix meowed.

"That's a good boy," Tim said, starting the car and throwing it in reverse. *"I'm going back to you, Kinzie."*

Tim didn't even bother calling his unit. They'd look at him as if he were crazy. Not that they already do. But that was not his taunt.

That was also a note clarifying someone's out there hurting Kinzie. And the letter 'B'. It might be for the beginning. It could also be burn. Or Brand. The killer is confessing the murders of these women. Tim continued thinking on the drive home.

......*

Michelle sat with Kinzie waiting for Tim's return. She felt refreshed after her nap. James will lay resting in the living room. Even though it's eight in the morning. That potion helped her so far, but hopefully she feels better. The house was quiet and still for now. But it's moments like this where she wished she could read. A perfect silence for concentration.

"Michelle," Kinzie's voice punctured the silence.

"Yes, I'm here," she replied softly.

"Is Tim back yet?"

"No, not yet. But I'm sure he'll be here soon," Michelle reassured her.

"Ah, okay,"she said, her voice sounding sad.

"What's the matter?" Michelle asked, getting up in front of the chair and seating herself next to her sister.

" Something isn't right. He seems upset. His energy changed all of a sudden."

"I'm sure we can ask him when he gets home or he'll tell us right away," Michelle replied, playing with Kinzie's hair.

"I know. I'm just worried," Kinzie put her head in Michelle's lap.

"I know hon, I know. And that's okay. It just shows you care. I know he feels the same way about you," Michelle replied, continuing to stroke her hair.

Kinzie's thoughts began to drown her emotions. She groaned in pain. It felt like her insides had hot pins and needles, poking from the inside out, "Can a girl catch a break?" Kinzie let out a cry.

"Kinzie what's wrong?" Michelle froze.

"Everything hurts," she replied as tears fell down her face.

Quinn hurried into the room and Michelle moved out of the way," Are you hot?" He asked.

Kinzie shook her head, "Pain, pins. Needles." Her cries became louder. James appeared next," What's happening?"

"James. Get some of the potion and mix it into a drink for Kinzie, please." Michelle responded quickly.

James nodded and hurried into the kitchen.

"Papa it hurts so bad," Kinzie cried

"I know sweety, I know," Quinn stroked her hair. Trying his best to help her keep calm.

"It feels like that time you found me. You know? In the caves."

"I'm so sorry. Do you want me to call Timothy? Find out where he is?"

"Yes... Please," Kinzie nodded. Her tears got heavier.

Quinn pulled out his cell phone and dialed Tim's number. One ring, "Hello?" Tim answered.

"Yes Timothy, how close are you to the house?"

"I'm almost to the main road. Why?"

"Kinzie needs you. She's in a lot of pain. Make haste."

"You got it," the line cut off.

"Quinn is Tim on his way?" Kinzie asked, her voice shaking.

"Yes, didn't you hear him?"

"Quinn, is he on his way?"

Quinn used his finger as if it was a pen and wrote, Y-E-S on her arm.

Kinzie nodded and cried harder. Burn marks appeared on her skin.

"Where is that coming from?" Quinn blurted.

Tim opened the front door and hurried to the bedroom, "Quinn, run some cold water! Quick!"

Quinn got up and rushed to the bathroom. The faucet came on the second Tim walked into the room Kinzie picked up his cent, "Tim." Her cries continued.

"I've gotcha, I've gotcha. Come on, let's get you in the tub," Tim picked her up. And carried her to the tub. Once she was submerged. The burn marks were gone.

He turned around, "What the hell happened?"

" We don't know, Tim. All we know is she was in pain and that the burn marks appeared," Michelle replied softly.

" I'm sorry for shouting or sounding harsh. But I found a note on my coffee table. I'll show you that in a sec. But first let me get my cat and other things from the car. I'll be back," Tim sighed and exited the bathroom

"Kinzie are you alright?" Quinn asked.

"No, but I'm better than I was. I'm in a lot less pain."

"Alright. Well, I'll wait here until Timothy gets back. Then I'll leave you two alone," Quinn replied with a Dad tone.

Tim came back in," Come on Felix, I want you to meet someone." Felix, entered the house and followed Tim to the bedroom.

Michelle beamed, "Awe! He's so cute!"

"Yes, Shelley, this is Felix."

"Nice to meet you Felix," Michelle smiled at him.

The cat meowed and looked up at Tim, "Alright buddy. This way,"Tim led him to the bathroom.

"Kinzie," Tim approached the tub, " This is Felix." The cat approached the tub.

"Awe. He's cute." Kinzie gave a slight smile. Quinn excused himself and took Michelle with him.

"Did we do something wrong?" Tim asked.

"No, he's just giving us our time alone," Kinzie replied, closing her eyes.

Tim went into the bedroom, and unpacked. After he was done he grabbed some of Kinzie's clothes, and walked back into the bathroom. He found Felix laying on the floor and watching Kinzie. She lay in the tub, with her eyes closed.

"Kin, are you asleep?"

"No," she replied," just resting my eyes.".

"Are you cool enough?" He asked, his voice filled with concern.

"Yes," she said softly, "Could you help me, please?"

"Sure. Felix, go ahead and explore," He replied looking down at Felix.

Felix got up and walked out of the bathroom. Tim got closer to the bathtub and pulled Kinzie up. He held his arm out and Kinzie stepped down and noticed the clothes, "Thank you for bringing those in by the way."

"No problem. Do you want me to wait in the bedroom while you change?"

"If you don't mind," Kinzie nodded

Tim shook his head," No I don't mind." He gave her a kiss on the cheek and left.

It's strange, twenty minutes ago she was in excruciating pain. But now it still hurts like hell. But it's tolerable. Barely. Her clothes are now soaked.She began to get more curious as to why these attacks are happening. And why is it so harsh? Why is someone attacking her? And who is attacking her? Why couldn't she hear for a short time? Whoever it is, it's personal. She peeled off her clothes and wrapped herself in a towel, and drained the tub. She grabbed another towel and wiped the water up off the floor. This is the most productive she's been in a while. She dried her hair and the rest of her body. And put on her clothes and grabbed her hair brush before leaving she rang the clothes out in the tub. She came out to find Tim and Felix on the bed, "Feel better?" He asked.

"Yeah, I guess. I have more energy than before and strength," Kinzie stretched herself on the bed next to him.

"Well that's good. Michelle dropped off some more potion for you," he said, grabbing the cup off the nightstand next to him.

"Thank you," she said with a slight smile. And took the cup, and drank. He fangs digging into her gums. The potion didn't taste the best. But it helped. She didn't notice but Tim was watching her this whole time. Usually she'd have home turned away. But he didn't care. All he wants is for her to feel better. After she was done drinking she put herself closer to Tim. He wrapped his arm around her and Felix moved to the edge of the bed. Kinzie apologized, and Felix gave a soft meow.

She told Tim about a cat that occasionally appears, and checks in. An all black cat by the name of Luna. They always have cat food at the ready. And occasionally they'll feed her some salmon or tuna. Tim already knew that cat was a happy one. They go crazy for some fresh fish. He asked Kinzie if she's tired. She shook her head and told him she doesn't want to sleep anymore. Which is understandable. Because all she does is sleep. She admitted she wanted to spend more time with Tim. Tim blushed a little and asked what she wanted to do. All she wants to do is talk. Anything to keep her mind off the events happening.

Most of the time Tim tried to bring up cases they could reminisce. Which was a lot. Until at last Kinzie could rest. Quinn entered the room to find her eyes closed at last.

"I'm so sorry you had to witness that Tim," His voice was filled with sympathy.

"No apology is necessary, Quinn. I love her, so I'm going to stay no matter what. As matter of fact if I recall correctly you requested that I do," Tim gave a smile, looked down at her and stroked her hair.

"I can see very clearly that you love her immensely. I also recall that conversation, thank you," Quinn smiled back. He was relieved to see that Kinzie found someone who accepted her for who she is. Truthfully he never thought she'd find someone because she is occupied most of the time with work and other things. However they do make such a great couple. And with that Quinn announced he was going to the office. And Tim nodded in understanding.

It took Quinn a moment to get there, but he made it. He too was weak from the lack of sleep, which everyone is suffering at the moment. Just out of pure concern. Though Quinn appreciated the fact that Tim stayed with Kinzie. And he knew Michelle felt the same way. He continued to look through the archives and still found nothing. The weight of his promise grew heavier. It was at that moment, Michelle knocked on the door and fed him dinner. Mashed potatoes, pork chops, and green beans with mushrooms that looked to be cooked and seasoned nicely. She sat on one of the couches, and stayed nearby, keeping him company. They talked for a little while and Michelle insisted she help look over the archives. Meanwhile James was in the kitchen cleaning.

Another long evening came before them. As they read and journeyed into the unknown.

Chapter Eight

Quinn decided this was a good time to go and get another opinion. And maybe even some answers. Being his age he knew many people with many specialities. Before leaving, he left a note in the vampire language for Kinzie before he left. Michelle and James were in the living room catching up on lost time. And Kinzie and Tim stayed in the guest bedroom. No one knew he left. The sun just started going down. He didn't find anything in the archives.

It was dark before Michelle noticed the silence, and tried to see if Quinn found anything in the archives. All she found was the note Quinn left for Kinzie. Folded neatly on the desk. Michelle grabbed the note and went to knock on the door.

"Come in," Tim answered.

Michelle entered, "Quinn's gone, he left this letter. I'm guessing it's for Kinzie." Tim and Kinzie lay wide awake on the bed. Kinzie reached her hand out, Michelle handed her the letter, and exited the room.

"Thank you," Kinzie called.

Kinzie unfolded the papers,

Kinzie, I'm trying to find answers and I can't find any in the archives. I'm convinced this began when your parents were killed. And someone is angry because you and Michelle survived. I wouldn't be surprised if she too became ill. As much as I don't want to say it, it's a likely possibility. The only thing I did find in the archives. The one that turned you into a vampire was also the one who went to see your father. He could be the one causing your cases to be as they are. I can't explain how it is. I came to that conclusion. I suspect Tim is going to be staying with us a bit longer. I'm worried, Kinzie. Something big is happening and I don't know what it is. Perhaps Tim can help. You two together can find the answers. I'll be back in a few days. Maybe longer. Keep an eye out on Michelle please.

Yours Truly,
Quinn

"Well that's interesting," Kinzie said, hardening her eyebrows.

"What is?" Tim asked.

"He's saying he's worried. He may have found our suspect in our archives. The one who killed my family. He suspects that someone's upset that Michelle and I are still alive. He might attack Michelle. Since neither of us died that terrible night."

"I've been wondering how she's still around. I know you're immortal but-"

"I've been trying to figure that out too," Her voice soft.

"He also said that you and I are the ones who can figure out how to solve this case," Kinzie announced.

" That's a lot of pages for a few words," Tim's voice filled with curiosity.

"Yes it's an incredibly complex language. And his writing has always been a bit large," Her voice trailed off.

"So it took almost twenty pages to say that?" Tim chuckled.

"Yes, because most symbols look similar so you have to add another five more symbols to explain. There can be up to fifteen to twenty per symbol. Does that explain the lengthy pages a bit better?"

"Yes, I suppose it does," Tim sighed, his head beginning to throb.

" Your head is hurting yet?" Kinzie looked over at him with a smile.

"Yes actually. Thank you for that," Tim let out a laugh.

" Sorry that wasn't meant to be offensive," Kinzie's eyes grew sensitive.

"I know. I suppose I'm agitated. I want to find the man who slaughters your family. And now is killing innocent women," Tim replied.

"Thank you for feeling this with me," Kinzie's eyes seemed to change color for a moment.

"I'll be back. I'm going to go smoke a cigarette," Tim gave her a kiss on the head.

"Alright I'll see you in a few," Kinzie smiled.

Tim continued to smile and exited the room. Michelle and James were sitting in the living room talking. And he continued to the patio. He was happy to see that Michelle found love. True love. Something that will last forever. He wished he had the same luxury with Kinzie. He began to think about what Quinn said, "we're the only ones who can figure out how to solve the case." It's true, their levels of thinking are different. And *that's* what makes them a good team. In addition to their personality types. Kinzie is a workaholic and Tim is more lax and doesn't pay any mind to negativity or stupidity.

But they both remain serious about their work. His left side started to ache, "It's going to rain. Lovely." Tim put out his cigarette when James stepped out back and lit his pipe.

"It's going to rain," he said.

"I know," Tim pointed to his arm.

"Ah, sorry. I didn't think that through." He said taking a puff. Pipe tobacco smelled a lot different than Tim expected.

"It's alright. Everything okay?" Tim asked.

"Yes, I think so," James replied, taking a seat.

"Okay. Well that's good. I'm gonna get back to Kinzie," Tim nodded.

James nodded. Tim opened the door, and went back to the bedroom only to find the bed empty and the shower running. He knocked on the bathroom door, " Kin you okay?"

"Yeah, you can come in," she called.

He had a wave of heat hit him. He shit the door behind him quickly.

"Join me?" She asked.

"Erm. Sure. I guess," Tim undressed and entered the shower only to see Kinzie washing her hair. The steam covered most of her body. But he did notice the small tattoos going down her spine. How did he not notice that?
Once she let her hair down to rinse it off, he figured it out. Her hair is long enough to cover the back.

"Where are your tattoos from?"

"Ranks after I became a vampire," she said,"I still hold rank even when I'm working in the human world."

"That's a lot of different ranks," he said looking down her spine. She put her hair back up. He pointed to onen on the back of her neck, "what's this one?"

" It gets me into the vampire realm and council," she replied before she put her head under water,"Ah I feel so much better. Do you want me to turn the water off?"

"No, I might as well take a shower while I'm in here," he smiled.

"Alright I'm stepping out," she said, pulling the shower curtain back.

Tim still couldn't see that much because of the steam. But what he did see was beautiful. He didn't want to disrespect her. He closed the curtain back.

"See you in the bedroom," she said smiling.

"Alright," he called back. He let the hot water run all the stress away.

Kinzie's favorite part of stepping out of the bathroom is the cold that hits you. Making you wake up. She went over to the closet and pulled out a black and red plaid leggings and black tank top. *"Thank you Shelly,"* she thought to herself. She brushed her hair, *"I wonder what other tattoos he noticed."* She remembered how many times she went to the tattooer. Or at least that's what they called him. The first time was the most painful. But after the 24th one it was effortless. She has over ,70 tattoos in total. All small, but all important to vampire culture. She has 50 down her spine. Three on the back of her neck, and 17 on her inner arm. Which are more complex than the others. And something she'd rather not go into.

Her hair was brushed thoroughly by the time Tim left the bathroom. She was waiting patiently on the bed. She tapped her fingers deep in thought. He ended up dressing. In a black t-shirt and tan cargo shorts. He asked what time it was.

"I'm not sure. My phone is dead and I was thinking about grabbing my laptop. But I'm not sure if the sun's out or not," she replied, still tapping her fingers.

"I can check to see if the sun's out if you'd like," Tim replied.

Kinzie nodded, "yes please."

"Alright," Turned to open the door, he peeked his head out and looked around,"No sunlight yet, love."

"Thanks," She replied, getting off the bed. She exited the room and went to the office. She grabbed her laptop, the cable and her phone charger and quickly made it back to the bedroom.

"What are you thinking about?" Tim asked. She was on the bed with Felix.

"My bills and seeing what we can find in the case," Kinzie replied, sitting in the bed next to them.

"Your skin tone looks better," Tim observed.

" How are my eyes?" Kinzie asked.

"Much better. Can you see more clearly?" Tim asked.

"Yes, my sight is almost back to normal," she said, plugging in her laptop cable and turning the device on.

A loud boom came from the living room, and James' voice cried out, "Michelle!" Kinzie jumped up and ran out of the room. Before Tim had time to process what just happened. Kinzie went out into the living room and found Michelle seizing on the floor. Kinzie was on her side and placed her head on her lap. A few moments later she stopped," James put her on the couch."

He picked her up gently and lay her down softly on the couch. He should have known better that he took care of her for a full year. Her diet requires more meat. But she hadn't had any in a few days. She's been so concerned about Kinzie. And James has been so distracted about Michelle he had forgotten all about her dietary needs. Kinzie too felt guilty.

"James, I feel guilty too. But that's not going to help anyone. We need to focus on Michelle right now. I know it's hard. Do what you need to, and pull yourself together," Kinzie said and sat next to her resting sister.

"I'm going to go smoke my pipe, then I'll make some steaks," James nodded.

"Do you mind if I join you?" Tim piped up.

James shook his head, " I'd appreciate the company."

Tim nodded and headed to the back door. James is not too far behind.

......*

The back door opened. Once they were both on the porch they sat across the table. James pulled out his pipe, and tobacco. Tim pulled out a cigarette and lit it.

"She'll be alright James," Tim said, exhaling the smoke.

" I know," he said, lighting his pipe, "she's stronger than she gives herself credit for."

"If you don't mind my asking. How bad were her injuries? She never talks about it. I don't blame her. I guess my curiosity is getting the best of me," Tim inhaled another toxic hit.

" No, I don't mind. She had 4th degree burns on her left side. From her upper thigh to her face. Frankly she was lucky to even be alive. When a strange woman brought her to our house she was couscous and in a lot of pain. Crying for her family. She had night terrors for three months. I sat with her every night. She kept apologizing for her screaming. I told her it's no problem. And all she could do was cry. One night she asked me to lay with her. Which was an honor because that's all I wanted to do. The night I lay with her. She didn't have a single night terror. But every day she got stronger."

"So why did she have a seizure? If you don't mind my asking," Tim asked, putting his cigarette out.

"You're fine. She has a high meat diet. I'm convinced it's because she could be a small amount of werewolf. But I'm not sure. If she doesn't have a lot. Well you saw what happened…"

"Don't beat yourself up, James. You've been focusing on Kinzie. And I know Michelle appreciates it," Tim replied, he completely understands the feeling.

"Appreciate that Tim. Let's get back to the girls," James said, dumping tobacco in the ashtray.

Tim nodded and got up. As soon as the two of them got inside thunder clapped and rain started to pour down. James went straight to the kitchen, and rummaged through the fridge. Tim went into the living room, and found Kinzie asleep sitting up on the couch. Michelle curled up in her lap.

"Kinzie," he whispered in his mind.

Her eyes opened. *"Hey"*

"If you're gonna go to sleep, you should probably get in bed," Tim replied, approaching the couch.

"If you could hand me that pillow, I'll take that suggestion," Kinzie pointed to the pillow resting in the chair across from her.

Tim grabbed and handed it over. Kinzie gently moved Michelle's head and replaced herself with the pillow. She and Tim slowly walked to the bedroom, careful not to wake her. Once the door shut Kinzie spoke up, "She just needs to rest."

"Shouldn't we have put a blanket on her or something?"

"No, James will do it," Kinzie replied, laying down.

Tim let out a laugh," I didn't know you're a matchmaker."

Kinzie laughed,"Don't Tell anyone. The last thing I need is a line of people at my door."

Tim seated himself next to her," I won't, I promise."

"Good," she smiled and placed her head in his lap.

"Rest well, love," Tim replied, stroking her hair.

If Kinzie had a heartbeat it would've pounded against her ribs. Despite Tim's attraction and tenderness, she wanted to take her time. She's seen too many people lose their lives. People she's loved and grown attracted to. She just wants to be ready for when that time comes. So desperately she wanted to kiss him, make love to him. She started to cry.

"Kin, what's wrong," his voice filled with concern.

"I just. I was thinking about how you're mortal and I'm immortal. And I want to kiss you and love you. But I don't know if I can bear the idea of losing you," her voice shook.

"Kin, look at me," his voice soft.

She sat up and looked at him.

" It would be an honor to die knowing I lived all of my life with you, I know you're immortal. I know you're different. And that's fine with me," he held his eye contact, "Can I kiss you?" He leaned closer.

She nodded. She closed her eyes. His lips are warm and gentle. She kissed him back. She heard his heart pounding against his ribs. He kissed her cheek, kissed her neck. Kinzie let out a soft Moan and took off her shirt. They continued to kiss as Tim cupped her breast. Kinzie pulled his shirt off and climbed in his lap. Tim kissed her neck down to her breast and pulled her pants off slowly. Kinzie let out another soft Moan. Hoping Michelle and James didn't hear. Tim pulled his pants down and gently pulled

Kinzie down. It was warm, and it throbbed. Kinzie bent down and kissed Tim's neck as she bounced slowly. She wanted him to last as long as he could. It felt good to be loved again. Euphoria hit her hard. She kissed his neck. And moved her affection up to his chin, his cheek then his lips. Tim held his breath and bit his lip. She knew he was close to an orgasim so she stopped. He pulled her to his chest. And thrusted hard. Kinzie bit her lip. To continue to thrust until the sexual tension is released. Kinzie rolled over lightly next to him.

"I hope I didn't hurt you,"he breathed.

Kinzie laughed," I'm a vampire, love. It would take more than several hard thrusts to hurt me."

"So... You like it rough?" Tim's voice trailed off.

"Hell yeah. Though I do enjoy the soft and slow occasionally," she smiled.

"Wow. You're perfect," Tim smiled.

"Why do you say that?" She lay her head on his chest.

"Because I've gotten complaints about my roughness, being a little too rough," Tim sighed.

"Well it's probably because you're slightly larger than average," Kinzie oveserved.

"Thanks for the explanation. I do feel better about myself now," Tim blushed.

"No problem. Thanks for the sexual release," Kinzie closed her eyes. She felt a bit better about the situation. He's not afraid of death and he's not afraid to accept people for who or what they are. If anything he's the one who's perfect.

......*

James got Michelle to eat something and carried her upstairs to her bedroom. He pulled up a chair next to her. And nodded off to sleep.

He re-entered his dream. Which didn't take long at all. He went back to the place where his father stood. Once again his heart ached.

"Hello my son," his father came closer.

"Hello," he replied softly.

"What's the matter?" His father asked.

"It's Michelle, she is not doing well at all. She's part werewolf and I completely forgot about her diet," James remained frozen.

" Ah, well it's been a while since you've seen her last. You can't blame yourself." His father's voice was soft.

"I suppose. Did you find out how she's still alive," James replied, hoping his father will change the topic.

"Yes, as a matter of fact I have," His father nodded, *"There's a spiritual bond that ties their life strings together."*

James' jaw dropped, *"Really?"*

"Yes. I'm not one hundred percent sure, but my best guess is that the reason is, Kinzie saved Michelle. They were both meant to die that night. But they both overcame death."

" Hmmm. Interesting. Is there a cure to Kinzie's illness?" James replied, raising an eyebrow.

"Yes. Continue giving her the potion you made, and find the answers as to who or what is causing this. But I have to go. You should tell Kinzie what I told you. And make another potion. She'll know what to do. I love you James." His father disappeared. As did he.

James' eyes snapped open, tears streamed down his face. He heard the words. At last. It was as if he was saying goodbye. But he didn't want it to be a goodbye. He wanted it to be a hello. Or I'll see you later. Why do goodbyes have to hurt? His heart pinged. Michelle sat up, "James."

"I'm sorry I didn't mean to wake you," he whispered. His voice did not allow him to speak any higher.

"It's alright. I feel better. Come here… " she patted the bed.

He did so. She pulled him to her chest. He allowed himself to cry. She stroked his hair. Once his tears slowed. He thanked her. She continued to hold him close. As they both drifted back to sleep.

Chapter Nine

Michelle's eyes fluttered open. Jame's Lay resting on her shoulder. She blushed and with a smile she started stroking his hair. Last night was precious. Of course Michelle won't say anything. In the bedroom, it's a safe haven. A space where you can express your emotions to your partner, and it's a space where no one can judge you. This is not the first time Michelle and James shared tears in a bedroom. She still remembers the nights that James would sit with her and bring her hot tea. Changing her bandages. Making her pain potions. Her burns didn't bother her as much anymore. They turned out a lot better than she thought they were going to. Her burn marks aren't as raised. They look as though a clay artist found a crack in her work and decided to put another piece, and try to smooth it over. As best as she could. Despite her horrible experience. She remains thankful for everything. Despite her disadvantage. She does hold an interest in sculpting.Just something about molding clay, and creating something from dirt and water and many other elements. She also had a fascination with carvings. Anything. Wood, stone, and marble. It's beautiful. She hadn't done it in a long time. But James introduced her into it. Helping ease her pain from being blind. Their history goes way back. It feels as it has from the beginning. That feeling of making your heart swell never left.

"Good morning beautiful," James yawned.

"Good morning my love," she replies, smiling.

"How did you sleep?" He said, rolling over to face her. He heard the smile in her voice. He just has to see it.

"I slept very well. How about you?" She asked leaning into him for a kiss.

Pecking her lips gently, "I slept well too. I'm glad you're doing better,"

" Am, I'm sorry for scaring all of you. I've just been so focused on Kinzie. I've nearly forgotten my dietary needs," Michelle sighed.

"The important thing is that You're alright. I'd be glad to help you with making meals and keeping up with your health. It's fine. I'm just glad you're alright," He said, putting a hand on her cheek. He's convinced the reason why they get along so well is due to them both wanting to help people.

"Thank you," She breathed. It feels good to have someone who is willing to take care of her. He always has. She appreciates all of his hard work He didn't have to help Kinzie. But he has. It feels good to have a full support system. So she can take care of herself, and she knows Kinizie is well taken care of. *"I wonder how she's feeling."* She thought to herself. James got up and insisted Michelle stay in bed. She still needs to rest from yesterday. She gives a nod in agreement, and James heads downstairs.

......*

Tim's been awake for a while. He can't help it. He's a heavy sleeper, so he didn't want to run the risk of anything happening. Fortunately it seems like the potion James gave her has helped tremendously. Even being asleep she looks better. She opened her eyes and jumped forward. If she had a heart it would pound against ribs in an attempt to escape out of her chest.

"Kinzie, It's okay," he whispered, reaching out to rub her back.

She calmed herself by burying herself into his chest, "I'm okay, I just need to calm down."

Tim kissed her head and rubbed her back, "Was it a bad dream?"

"More like a memory," She replied, pulling away.

"You would like to talk about it?" Tim whispered.

She paused, "I was being tortured for information, and as you know drowning won't work. Or cutting off limbs. It's the sun.

The less you feed the worse it hurts," A lump started growing in Kinzie, " I was at the point of starvation,"

"Which hurts your regeneration," Tim said softly. His heart pinged.

"Exactly," Kinzie's voice was almost inaudible, " I don't remember the room because I was blindfolded. But all I remember was a temperature hotter than fire. Running through me. My screams weren't even recognizable. He must have had a window or a latch where he could access the sun and hide it again. Thankfully on the fourth day Quinn found me. It just surprises me that I survived. And now I'm a successful *young* detective. Living in a huge house with my sister," She replied wishing she could sigh.

"I'm so sorry Kin," He says, rubbing her back.

"Thank you., It was over fifty years ago. I'm glad to be alive, so I can save people. I'm just lonely," She looked up at him, "Thank you, Tim."

"You're welcome, love. I hope you're not lonely now," Tim Smiled.

"Of course not," Kinzie let out a laugh.

Tim's mind began to wander. He knew that was one of her many dark secrets, she's withheld from Michelle. Michelle's heart would ache. Tim knows she's strong, but not like that. *"Hotter than fire,"* Kinzie's voice rang in his mind. Fire can vary from 750 degrees fahrenheit, ato 1,000 degrees fahrenheit. The lower it is to the base of a match. The cooler. A human would die within minutes, Maybe even seconds. Since she's a vampire, and doesn't need to breathe smoke inhalation is not a concern. But the burns, and the pain. He couldn't help but wonder why? What could that person want so badly to torture someone for that long? How long would it take for a vampire to recover from something like that? Tim looked over and found Kinzie fast asleep. He wonders if she remembered the voice. Too bad Quinn left, he would've talked to him more about what happened to Kinzie. He'll probably talk to him about it when he gets back.

Tim's thoughts began to race. *What if the man that tortured her, is the one who caused this? Someone that sick in the head to torture for information, could be twisted enough to hunt her down. Who was it? What did he want to know so badly? If it is the same person, they've only just begun.*When Kinzie wakes up Tim's going to review a timeline, and ask her questions. It could be someone else. But the feeling in his gut is strong. It's never been wrong. After years of working as a police officer, then a detective. You learn to trust your instincts. And those gut feelings can eventually lead to saving a life. That's how Kinzie saved him. One night Tim and Kinzie got a call about a suspect holding hostages at a local Food shop. Kinzie and Tim got summoned separately. Kinzie was still at the office doing dome re-search. Tim was already out. He couldn't remember why.

Tim arrived first. It was a hot mess. Traffic was blocked by Police and there were Six cars ready and waiting. He asked if they notified Kinzie. They said yes. Kinzie read the files as she walked to her car. She studied this guy. He's robbed several places and Killed many people. If he didn't want to get caught, why is he in the downtown area? Suicide by cop? She got into her car, and reversed. If she had a heartbeat it would pound. She took a deep breath in her mind, keeping it clear, she needs to be ready for anything. She arrived on the scene. Tim wasn't there.

"What happened?" She snapped.

"Bryte, went inside to try and negotiate…"

"Stay here, and stay behind the cars!" She replied, and withdrew her gun from her holster and pointed it low.
The officers obeyed her orders. And stood behind the cars. She approached slowly, and opened the door. Tim had his hands raised facing the suspect. The hostages were sitting on the floor. Fortunately they weren't tied up.

"Please leave," A shaky voice rose. He sounded like he was in his late twenties. She heard a soft and low beeb. But no one else heard it.

"I'm just checking on my friend here. And just making sure everyone is alright,"Kinzie replied with a cool voice.

" Yes, everyone is fine," the man replied.

"You don't seem to be," She replied, trying to make her voice sound concerned even though her blood was boiling.

"Well, I am," He replied, turning the gun to her.

"Okay, I'm sorry. Maybe you and I can work this out. We don't need all these people here, do we?" Kinzie stood steady.

"No, we don't. I suppose you're correct. Everyone else can go, you two can stay 'while we talk,'" He laughed. All the hostages got up and ran out the door. His voice wasn't shaky.

"What the hell? This guy is having a psychotic break.*" Kinzie thought to herself. Usually in these types of situations it can either go really good, or really bad.*

"What would you like to discuss with us?" Tim asked, still holding his hands in the air.

"Oh stop acting like you care. I just want to see the world burn, and I want you both to be in the middle of it," He growled and pulled a small button out of his pocket.

"What did we do?" Kinzie asked.

"You continue the justice. The justice that let the man go that killed my sister!" He shouted. And pressed the button.

Tim was standing too close to the explosion, and let out a scream. There was no time, Kinzie scooped him up, she was under his right shoulder and held his body weight. They both came outside, and hurried behind a car. Another loud explosion came from the building Flames carried themselves above their head. She tore off a piece of her shirt and wrapped it tightly around Tim's injury. Making certain his wound won't get infected, or be exposed to shrapnel. The Doctor was already waiting outside just in case. She sat with Tim Until the Medical came over. He got into the back of the ambulance with him. This is one of the better outcomes. Only one life was lost. It took Tim a while to accept the loss of his arm.The physical therapy, and the day to day tasks seemed like such a chore. But, now he's better. It's better to lose a limb, than a life.

And if anything this has made him stronger. At first it was terrible, the pain, the feeling of having an arm still. Until the physical therapy, He didn't know how important it was to have both arms to have proper balance. He was out of work for the better part of the year. Two months in the hospital. And the remaining time in the McCoy house. As a matter of fact Kinzie

Built the downstairs bedroom while he was in the hospital. She asked the doctor what all he needed. And she made sure he got it.

She didn't want him to be alone. Michelle took the day shift. Kinzie took the night shift. Giving him medicine. Making sure he did his physical therapy. Changing his bandages. She held him close when he cried from the pain. Kissed his head in comfort. I guess you could say she always loved him. She didn't say it. But he felt it. The three letter words weren't exchanged prior. But it was slowly built. That's for sure. She trusts him with her life. And vice versa. They've saved one another more times than they'd like to admit. Like a hero love story. But nothing like superman. Just two police officers doing their job. Kinzie having more hand to hand combat experience than Tim. But he's well trained in a wide spectrum of shooting and safety tactics. Tim's thoughts grew deeper. When Kinzie's better he's hoping to see what she's capable of as far as hand to hand combat. Still deep in his thoughts a smell filled the air. *"Ohhh bacon, and steak.."*

Tim got up and carefully exited the room. Finding James in the kitchen, "Good morning." he announced.

"Good morning, How's Kinzie doing?" James asked, adding some seasoning to the cast iron pan.

"She's doing alright. Had a night terror, but she's alright. How's Shell doing?" Tim asked, leaning against the doorway.

"She's doing much better also. Upstairs resting. I'm making her this for breakfast," He replied waving the spatula.

"She's going to love it. I'll tell you that much," Tim nodded in approval, "Do you mind if I make some coffee?"

James shook his head, "Go for it. We're going to need a cup anyway,"

"Alright," Tim nodded, and entered the kitchen. He removed 3 mugs from the cabinet, and changed the coffee filter, And poured cups worth of coffee of water, and filled the filter with the Folgers dark coffee that rested on the counter. Once the coffee started brewing, he went out to the patio to smoke a cigarette. *I wonder when Kinzie's going to wake up again?"*

Inhaling his preferred poinsion, his thoughts continued. Hopefully Quinn found something.

......*

James finished making the plates, and poured coffee. He rummaged through the kitchen. Tim came back inside, "What are you looking for?"

"A tray," James continued to open cabinets.
"Oh, I gotcha," Tim replied, and wandered over to the panty and pulled out the tray he remembers so well.

"Thank you," James replied with a smile, and took it.

"You're welcome.Thank you for taking care of Shell," He replied with a half smile, and went to the bedroom.

James smiled and set up the breakfast tray. He went upstairs and pushed the door open. Michelle was looking out the window admitring the birds. She is so beautiful... "Breakfast," James said, placing the tray on the bed.

"It smells amazing," she smiled.

"Thank you," James seated himself next to her.

"You're welcome," She said, picking up her plate, and a fork. He made scrambled eggs, bacon, and steak, which he cut neatly into slices. Beautifully seasoned. And the smell is amazing. First she tried the bacon. The crunch and flavor sparked her taste buds. He used a bit of salt, "Salt," she said. When she was in recovery James had her tell him the ingredients in the food, including the seasoning. It was challenging at first. But she got it.

James looked over and smiled, "I can't believe you remember! God that was years ago!"

Michelle laughed," How could I forget?" She took another note of bacon. Before she knew it, she ate it all and pouted.

"What's the matter?" James asked

"It was so good I wanted more!" She sighed.

"Well there's still steak and eggs," James chuckled. God she's cute!

"Fine," she dug into the eggs, and chewed, "Salt, pepper, extra sharp cheddar cheese, sriracha, mushrooms, onions, and garlic."

"What kind of onion," James leaned into her hair.

"Green onion," She laughed tilting her head. His breath in her neck is so warm.

"Try the steak,"James nudged her shoulder.

She did so, nice slow chews, " Worcestershire sauce, the expensive one, salt, pepper, lemon zest, and a hint of rosemary. Who knew such simple ingredients would make something taste so damn good?

They continued talking and eating. Just like old times. A wave of relief came over Michelle. It felt refreshing to have company. Old company from many years ago. Things have changed so much over the years. But it's nice to know things can still remain the same. After eating they just sat and drank coffee. Talking. And

Michelle admittedly enjoyed doing nothing. There's no shame. Because everyone needs a day off and for themselves.

……*

Many hours later, Kinzie's eyes opened. Her sight is clearer than before. She felt refreshed, energized, and filled with relief. One step closer to being "normal." She stretched, hand searching for Tim. She felt his shoulder.

"Hello, beautiful. How did you sleep?" He chuckled.

"Very well, how did you sleep?"

"I slept great," Tim replied smiling.

"Good, I'm glad," She sat up and reached for her laptop. The top of her hair is a little messy.

"Whatcha doin?"

"I've been meaning to check my accounts, but since Michelle got sick. I just haven't had the chance. And I've been meaning to order you a keyboard," Kinzie replied,turning the laptop on. And rubbing her eyes shortly after.

"Kin,, you don't have to, re-"

" I know but I want to," she said typing in her password.

"Alright if you insist. I just don't want you to spend too much on me," Tim's voice trailed off.

" I don't consider getting something you need, 'spending money on you." She said logging into her bank account.

"Actually, would you mind me being nosy? I've always wondered how much money vampires have," Tim scooted closer to her.

She shrugged "I don't care."

Tim's jaw dropped, "Holy shit."

"What?" Kinzie replied

"I'm just surprised."

"Tim, I've been working for over 500 years," She laughed.

" Good point," He smiled.

"Alright, all the bills are paid, now let's see if we can find the perfect keyboard," She replied, pulling up another web browser. And went on google.

"Thank you for this Kin,"He said softly in her ear.

"No problem at all," She replied gently, handing Him the laptop, "Just don't spend all of the money."

Tim let out a laugh. There's no way. She had enough money for ten or more life times, or more. Billions of dollars accumulated over many, many years of working. There's no way he could spend it all in one sitting. Even if he tried. She used to travel a lot more. But not as much as she used to. Ever since she returned to being a detective. But soon she's going to want to take a vacation soon. Maybe add on to her "recovery."It's also way too soon, and dangerous. It would be nice to show Tim the places she's been. Show the different sides to her personality. But all in good time.

In the three years they've worked together, he's seen Kinzie mad once, "Hey Tim, do you remember the day I lost my mind when I came to a crime scene?"

"Yes. We arrived and you had to tell everyone to back off. You were fisty that day. And I honestly thought we would need some more caution tape," Tim laughed.

"I was so close. I have no idea how I kept my composure but good Gods, I wanted to strangle someone," Kinzie laughed.

"What made you more upset? The fact that they were walking all over it, or the fact that they let the press take a walk through?"

"Both! You're supposed to *sit* there and *not* let anyone inside the tape. Don't take pictures, and keep the press away. It's supposed to look like the original incident. The way it happened. But whoever stood guard waiting for us to arrive were idiots. The forensic team hadn't even arrived yet. But oooh my patients was thin that day," she lifted her hands and scrunched her fists.

"I know, then someone had to talk to the press," Tim replied, still looking for the keyboard.

"And I wasn't going to do it," Kinzie laughed. She leaned in to see what he's looking at, "Any luck?"

"Almost. I just want to change the color, and the length of the keys," Tim nodded.

"Awesome. I like the mouse feature on that. Have a laptop mouse. I also like the fact that it's smaller than the average keyboard. It's easy to type single handed," Kinzie said reading the description box.

"Oh and the bottom of the keyboard and I can hand write anything and it'll convert the words from written to typed," Tim replied.

"Awesome. I would suggest ordering two of them and make sure that it has insurance on it," Kinzie replied.

"Yeah, I thought about it," Tim said with a smile.

"Alright," she smiled and went to the bathroom. She noticed her hair in the mirror, and brushed it down. And since she's already in the bathroom, she brushed her teeth. She noticed her eye color, it looked a lot better. Almost back to normal. She smiled, felt the stress fade from her shoulders. After she exited the bathroom she went to the closet. Grabbed a change of clothes, and undressed. Tim couldn't help himself, and a whistle escaped his lips.

"Aren't you supposed to be looking for your keyboard?" Kin Retorted playfully.

"Already ordered," Tim chuckled.

"Alright then," She smiled, and continued getting dressed.

"Can I look at your playlist?" Tim asked.

"Sure," Kinzie shrugged.

TIm pulled up her playlist on Spotify, and dropped his jaw There were a lot of musical interests. Mostly rock, classical, pop, jazz, and more. A lot of similar interests, "Wow, I didn't realize we had such similar music interests."

"There's a lot most people don't know about me and I like to keep it that way," she replied sitting next to him.

"I can understand," Tim smiled, " I have another question. If you say no, I'll respect it."

"What's the question?" Kinzie asked.

"Can I see your fangs?" Tim exhaled.

"Why?" She asked in a low whisper.

"Because I love you. And I'm not afraid. I want to see the side of you that you've hidden for so long. I'm sure there are positive sides to being a vampire. But regardless this is part of you. And I'd like to see it," Tim's voice was soft and gentle.

Finally someone who accepts her for who and what she is. She nodded. Tim watched carefully, and saw Kinzie's fangs. His eyes grew large. Knizie separated her lips so he could have a better look.

"It's not that scary," Tim smiled

Kinzie smiled back at him, fangs gone, "Really?"

"Really. You're not scary Kin. Because the good part of you is far more visible. Your Kindness overrides any bad part of you," Tim replied softly stroking her cheek.

"I'm so relieved to hear that," She whispered. Doing her best to hold back the tears she's buried for so long.

"No, no, if you need to cry. Please do so," Tim said, pulling her closer. Those words pushed her emotions over the edge. And before she knew it, tears started to roll down her face. Tim pulled her close and stroked her hair. He kissed her cheek. And just held her close. To Kinzie this was strange. Only Michelle and Quinn have seen her vulnerable side. It's moments like this anyone longs for. Behind the door of the couple's bedroom you'll find truths, fights, and most importantly, the vulnerability of someone's soul. It's not easy to reveal one's dark side or emotional side. But in moments like this, it's the most wonderful thing anyone could experience. After Kinzie calmed herself, Tim wiped her tears away. She Smiled. Then they heard a knock on the door. Tim and Kinzie giving permission simultaneously, James entered the room, cup in hand. He gave it to Kinzie and asked Tim if he wanted anything to eat. Tim noedded. James gave a slight nod and exited the room. Shutting the door behind him. Kinzie was glad to know James is helping Michelle out and allowing her to rest, just as Tim is. She's earned it.

......*

Quinn walked down a brick sidewalk with some old mansion homes on either side of the street. Humming an old tune from his war days from long ago. Hoping someone he knows will come along or maybe bring a sign. His shoes continued to click softly on the bricks. He always loved brick roads. A true labor in the olden days. The designs themselves were so surpurbe back then. Still humming, he saw a woman approaching. He couldn't see her face, because of the long black cloaked hood. But she seems to be of average height and weight. Though she was a little bit taller, due to her thigh high leather heels. Long red hair curled down her chest. She started humming too, and approaching slowly. Once face to face they stopped,

"Hello Quinn," She said softly, her british accent ringing in Quinn's ears.

"Hello Anna. How have you been?" He asked, gesturing a slight bow.

"I've been alright. What do I owe the pleasure of this visit?" She replied putting a hand on her hip. She was wearing a long cloak, fitting leather pants and a black corset.

"I need some help. If you cannot assist me, I need a reference,"Quinn locked eyes with hers.

"Come then, We'll speak in private. Is everything alright?" Anna said and turned around.

"No, old friend. Not even in the slightest," Quinn followed. His hope runs deep that he'll find someone who can help Kinzie. And answer the question as to who can over power a vampire Kinzie's age. Since she's so mature, it wouldn't be as easy as one, two, three. There's a lot of power and planning behind it. Kinzie is a great detective and is well known in the public eye. Another question would be, why? Is it personal? Or is it just that someone wants to take her out of the public eye? Maybe both? Quinn's thoughts stopped when he saw an old Victorian house, which he remembers well. It had a concrete stairway that led up to the stairs on the porch. Matching bushes aligned on either side of the stairs. The porch had a wood pilla, and a welcoming deep wooden door, With a half circle of stained glass window above it.

"Ah, the old manor house," Quinn smiled

"Yes, indeed," She replied softly.

This house held so many memories within these walls. Anna started walking up the stairs, Quinn not too far behind. The house was three stories. Nine bedrooms and eight bathrooms. *"I wonder if it's the same inside?"* Quinn thought to himself. After a few moments they approached the front door.

"Is anyone else here tonight?" Quinn asked quietly.

"No, everyone's out on a mission," Anna replied, rummaging through her pockets. Had someone else been home she would've kept the door unlocked.

"Ah, so you were on your rounds, when I came along then?"

"Yes, there's been a lot more activity recently. Ah, there they are," She said, removing the key and quickly opening the front door. Quinn followed her in. Once the door was shut Anna asked, "So, what's been happening?"

"It's Kinzie, she's ill," Quinn walked into the living room.

"But, I don't understand. She's a 500 year old vampire. There's no way," Anna removed her hood, and sat across from Quinn.

"That's exactly why I'm here. I don't know either. I wish I did," Quinn's voice trailed off, " We think it's a powerful witch or warlock. I came to see what your thoughts were and if you had any other suggestions."

"Of course, erm. How bad is her condition?"

"It was pretty awful. But Michelle's healer came to the house and helped make a potion that seems to be making it better. But I don't know how long it will last. Before, she couldn't drink any blood. She'd vomit, she wouldn't sleep at all, or she would sleep too much," Quinn let out a sigh and sank into the couch, " I feel so helpless Anna. I promised the McCoy's I'd protect them. But I don't know how. After all these years on this planet you would think I'd come up with something."

"We'll come up with something, Quinn. But it seems like you have a good hunch so far. You know there's a lot of powerful people that work for the council," Anna replied, taking off her cloak and crossing her legs.

"But that's just it, We sent a message to the council, and we have yet to receive a response. And in case you're wondering, James opened a portal that would take the letter to the vampire realm," Quinn began to rub his temples.

"Thanks for reading my mind. I've been wondering what's happening with the council, I've tried to contact them as well, and I haven't heard anything back from them," Anna tapped her fingers on the arm of the couch.

"Oh good lord," Quinn sat straight up.

"What is it?"

"I just had a terrifying thought,"

"Quinn, what is it?"

"What if something actually did happen to the council? And they are corrupted. We just sent them a letter confirming their attacks and methods on Kinzie are working,"

"Oh, shit," Anna breathed.

"Yes, my thoughts exactly," Quinn replied.

"Quinn, if the council is being corrupted, You must go. I'm sure from there You'll figure out what's happening," Anna replied, locking eyes.

"Kinzie is in no condition to travel," Quinn sighed sadly.

"Well what about the one who created the portal?"

"Hmm, I'm not sure. He's capable of traveling. I'm just not sure if he'll want to be away from Michelle," Quinn replied, shaking his head.

"Has she been harmed as well?" Anna raised an eyebrow.

"Yes, she… Had a eplipeptic reaction, from lack of nutrition. Or perhaps that's what they wanted us to think. I only found out about that through a telephone call," Quinn sighed.

"I'm sure that's what they wanted you to think. The McCoy sisters are quietly being attacked. I would suggest you and the healer go to the realm of the vampires, and find out what's happening. If there is something strange going on. There will be a cure somewhere," Anna's eyebrow hardened.

"Do you have any clue as to what the cure is?" Quinn asked.

"No, unfortunately. I wish I did. But it's late. You should get some rest. When you return back to the McCoy manor. Tell everyone what happened. I'm sure the healer will volunteer to help. And that will give the girls some time to find some answers as well. Be warned Quinn, time is of the essence," Anna rose from the couch.

"Thank you my old friend," Quinn stood and took a bow.

"You're more than welcome. Please feel free to use one of the guest bedrooms on the east side. I need to go back to my rounds," She gave a slight nod of the head.

"Please be safe," Quinn blurted.

"Always," She said putting on her cloak

Quinn wandered up the stairs deep in thought. He was glad to find an answer, but that wasn't the answer he was hoping for. Anna is a few years older than he is, and still as beautiful and as smart as ever. What could the cure be? And how is this connected to Kinzie and Michelle? It took him forever, but he arrived at one of the guest bedrooms. The sheets were fresh, and the room was clean. Quinn took off his shoes and lay himself down. Before he knew it. Darkness took him. It's been days since he slept well.

......*

Kinzie's head began to spin, and lightheadedness. Michelle and James came downstairs and everyone was in the office. Going over all the cases and what could be happening in the vampire council. She felt fine earlier. Tim's anger keeps rising, he's impatient and wants Quinn to return with some news.

"Kinzie can't wait much longer!," Tim continued to pace.

"Tim," Kinzie croaked. What happened to her voice?

"No, no, don't Tim me!" his stomps became louder.

"Tim, stop! Her condition is delicate. If you're that pissed off about it, go have a cigarette," Michelle snapped.

"Please, all of you, sto-" The lightheaded feeling overwhelmed her. Her eyes rolled into the back of her head, and she slumped down into her chair.

"Kin!" Tim tried to rush over, but Michlle stepped in the way.

"You and I are going outside. James please put Kinzie on the couch," Michelle said firmly.

"But Shell," Tim stammered.

"She will be fine, I promise. We both need to calm down. Do it for her," Michelle locked contact with Tim.

"Alright, alright," Tim replied with a sigh. His heart swelled. Breathing seemed to hurt. He wanted it to be him who's suffering. He stepped out onto the patio and lit a cigarette. Michelle lingered behind him and shut the door.

"Please sit Tim. We need to talk," Michelle said softly. The moon is shining down on both of them.

Tim nodded and slouched down into the chair. His heart sank into the bottom of his stomach. He felt like it was his fault. If he would've listened.

"Stop beating yourself up Tim. It's no one's fault. Or at least no one here," Michelle sighed, and seated herself across the table.

"You mean the vampire council that I didn't know existed? It's their fault?"

"Something like that. I'm guessing that someone has somehow overcome the council. It would take a high power of magic. Just like it would take a lot to injure Kinzie," Michelle looked him in the eye.

" How did you come to figure this out?"

"I suspected something was going on, when we didn't get a response from the council. They're usually very good about responding rather promptly. But since it's been quiet it's safe to assume something happened," Michelle replied leaning back into her chair.

"But Kinzie is a perfect citizen. Why would anyone attack her?" Tim inhaled his cigarette.

"There isn't any reason. That's why it's so strange, and that's also why I think they're being manipulated somehow."

"So what are we going to do?"

"Find the source of evil and tear it down," Michelle's voice grew dark. Tim, in that moment realized she too is hiding the anger inside.

"Alright, sounds good. But one last question, how bad is this?"

"Well they're trying to disable the highest ranking detective and one of a few vampires who are in good relations with the council and work closely with them. So you tell me," She said, trying to relax the tension in her muscles.

" Well the crime rates would increase, and there would just be chaos everywhere," Tim exhaled the last of his cigarette and put it in the ashtray.

"And if there's no detectives or police to help resolve the issues, what will happen?"

"Anarchy and world domination," Tim's voice trailed off.

"Alright, let's get to work. Oh, before I forget, try not to express any more feelings of irritation, or any negative emotions. I only say that because it feeds into whatever Kinzie spell is under, and makes her weaker," Michelle said standing up.

"Got it. Thanks Shell for the sit down, calm down gesture," Tim stood.

"Anytime. It's not easy for me either. But if you want to talk, I'm here," She said walking over to the door. Tim came behind her, and followed inside. Once they enter, the house somehow feels heavier. They walked into the office. James did as he was asked, and moved Kinzie to the couch. Tim's heart slowed.

" We should probably move her to Tim's room," James said, barely audible. It was as if somehow anyone spoke too loudly Kinzie would shatter.

"Can I do it?" Tim blurted.

"Yes," James nodded.

Tim gestured his head with a nod. He wanted to say thank you, but he couldn't. He approached Kinzie quietly and knelt down, sliding his injured arm under her head, and his regular arm under her knees. Strands of her hair stuck to the back of her neck, and her skin went back to being slightly gray. His muscles wrapped around her gently, just as gently as two fingers picking a flower from a cherry blossom tree. It was an honor to carry her, and care for her. Just as she did from him. Time seemed to slow down as Tim took each step to the bedroom door. He doesn't have anyone else to cling to. Both of his parents are dead. All he has is a brother, but they rarely speak. He lay her down on the bed. And went to the bathroom and rinsed a clean rag under cold water. He returned back to the bed, dabbing her head with the cold rag.

"Thank you," Kinzie's voice rang in his head.

"You're welcome. Is there anything else I can do to help?"

"Just stay with me," She replied weakly.

"Always, go ahead and sleep, love," Tim whispered, "I'll be here when you wake up."

"Okay, I love you," Kinzie breathed.

"I love you, too," Tim kissed her head. And started stroking her hair. From then on silence. Tim kept the cold cloth on her head. And once it lost its temperature, he continued to run cold water on it. He held her closely, and waited patiently. While doing so he pulled out Kinzie's laptop, thankfully her password. She notes already on the cases and how they could be connected. The house phone rang, and Tim heard Michelle's voice.

......*

"Hello?" Michelle answered

"Hello, Shelly," Quinn's voice was on the other line.

"Hello, papa. How are things?"

"They're alright. I'm at one of my contacts' house now," Quinn's voice replied.

Michelle paused. It was Quinn's voice. But it wasn't him. His vocabulary is more complex than that. Michelle's heart began to pound. James came around the corner and mouthed, " Are you okay?"

Michelle shook her head.

"Really? Which one?" Michelle replied.

"Oh, you don't know her. She's a very nice lady though. Very helpful," Quinn's voice replied.

Michelle's hair stood on the back of her neck, "I'm so glad. Hopefully you got the information you've been wanting to find."

"Yes, I think I have," Quinn's voice sighed into the phone, "How's Kinzie?"

"She's fine. She's asleep at the moment," Michelle replied calmly. She's trying to get the person on the other line to admit what their intentions are.

"Ah alright then."

Tim came out of the bedroom and quietly walked over to Michelle. She gave him a worried look. "Is that Quinn?" He mouthed.

She shook her head, and mouthed back, "He's pretending to be him."

"Michelle, are you still there?"

"Yes, papa. I'm sorry. I'm just trying to decide what to make for breakfast. Should I let you go, and you can call back later?"

"Sure, no problem. I'll talk to you later then," The man was smiling on the other end of the phone.

"Alright, talk to you later. Safe travels papa. Bye," Michelle hung up and exhaled.

"What the hell?" Tim said softly.

"He was calling to ask how Kinzie was doing. And of course I lied and said that she was fine," Michelle replied quickly.

"How do you know it's not Him?" Tim asked.

"Tim, in the time you've known Quinn, have you ever heard him say, 'They're alright. I'm at one of my contact houses now.'?"

"No he'd have a long drawn out pronunciation and different phrases that aren't so modern," Tim shrugged.

"Exactly!" Michelle replied quietly trying no to wake Kinzie.

"Who do you think would've done this?" Tim asked.

Michelle shrugged, " I don't know."

"When Kinzie wakes up I'll ask her. Not that she needs the stress. But we need to know who this is." Tim said softly.

Michelle let out a sigh, "I'm going to go rest on the couch and watch some criminal minds."

"I'll join you," James said, rubbing her back.

Tim let out a sigh, "Alright. I'll stay with Kinzie. I'm probably going to make lots of coffee."

They both nodded. TIm sighed, feeling heavier than before, he walked back into the bedroom. Kinzie was tossing and turning, "Shhh, shhh. It's okay, it's okay," Tim said softly, he rushed to the bed and started to stroke her hair, while sitting himself next to her.

"Tim, can you pull me into your lap?," Kinzie's voice was trembling. He lifted her gently and pulled her close. He lay her head down on his lap and pulled the hair from her face. He didn't stop stroking her hair. *"Thank you."*

"Hey, So Quick question. Do you know who would potentially attack Quinn?"

"The same person who is attacking us. Why? Did something happen?"

"Well Shell answered a call that sounded like Quinn. But it wasn't him. Do you know anyone who would be able to do that," Tim asked softly.

"Yes. One, his name is William. You know the man who tortured me. I just hope Quinn is alright," Kinzie replied with a sigh shortly after.

"I'm sure he is," Tim replied, wishing he could be more confident.

......*

Quinn lay in the same room as before, unable to move. Or open his eyes. There was however a stranger in the room. Pacing back and forth.

"Well old man, now that you're just lying there...Why don't we have a little chat?" An angry male voice said, " I am sick of your God-daughter. I am sick of being the tiny spec in her shadow. Now I'm going to defeat you one by one! And you will all one day bow to me! You will one day see tha "

The door busted open and Quinn heard a struggle. He heard Anna curse and put up a fight. The sound of glass shattered and footsteps.

"Damn that man," Anna sighed. She got up and leaned over Quinn, "I'll be back, I know how to reverse this." Footsteps exited the room. A few minutes later she returned and opened his mouth. She poured a warm, heavily seasoned liquid and waited.

It felt like several hours. Maybe it has been. Who knows. All Quinn was ready to do was have Anna call and tell Michelle and Kinzie what happened. And have Kinzie and Tim travel to the Vampire realm. All this time William has driven into madness. Everyone has people who dislike them. But this gives a whole new meaning to hate. But why? Maybe he was the one who wanted Kinzie, all those years ago. Maybe he wanted her to submit to her after turning her into a vampire. Clearly he doesn't know her. He never did.

Kinzie doesn't submit to anyone. No matter the pain, or the cause. That's why she was tortured for four days. Quinn and one of her trusted healers fought them off. And it took Kinzie two weeks to heal. Which is unusual for a vampire. Gold is their weakness. It is believed that gold is a curse to vampires because it resembles the sun. And silver to werewolves is silver because it resembles the moon. No one is sure why. But that's how it always has been.

Anna waited patiently next to his side, before Quinn opened his eyes, he said, "Call Kinzie, tell her to go to the realm." Anna got up and quickly followed instructions. Dialing the McCoy house as fast as her fingers would allow.

......*

The phone rang loudly. Michelle answered, "Hello?"

A woman on the other end of the phone replied, "Hello is this Kinzie?"

"No, But this is her sister. How can I help you Ma'am?"

"Quinn asked me to send her a message. Go to the realm. Whatever that means," She replied with a sigh.

"Is he alright?"

"Yes, William broke into his room and put him in a paralysis spell. But he seems to be coming out of it now. I'm not sure where William went. But he took a portal and broke some other things."

"What's your name?" Michelle asked.

"Anna," She replied shortly.

"Thank you, Anna. Take care of him. We can take the rest from here. Be well," Michelle replied.

" Thank you, and same to you," She said then the dial tone rang.

Michelle ended the call and sighed in relief, and rose from the couch. James had his head tilted back and his eyes closed. She smiled and proceeded to Tim's room, and knocked on the door.

" Come in," Tim's groggy voice called.

"I got a call from Quinns contact. He said to tell Kinzie to go to the realm," Michelle said after opening the door.

Kinzie sat up, "Are you sure that's what he said?"

"Positive. He's alright. His contact is with him now," Michelle leaned up against the wall.

"Alright," Kinzie replied, staring off into space. She hadn't been there in a long time.

Tim sat up, "Are you sure about this?"

"We have to go to the vampire realm ourselves. There are people there who can help me. And that I trust with everything." Kinzie croaked.

Her condition is only getting worse. So Tim had no choice but to nod and agree, "Alright. We'll go "

"Only you can come with me, Tim. Michelle and James have to stay. I'm only allowed one person to come with me. And, you want to know more about me, right?" Kinzie tried to give a smile.

"I appreciate your efforts in trying to make me laugh. But this is serious. I don't know where I'm going . And I am a *human* going into a *vampire* realm. I might as well be bate."

Kinzie exited a laugh from her lips, "No one is going to eat you. Forget anything you've seen in the movies. Most of them are inaccurate and they're garbage."

"Alright. I trust you," Tim sighed. He doesn't do too well with the rest of the unknown. A whole nother realm. How do they get back? How do they get there?"

"Alright, Tim. We are going to walk through a portal. That being said, stay close to me. Don't talk to anyone," Kinzie said softly.

"Where are we walking to?," Tim asked.

"This," Kinzie said, revealing a glass bottle.

"And what do we do with that?"Tim Asked.

"We break it in front of a mirror. It'll create an entryway," Kinzie replied.

"Do you have a specific person in mind?"

"Yes. A very good friend. His name is Bron. He's one of the best healers and the most knowledgeable among the Vampire community." Kinzie replied.

"Alright. Let's pack a bag. And make sure you have extra clothes and plenty of blood bags," Tim replied.

"Alright. Let's move quickly," Kinzie replied softly. Her voice wasn't getting any better, " Also bring as much of the potion as we can carry. He Bron is going to want a sample."

"Kinzie, hon. I love you dearly. But I've got it. Please rest your voice and your body. I'll go over everything before we leave," Tim replied gently. Since the sun was down, he wandered around the house freely. He went upstairs to Kinzie's closet, to get a backpack large enough to carry everything. Once he found one.

He folded four days of clothes and made sure she had an extra pair of shoes. Then he hurried downstairs and packed himself the same. Michelle came around the corner and gave him a Carton of cigarettes and a plastic bag. She also handed him a fabric bag with blood bags, non perishable products, and a water bottle of the potion.

"Take care of her, will you please?" Michelle pleaded.

" Of course," Tim took the kind gestures and packed them. Once he closed the bag, he pulled Shell into a hug, "It's okay, you take care of yourself. I promise I won't let anything bad happen."

"Okay. I will," Michelle patted his back and pulled away, " see you when you get back."

"Alright," Tim smiled. He went back into the office. And did as he promised, " Alright, you have a few blood bags, a water bottle of the potion. I have a few snacks, and we each have four days of clothes. And I brought you an extra pair of shoes."

"Alright. Let's go," Kinzie nodded and sat up. Tim put his arm around her. They walked over to the desk and she opened the bottom left drawer. There was a wooden box with velvet inside and it held six glass bottles. The velvet held their shape. Kinzie pulled out a mirror from a crack in between the bookshelves. And Chanted Brons name it what Tim assumed to be the vampire language. Then broke the glass at the bottom of the mirror. The mirror's reflection was no longer the office, but of a living room with a stone floor and a fur carpet.

Kinzie started to move forward. And Tim walked with her. For a moment they felt wet and then they entered what looked to be Bron's living room. A heavily tattooed vampire came around the corner. Black hair and honey gold eyes. He had to be six feet tall. He was muscular. He had a strong jaw and a very pissed off look on his face, when he saw Tim. But then he looked down at Kinzie," Sweet God's Kinzie what happened?" He came over and looked at her eyes.

"I don't know. But could you take us in please? I need your help," Kinzie replied. Her voice was so broken you could barely understand her.

"Yes, of course. Here let me take your bag," he reached out to Tim. He handed it to him.

"Sorry to startle you, I'm Tim," He nodded.

"And I'm Bron. Nice to meet you. Sorry for the sour look. It's just a lot that has been going on lately. And I wanted to make sure no stranger was walking through my portal," he replied, setting the bag down on a wooden couch.

Tim and Kinzie made their way slowly to the couch. He seated her first, "I understand. I'd be the same way."

"What's going on with Kinzie?" Bron asked. .

"I'm right here!" Kinzie croaked.

"Your voice is cracking and you need to rest. I know you're here. I just don't want you to over do it,"Bron said sternly

"Love you too," she muttered under her breath.

Bron looked at her and squinted his eyes. Kinzie put her hands up in surrender. Bron noded and gave his attention to Tim.

"Well she's been sick for a while now. She's been vomiting, she can't maintain her own balance. And a friend of ours made a potion that seemed to help. But she's only getting worse. We've tried contacting the council but they didn't reply. And we think that William is after her. We've tried everything," Tim sighed.

"Alright. Do you think William is taking control of the council?"

" Yes," Tim nodded.

"Then that would explain the chaos happening around here," Bron replied, walking over to examine Kinzie. He crouched down and put his hand on her forehead. Then he gently pulled the lid of her eye up.

"What's been happening here?," Tim asked.

"Well the council is just silent. Usually they're more involved. They're up in the castle all day everyday. Anyone who tries to talk to them is told to come back later. And we're all thinking that someone is manipulating the council. Or something," Bron replied. Stroking Kinzie's hair.

"Interesting,"Tim's voice trailed off.

"Very well. Kinzie, you are going to rest in the guest bedroom, "Bron said standing up.

Kinzie just nodded and reached her arms up. Bron turned to look at Tim, " Do you mind if I?"

Tim shook his head, " No not at all. You haven't seen each other in a while. Do you mind if I smoke? "

"No, go ahead. Come on Kid," Bron reached down and scooped her up. Carrying her bridal style out of the room. For a moment Tim was jealous. But he knows Kinzie loves him. He pulled the carton and tore his way to pull out a cigarette. Once he lit it Bron came back. And sat next to him, he pulled out a clay ashtray from a shelf, and handed it to Tim.

"Oh thanks," Tim smiled and put it on his lap.

"No problem," Bron paused, " How long have you known Kinzie?"

"Three years. You?"

"Since she turned. I'm a couple hundred years older than she is. That's why I call her Kid," Bron smiled wide.

"Ah. I see," Tim exhaled.

"What's your story?" Bron asked.

" What do you mean?" Tim ashed his cigarette.

"I mean, who are you? Where did you grow up?"

"I'd really prefer not to talk about it," Tim exhaled again and put his cigarette in the tray.

"Alright, I'm sorry. I don't mean to make you uncomfortable," Bron.

"Actually, if you don't mind, I could use some rest too," Tim sighed.

"Alright. I'll show you where the bedroom is," Bron stood up.

"Thank you,"Tim stood up and followed him. He walked him directly to Kinzie. She lay curled up and comfortable on one side of the mattress.

"You're welcome, I hope you rest well," Bron turned and walked away.

Tim didn't mean to be short or snippy. But his past is very sensitive to him. His father died young and his mother died a few months after he joined Kinzie. One of the few people in the world who knows him inside and out, gone. Just like that. No warning. It feels so empty. Kinzie stayed up late with him when he couldn't sleep. He didn't understand how. But now he does. She's a worrier just like him. Riding the waves of life. And embraces peace when it comes. Tim lay on the mattress next to her and closed his eyes. Any rest would be nice.

If Bron had a heart it would've pounded the second he saw Kinzie. He's never seen her like this before. But it was nice to have her in his house again. He remembers the nights she stayed here. His story is long. But a painful one. His father was drunk often and his mother was no more. He worked as a black Smith which is why he's so muscular. Later on when he was older he confronted his father and left. One night he went out walking in the woods. And the next thing he knew he felt a shooting pain in his neck that felt like hot daggers.

That's the short version. That's all he can afford to remember. The rest is much too painful. He got some firewood and lit the fireplace. Afterwards he remembered the day he met Kinzie.

She was unconscious. Bloody neck and had Ash all over her. In her hair. Her breathing was slow. But her heartbeat was the exact opposite. Pounding so hard you would think her ribs would've broken. The head master asked Bron to look after her until she rose. He did so.

" I know you can hear me. I'm sure you're scared but there's no need. It'll be alright, I hope you don't mind if I wash your hair," you're too beautiful to have ash in it," Bron said softly.

He took a bucket of hot water, a rag and a metal comb and washed her hair. He noticed when he combed it her heartbeat slowed. He continued to do this until the ash was gone.

"There that's better," Bron whispered. Her hair trickled down the side of the couch.

"If you're feeling any pain, it's normal. I'm going to move you to a place more comfortable," Bron said softly. He picked her up gently. She was tiny compared to him. He carried her to the hay mattress he made.

◇...◇...◇

A feeling in the air snapped him out of his moment of memory. He got up and rushed to the bedroom, Tim looked up, "I was about to call for you."

"What's the matter?" Bron replied, walking around the bed.

" She just vomited and she's not responding," Tim replied quickly.

Bron looked down at the floor. He felt her forehead, "She's burning up. Kinzie, hold on." He closed his eyes and tried talking to her through his mind. That failed. Then he connected to her mind.

"Kinzie?" Bron called.

"Yes?" Her voice replied crying.

"What's wrong?" Bron replied following the sound of her voice.

" My stomach hurts," she cried. ," From the time that I was stabbed."

"Come to me, please. I need to see it," Bron called back.

Kinzie appeared before him slowly. She held her left rib cage. And limped closer and closer. Once she was in front of him she revealed her wound. A scar appeared on her abdomen under her right breast.

" Okay, okay. I know what to do. I'll be back,"
Bron exited her mind. His eyes snapped open and he picked her up and carried her to the bathroom.

Tim already suspected that he'd be giving her a cold bath "is there anything I can do to help?"

"Yes, actually take those buckets by the door. And fill them up with water and bring them back here. Please," Bron replied, rummaging through the cabinet.

Tim moved quickly. He picked up both buckets with one hand. Filled them up and brought them inside one handed. He didn't know how. But he brought them to Bron. Bron poured one bucket in the bathtub. And lifted her shirt. A red mark appeared where she was stabbed. Tim's eyes widened.
"What the hell is that?"

"Look, Tim. I'll tell you all you'd like to know. But Kinzie comes first. We need to cool down her body heat. Once she's comfortable I'll tell you. Okay," Bron lowered her shirt. Felt her forehead and arms. And for a moment he locked eyes with Tim.

"Alright," Tim exhaled a sigh.

"Kinzie," Bron spoke while lifting her eyelids, "Come on Kid. Come back to us."

Tim approached the bathtub and got down on his knees. He stroked her hair, "Kinzie I know you're trying. You can do this. Just feel my touch. And hear my voice. Come back."

"What the hell?" Bron looked confused.

"What?" Tim raised an eyebrow.

"I just heard a heartbeat,"Bron stammered for a reply.

"Well yeah I'm right here," Tim laughed sarcastically.

"No. I can hear yours. I mean I heard one beat," Bron replied and widened his eyes. And looked at Kinzie. Kinzie's eyes snapped open.

"What happened?" She croaked.

"You were overheating, you vomited and your old scar started turning red," Bron replied.

"Which one," Kinzie asked, closing her eyes.

" The one you and William fought before he got banished," Bron's voice got softer.

"Sensitive topic got it," Tim thought.

"Oh," Kinzie opened her eyes. Tears started to swell.

"Hey Tim, erm. Can you get Kinzie a change of clothes? And maybe smoke a cigarette. We're gonna talk for a sec," Bron replied. His voice was hesitant. And hurt.

"Sure, bud. I'll be back, love," Tim replied standing up. He exited the room and closed the door behind him.

Once the door was shut Bron turned to look at her, "You know it's not your fault."

"I know. I haven't told him that part of my past yet. It's just too painful," Kinzie, a tear rolled down her face.

" Hey, it's okay. If you'd like I can tell him about it," Bron hated seeing her cry. She doesn't do it often, when she does. Her soul can't handle it anymore.

"Please, that would be great," She nodded.

"Alright. I'll do that once we get you back in bed," Bron nodded, "Hey Tim!" He called.

Tim came in a few moments later,clothes in hand," Hey."

"Alright go ahead and get her dressed,and take her to the bedroom. I will tell you what happened," Bron Replied leaving the room.

"Are you okay?" Tim asked, helping her out of the tub.

"No. I'm just emotional and weak. Bron will tell you why. I just need to rest," Kinzie replied, drying off, and getting dressed. Using Tim's shoulder for balance.

"Okay. Sounds good," Tim replied gently rubbing her back.

" Okay. I'm ready," Kinzie replied leaning against the wall.

"Alright, I've got you," Tim leaned down and scooped her up gently. She opened the door, and Tim carried her to the bedroom. And lay her down delicately, "I'll see you soon." He whispered. Kinzie nodded and rolled over.

Tim found Bron was waiting in the living room. Tim seated himself in an older upholstered chair across from him. Bron looked at the fireplace wondering where to start. The crackle of the fire was a welcoming reminder of what once was.

"Kinzie and William have always been enemies. They never saw eye to eye. Kinzie was a vampire who wanted to save lives. William was the vampire who was dark and angry. Wanted to see death upon the humans. He did terrible things. And Kinzie fought him to protect the humans. But it failed. He stabbed her with a Golden sword. And detonated a device that killed 11,000 humans, maybe more. Kinzie was the highest in command. She's lucky to have survived. He made her so weak she couldn't move. So I went out to find her. The sun was rising. And at last I found her. It took her about two weeks to recover from that. But she'll never forget the screams that came from that place. The cries for help. Men, women, children are all dead. And to this day she's convinced it's her fault. But it's not. She did everything she could. Weeks after that she cried, not from the pain. But for the lives lost. She's seen the worst in people, but she still holds hope," Bron paused. Tears filled his eyes.

"I'm sorry," Tim's voice barely audible.

"Thank you," Bron choked on his reply.

"Can you show me?" Tim asked, " I want to see."

"No you don't," Bron shook his head, tears still streaming down his cheek, " I appreciate your sympathy Tim. I really do. But please trust me. You don't want to carry that burden of memory."

"I used to serve in the army. So I've seen my fair share of terrors. But I trust you. I'm so sorry," Tim replied softly. He saw Kinzie linger in the hallway. She shuffled over to bron and got on her knees. Opening her arms.

Bron took her embrace and cried. The motherly gesture was beautiful to say the least. She rubbed his back with one hand and held his head with the other. He squeezed her tight. Tears are still falling. There's something about a woman who embraces a man's emotions that is so attractive. Someone who can feel with you. It took a moment to realize Kinzie was crying with him. Tim knows how comforting that is, and he was glad to know she does the same with everyone.

"I'm sorry. For both of you," Tim said softly. He couldn't imagine seeing such horror. A part of him still wanted him to see. But at the same time he knew Bron was doing him a favor.

Kinzie pulled away and kissed Bron on the head, "Thank you, Tim." She turned back and her face was damp from the tears she cried.

She came over and sat in his lap. She curled up into his chest, "There have been good times too. But the bad weighs heavier than the good."

"Oh are you talking about that one time you led a few of us to a town and we acted like humans for a night. We went out drinking," Bron laughed.

"Yeah," Kinzie laughed.

"So you guys have literally known each other forever," Tim looked down at her.

"Yes," Bron nodded.

"God, you guys are making me feel so old," Kinzie laughed again and covered her face.

"I'm right there with you sister. Keep in mind I'm a couple hundred years older than you," Bron replied, pointing his finger.

"So do you guys have special abilities?" Tim asked.

"Not like most people think. Our senses get heightened. And some can sense some things stronger than others," Bron shrugged, "For example. I could sense Kinzie was ill before you said anything."

"I can sense the atmosphere around us when we were looking at crime scenes," Kinzie looked up at him.

"Ah, so that's why you're so good at your job," Tim smiled and put his arms around her.

"What have you seen?" Bron asked.

"I'd rather not talk about it," Tim sighed.

"You're not much of a talker about your past," Bron observed.

"Nope," Tim said honestly. Not meaning to be short or snippy.

"It's alright. I can understand that," Bron smiled. He didn't realize he and Tim were so similar until just now. Both are tall. Both don't talk about their past. And both love Kinzie. And both have had the best bright out of them through Kinzie.

"I appreciate that," Tim replied with a slight nod.

"I'm going to go back and get some rest," Kinzie said, giving Tim a kiss on the cheek.

"Wise idea, rest well," Bron said.

"I will," She replied, getting up and exiting the room.

"I'll be right there," Tim said smiling.

Bron sat quietly on the couch deep in thought. *How is William attacking her? He doesn't possess any magical abilities. Maybe he created an army. Or manipulated someone who does? And why? Is he still holding a grudge from so many years ago?* He didn't understand the details. All he knew was that someone was attacking Kinzie. Take William out and Kinzie will get better.

Meanwhile Tim remembered when she first went into a club undercover.

◇...◇...◇

Kinzie was wearing dark eyeshadow and black stilettos. She wore a red dress that came just above her mid thigh. Tim saw her and bit his lip. When she approached, "Damn girl," exited his lips. Kinzie smiled. She was wearing matching red lipstick. And kept walking. The man she was walking towards was dangerous. He was one of the biggest gun dealers in the area. Powerful and doesn't give a damn about any lives that turn against him. He also has a prostiton ring.

"Hello," he said.

"Hello," Kinzie replied in a british accent.

"You're gorgeous, what's your name?" He said, sipping his whisky.

"Sarah," She replied.

"You're the lady in red?"

"Yes darling. I was wondering if you want to dance?" She asked, lowering her head and biting her lip. It wasn't the first time she had to seduce a man to arrest him.

"Yes ma'am I'd love to," He stood up and grabbed her hand.

"Lets go," She reached her hand out.

He took it, and followed her to the dance floor. Once they arrived at the center, she shook her hips to the beat. And pushing herself up against him. He turned her around and pulled her closer, Kinzie looked around and found Tim and the other plainly clothed officers, "This is a beautiful club you've got," she said. And shook her hips while lowering herself down. She shook hips, and came back to a stance and looked him deep in his eyes.

"So, are you the one who has the connections?" He asked. His black eyes glistened.

"I am," She replied smiling.

" Oh alright. I'm holding an auction on Friday. And I'd like you to be there," he replied.

"Alright I'll be there. I assume you're going to send me an invitation in private," She stood on her tiptoes, and whispered in his ear.

He shivered, " Yes ma'am."

"Alright then," She leaned in and kissed him. A sign of respect. And locking a deal with the devil. If there's anyone you don't want to mess with, it's the lady in red. He kissed back.

"I'll see you Friday then darling," She said and exited the club swishing her hips as she walked out. She could feel him staring at her as she left.

The lady in red is an alias that she used to trap the man. Sarah Jones, She has connections to class three weapons, and has connections to perverts that will bet on women who are in the ring. Sex slaves. This man hasn't been caught ever. He's been running this business for over 20 years. Once she and Tim got in the car. And drove off. She forced a sigh.

"What's wrong?" Tim asked.

"I feel disgusting," She replied, admiring the moon out the window.

"Why?" Tima asked.

"I kissed a man who killed 20 women for disobeying him and 15 men for a deal gone wrong. Why do you think so?"

"I'm sorry I didn't see you Kiss him. But we're one step closer," Tim replied, hardening his eyebrows.

"It's not your fault," She replied softly.

"Do you wanna go back home?" Tim asked.

Kinzie shook her head, and tears started to fall from her face.

"You want to stay with me?"

She nodded and sniffled.

"I wonder what she's thinking right now," *Tim thought to himself.*

She stayed silent, still looking at the moon. Her comfort and her oldest of friends.

"You can sleep in the bed and I'll stay on the couch," He replied softly.

"I don't want to be alone. Please, I'll stay on one side of the bed," Kinzie whispered.

"Okay," Tim nodded.

Friday came, and they caught him.

Tim smiled, "I'm going to lie down with Kinzie."

"I'm going to take a walk. Go ahead and make love to her," Bron stook up.

Tim laughed, "Yessir."

Bron exited the room, closing the front door behind him. And Tim rushed to the bedroom. Kinzie waited for him undressed, "I heard. I'm ready."

Tim undressed and climbed on top of her. He kissed her neck and her lips. Kinzie let out a moan. Tim hovered over her opening, and slowly inserted himself inside slowly. Kinzie moaned louder. Tim started to thrust slowly, and let out a soft moan. Kinzie clawed his back. And gripped his shoulders. Tim's pace quickened. Kinzie's moans grew louder. She bit her lip and her temple began to show. Tim's skin slapped against Kinzie's. He pulled her closer and breathed into her neck. Kinzie's moans got louder. Tim kissed her neck and his hand slid down her stomach, he placed his thumb on her clitrus and started rubbing the sweets spot. Kinzie moaned the loudest. Tim bent down and kissed her deeply. Continuing the rubs and slapping of the skin. This continues for longer than five minutes. And before Kinzie knew it bliss showered over her. Soon after Tim finished too. He fell down to her side, breathing heavy. "Come here," and pulled her closer. She scooted herself close to him. And smiled. Satisfied and supported. Kinzie fell asleep quickly. Tim however stayed up. Watching her lie in the stillness lifeless. Motionless. Not even breathing. But he knows she isn't dead. Just still as can be. Still lethargic. And slowly getting worse. She's stronger than she looks though. That's for certain. The moonlight peered through the window and Tim found himself staring at the woman he just made love to. He couldn't sleep. Not yet. And finally that night. Tim got some sleep.

The next evening Kinzie woke up mildly more refreshed than the day prior. It might have something to do with the activities the night before. But it felt good not having to rely. On anyone for support or to carry her. After slowly shutting the door behind her she tiptoed into the living room and sat on the couch. The house was quiet. Bron was probably still asleep. So she pulled out a pen and some paper from the end table next to her and started drawing memories of her old life. Her house and the farm. And her horse that saved her sister. It helped her forget that she was sick. Just for a moment. Until three hours later the door to Brons room opened.

"Morning," she said.

"Kinzie, why are you up so early?" Bron groaned.

"I couldn't sleep anymore," she said quietly.

"And Tim?" Bron asked, rubbing his eyes.

"Knocked out cold. Which is good. He needs the rest," she replied. Her voice is still miserable. Bron's just gotten used to it now.

"I bet," He chuckled in reply.

" Why are you up so early?" She retorted.

"Nightmare," Bron replied shortly.

" Wanna come give me company in case I pass out or something?" Kinzie replied jokingly. She knew it would pluck Bron's nerves. Acting like her life doesn't matter.

"Sure, why not?" He replied through his teeth. He moved the drawing in the seat next to her. He glanced at a few of them and smiled.

"What?" Kinzie asked, looking up at him.

"Nothing," He chuckled, sitting next to her.

"Yeah? You're blushing," She replied, nudging his arm.

"I'm just amazed at how talented you are," Bron locked eyes with her, he paused, "Are you feeling alright?"

"A little weak and light headed. But that seems like the usual now other than that. I'm fine. Why do you ask?"

"Your irises aren't the same color as before. They're a darker color. I can't describe it," He leaned in looking closer.

"Bucket," Kinzie croaked, covering her mouth.

Bron disappeared and reappeared with a bucket in hand. Kinzie took it and let it all out. Bron sat next to her and felt her forehead, then pulled her head back.

"Do you want me to get Tim?" He asked. Kinzie shook her head.

"He needs to re-" She vomited again.

"Yeah, But he also needs to know what's happening," Bron kept her hair back.

Kinzie still shook her head.

"Damn it Kid! Stop being so stubborn. He would want to know! I would like to know. Screw this, Tim!" Bron yelled.

Kinzie looked up at him with glossy eyes. She wasn't shocked because he went against her wishes. She wasn't even angry. She was surprised because he admitted that he still loves her. Tim's heavy footsteps approached closer.

"What's going on?" Tim asked. He approached with shorts. And nothing else.

"She's vomiting again. And her irises aren't blue. They're darker somehow," Bron replied quickly.

"Thanks for getting me," He replied, kneeling down in front of her.

"No problem, " Bron nooded.

"Kinzie, look at me," Tim looked into her eyes. Bron was right. Her irises shifted from a navy blue to black. Or so it seemed, "Is there anything we can do?"

"Not right now. The best thing we can do is to get her to rest, and give her cool baths. That is while we figure out the root of her illness. And take it out," Bron replied.

"Well William from what I understand is the cause. So we might need to bate him into coming into the realm," Tim put his hand on Kinzie's head.

"That's not a bad idea," Bron agreed.

"Alright, then. Hopefully he'll respond before anything else happens," Tim replied with a sigh.

"Do you want to try the potion?" Bron asked.

Kinzie shook her head, "I don't want to vomit anymore."

"You need something in your system, love," Tim replied.

"Alright. Let's do half a blood bag, with the potion and see," Kinzie replied leaning her head back.

Tim nodded and got up to go into the bedroom. His heart sank while he rummaged through the bag. Once he grabbed everything He came back into the room, "Do you have any cups?"

"Yeah, I'll take that," Bron reached out his hand. Tim handed it to him and went around waiting for Bron to stand up. Then they traded places. Kinzie rested her head on Tim's shoulder. He kissed the top of her head.

"It'll be okay," He whispered.
Kinzie just nodded. She's been through much worse than this. All she could think about was Michelle, James and Quinn. She would rather be the target than anyone else. It's not a hero complex. It's just protecting the ones she loves the most. Michelle is all that she has left as far as blood. Quinn has always been around and considers him a father. And James is in love with Michelle. Therefore she considers him a brother. And Tim has always been there. She's always loved him.

Chapter Ten

Michelle lingered in the living room facing the window, a hot cup of tea steaming in her hand. James came from behind her and hugged her waist. He knew that her mind weighed heavily on her sister. It's already been three days. *Why would anyone want to do this to her?* she thought to herself while sipping her tea. She doesn't know how long she's been standing there. She's always been a worry wart. But this is a whole new level of worry. The fact that someone is actually trying to kill Kinzie, gives a good reason. A sense of hopelessness lingered in the air. Just the thought of losing Kinzie makes her chest tense. Making it harder to breathe.

"Shell?" James said softly.

"Yes," Michelle breathed.

"Why don't we go upstairs and lie down?" James asked.

"I don't know if I can sleep," Michelle sighed.

"Stop fighting it. You're allowed to be emotional. Come here," James gently tugged her shoulders, to try and get her to turn around.

Michelle buried her head into his ribs and cried. The sobbing made her hands shake, and her teacup dropped and shattered. The sound of her heart. James pulled her in closer. For so long she's been strong and certain. But now she's weak and vulnerable emotionally. Like she once was. But James wasn't wrong. She hides her emotions, and very well. But today she saw them peek through the cracks. If there's anyone strong enough to endure this kind of attack. It's Kinzie. Somehow she knew Kin grows weaker. James just held her and gave full support. He gently pulled her bare feet away from the glass. He started humming and kissing the top of her head. How does he remember so much about her?

"It's going to be alright," James said softly.

"Thank you," She breathed.

"Always," James Kissed her head. "I'll get the mug,"

"Thanks, I think I'm going to sit and try and watch something. I need to get my mind off of everything," Michelle replied, nodding and seating herself on the couch. James went into the kitchen to get the broom. Hearing sounds from the TV, he swept up the mug and looked up to find Michelle asleep on the couch. James felt a smile appear. She was so stubborn for no reason. Or so it seemed. She couldn't sleep, because she was too worried. James has seen that before. According to her, only he knew how to break down her emotional barriers. After he cleaned the remaining tea. He seated himself where Michelle's feet rested. He too drifted off to sleep.

......*

Quinn was sitting up in bed taking a sip of tea. Anna sitting with him, "I'm glad you're alright."

'I am also, but I worry for Kinzie," he sighed, placing his empty tea cup on the night table.

"She's more capable than you think Quinn," Anna reassured him.

"I know..it's just this whole thing is so complex. And it's that way on purpose. However it seems as though Michelle is alright," Quinn murmured, his voice trailing off.

"Keep in mind Quinn. Kinzie is his primary target. Michelle is only going to suffer because Kinzie is. They are spirit bound. That being said, he's trying to cover his tracks. But everyone knows the council. He must have some powerful friends for them to be Manipulated," Anna said.

"Yes, but the solution to that is simple, and Kinzie knows it," Quinn continued mouthing. And thinking.

"Then what about Kinzie's life long term? Is he trying to kill Kinzie?" Anna asked.

"No, no. Nothing like that at all," Quinn waved his hands. Most would think Quinn was in a state of madness. But Anna knew what he was doing. He was trying to solve the puzzle. They both know why William was doing what he was doing? They wanted to know how. What kind of contacts does he possess? Who could possibly brainwash six members on the vampire council, and make an older vampire ill? It could be just him. He would've had the time to develop his powers and grow them. And master dangerous skills. However there has never been a vampire in history to hold this level of magic.

"Then what's happening?" Anna asked.

" He's trying to create an anarchy," Quinn whispered. Kinzie is one of the few with the skills and the experience disable him. If she and the council vanished. Vampires would be free to roam. Go to other world's. Especially the rogues.

Anna's eyes widened,"That does make perfect sense."

" We thought it would be anarchy in the human world only but in all honesty. He would have access everywhere. Oh my God," Quinn gasped. Kinzie was headmaster of the vampires and banished him. And This is what he does? How mad would a vampire have to be to even attempt such a thing?

"I need to call Michelle and see if she can contact Tim. They need to be informed of this madness," Quinn spoke. Barely audible. Anna just nodded, she handed him her cellphone. After dialing a number he didn't even have to think about. The line rang.

......*

The house phone rang. Michelle jerked up from the couch and reached for the wireless phone nesting on the table next to the couch, she cleared her throat and answered, " Hello?"

"Hello Shelly, I apologize that I woke you but I have important information," Quinn replied.

"Oh papa! Thank God you're alright. I'm listening," She let out a sigh.

"William isn't just trying to take over the human race. He's trying to take control of all worlds. That's the only explanation I can provide. Disable the Higher Power, and you're free to roam and cause chaos and anarchy," Quinn sighed. He sounded exhausted.

"Of course he would be crazy and stupid enough to make such an attempt. I'm sure Kinzie and Tim will figure that out," Michelle yawned.

" Speaking of Timothy, I was going to ask you if you could phone him and let him know what's happening," Quinn asked.

"I can try. I'm not sure if he'll get a signal there, and if they're hiding I don't want to give them away," Michelle replied.

"Alright thank you Shelly. I should arrive there in a few days. Goodbye," Quinn replied.

"Bye," she ended the call. She picked up her cell phone and messaged Tim. Then rolled over and went back to sleep.

......*

Tim ran his fingers through her hair as she lay resting on his lap. Bron sat across from then in the chair rubbing his temples. He froze, " Erm, Tim. Something just vibrated in your bedroom."

"Oh! That's my phone. I didn't think I'd get a signal here. Bron, would you mind sitting with her while I go get it?"

"No," Bron shook his head and stood up.

Tim stood up gently and held Kinzie's head. Bron sat and slid his leg underneath. Tim turned around and walked down the hall.

He checked his phone, "message from. Shell McCoy "

Tim,
Quinn just called and he's fine. He said that William isn't trying to
create an anarchy in the human realm. He's trying to have access
to all portals, All realms and The human world happens to be one
of them. I didn't want to call in case you were hiding. Keep Kinzie
safe. Hope to hear from you soon,
Much love
-Shell.

Tim's thoughts began to flood. So many more questions rather
than answers. The only other person who can help is Bron. Tin
sighed. And went back out onto the living room. Only to find
Bron spacing out.

"Hey, you okay?" Tim asked.

"Yeah. Just my mind wandering off a bit," Bron cleared his throat.

" So Michelle messaged me and let me know some thoughts. She
said that Quinn is thinking that William is doing what he's doing
because he wants to access all worlds and portals. So basically
take out the people who can stop him, then do what he wants,"
Tim sighed. And sat in the chair.

"Do you want to come back over here?" Bron asked, raising an eyebrow.

"No, I need to think. Plus I think it's fair that you spend time with her. You haven't seen her in so long," Tim pulled out a cigarette and lit it.

" Thank you," Bron smiled.

"No problem. Man. I'll be back," Tim said walking into the bedroom once Bron heard the door close, he felt a wave of guilt.

"Stop it," Kinzie croaked.

How did she always know what he was thinking? "I can't help it right now."

"He'll be back out. He's not upset at you. He just needs time to process alone. And sometimes that's the best way to find the answers you're looking for," Kinzie replied, her eyes still closed.

"I understand," He said softly, "Kinzie, I'm sorry."

"For what?" Kinzie asked, eyes still closed.

" For not being in the human world. I know you begged me to come with you. I just hate seeing you like this. I just wish there's more that I can do," Bron's heart sank as he spoke.

"Stay strong, We'll figure this out. I would rather be the one suffering than Michelle, Tim, you, James or Quinn. I know my life is at risk and I have some Idea of what William is capable of, But one of the important things also is getting the council to see who William is. But first I'm going to rest," Kinzie replied feeling light headed. She could feel herself fading fast.

"Alright. I'll be here," Bron said, stroking her hair. With each time her body felt heavier. Until at last she was asleep. He was glad to see that she's finally getting some rest. He didn't stop stroking her hair. And tried to push his thoughts out of his mind. It was no use. The memory of the day they found Kinzie, when she was being tortured. Flooded his mind.

The day he and Quinn found her she was hanging still on golden shackles. Made to make it hurt worse. There were dark spots all over her arms and neck. Luckily her face hadn't been touched. She might've gone blind or something. He looked across and saw a string go behind a door. But the string was attached to a window which was blacked out with some kind of paint. But behind the door were security camera footage. Bron couldn't help himself. He rewinded the tape and heard everything. Kinzie's voice screaming in agony. Bron cried, loudly. Just for a moment. And composed himself so he could free Kinzie quickly.

Which he did. He brought her here. And watched her sleep for almost two weeks. Making sure she feeds, and bandaging her wounds. Which took about a week to heal. But in that time he never left her side. The first night Kinzie woke up she cried in his arms. There's always been a bond between them. One they didn't know how to define. That has no relevance. The bond is there. That's all either of them needed to know.

She looks so tired and weak like she did then. Why does this feel so helpless? She doesn't even love him anymore. But he loved her. More than he'd like to admit. However he is glad to find Tim despite him being a mortal. Had made her happy. That's all a man ever wants. To have a woman he truly loves is happy.

Kinzie slept for a while. Bron began to question how long. Until Tim opened the door. To the bedroom. Once he entered the living room he lit a cigarette, "Has she been resting all night?"

Bron nodded.

"Good. I've been trying to think about how William would have done this all by himself. But it's impossible. Yes, he could have gotten powerful one way or another. But he needs followers to monitor all locations. So technically it wouldn't be an anarchy, but nevertheless. That doesn't make him any less dangerous. I vaguely remember a symbol that could help us. It causes people under manipulation, or some sort of spell to see that there's an enemy. Maybe he didn't hurt the council. Maybe he had other people come in assist the council and put them under some sort of hypnotic spell. Who knows," Tim shrugged, " but we should continue to find more information here. While getting a hold of William."

"Wow, Tim. Thanks. That's Incredible, scary, and perceptive of you," Bron smiled.

"Thank you," Tim smiled back, " it's my job. Anyway, do you have anyone here that you trust to give us some information? And maybe they could suggest a few things to help Kinzie too."

"I was hoping we wouldn't leave at all. Since things have gotten so strange. But you do present a fair point. Alright Tim. We'll go see an old friend of ours," Bron looked down at Kinzie, "But let's let Kinzie rest a while."

Tim nodded in agreement, "Fair enough."

......*

Michelle rose from her slumber, stomach churning and liquid coming up her throat. As she rushed to the bathroom, James jolted up. He didn't even bother asking if Michelle was alright, because he already knew she wasn't. He went straight to the bathroom and held back her hair. He felt her forehead. *Damn she's burning up!* James thought. Once Michelle was through, James carried her to bed.

"I think whatever's happening to Kinzie is happening to me," she sighed.

" I'm so sorry, Shell. I know you hate being sick," James replied, grabbing a rag from the bathroom, running cold water over it.

"But I can't complain too much, I have a hot medicine man taking such good care of me," Michelle tried to make James smile. But instead, got silence and a cool damp feeling all around her face. She had almost forgotten how fast he's able to move. The cloth felt good.

"You know you need to tell Tim, right?" James said sadly.

"Yes, I do know. I don't want to. He doesn't need the worry or the stress," Michelle closed her eyes.

"He doesn't need to worry. He chooses to be worried. Just like he chooses to be stressed. He only does those things because he cares about you. Just like we all do. The one you need to worry about Knowing, is Kinzie. Since you two are affected by one other," James lay next Michelle rubbed her back in reassurance.

"You're right. Thank you my love," Michelle smiled, and pulled out her cellphone. And once again texted Tim.

Hey Tim,

I hate to tell you this at such an awful time. But I'm ill. I vomited a few minutes ago. And my body is spiking a fever. I'm alright for now. But Kinzie cannot know. She needs to focus on getting better. Remember I have James here with me. So I'll be alright. Love you both. And please stay safe.

-Michelle

James read it as she was typing. "Short, sweet, to the point. Very nice. How do you think he's gonna handle the news?" James asked.

" He's probably going to sigh and mutter under his breath. But he won't dwell on it. Because there's no point in dwelling," Michelle replied with a yawn," I'm gonna go back to sleep. I have a feeling I'm going to need the rest. "

"Wise idea. Sleep well love," James replied burying his face into her hair. It smelled like honey and flowers. And she did. Since James held her so closely. His body heat calms her nerves. The world seemed to start to spin.

Then waking into her forest of memory, she visited her days in England. Being a barkeep has its ups and downs. If you're attractive, you can get great tips. But ever since the night of the accident, Michelle never felt pretty. Even though people said she

was. She would just nod and say thank you. But internally she would scream, " How do you think I'm pretty?"

For the first time ever she actually felt pretty. And that's because James sees her for her raw beauty within. Strong, emotional, caring, stubborn, loving, and trustworthy. The way James Holds her close to him. It's as though he's cherishing her body. And her mind.

But before that. After she left where she recovered. She hated herself. She had wished Kinzie let her die in the fire. Her burn marks ran deep and covered a good majority of her body. Later on she realized how lucky she was. A woman came into the bar. She was one out of five people. But it was still the afternoon so it kind of ran slow.

"Two whisky shots please," the lady said softly. Tears filling her eyes.

" Coming right up," Michelle replied with a soft smile.

She was a pretty lady. Long brunette hair, blue eyes and kind of pale. But pretty. She was wearing red lipstick.

"I hope you don't mind my asking but, how did you get those?" She gestured her hand pointing to her own face and arm. Back when she could see.

"Erm. My parents died in a house fire along with my three brothers and I was upstairs. I had no idea.My sister saved me," Michelle replied, putting two shot glasses on the counter, and pouring the alcohol to the top. They were small. But who knows. Maybe this woman can handle her liquor.

" I am so sorry. You're lucky," she sighed before throwing back both shots.

" Thank you," Michelle smiled.

" Why don't you feel lucky?" She asked.

"Wait, how did you?-"Michelle looked at her confused.

"Know what you were feeling. It's simple dear. I'm a sencer. I can feel what other people are feeling," she pulled out a pack of cigarettes from her pocket and retrieved one. And lit her cigarette

"Because I carry the scars with me everywhere I go," Michelle replied politely.

"Well it's better than being carried in a box. And never seen or heard from again. That's what happened to my son Recently. I'd rather see him with the battle scars, than watch him be lowered into the ground. But that's just me," tears streamed gently down her face. She inhaled the cigarette.

Michelle was moved, "I'm so sorry. Thank you for sharing your story. It helps put things in perspective."

"I'm glad. Thank you for the Drinks," She smiled. "By the way I think you look like a warrior. A beautiful woman who overcame death." She put down her payment in coins, and left quickly. Wiping her tears away,

Michelle put the money away, still taking in what that customer said. Maybe that's what people saw. She just wanted to be normal again, But that wasn't going to happen. So the best thing to do is accept what has been. And not to predict what will be. She became a stronger, better version of herself since that day.

Michelle's body felt heavy. She tried to open her eyes. Her efforts made her body feel heavier. Why does it feel like an elephant is on her chest? With every breath, there was an ache, "James?" She whispered.

"Hey Shell. I'm here," She heard his voice and felt his hand on her head.

"What's happening?" She coughed.

"Your fever is spiking, and your breathing is irregular," James' voice filled with concern.

"Am I copying Kinzie's symptoms?" Michelle whispered. It seemed like that's the only way she could talk. Why did it hurt so badly to breathe?

"Yes, it appears that way. I need to have someone bring oxygen to the house. You're having trouble breathing on your own," James replied.

"You don't need to. There are oxygen tanks in the basement, along with the sterile tubes. I had ordered extra in case Tim Needed some," Her voice trailed off.

"Alright, I'll be back," James said quickly.

She felt herself fading fast. Why is this happening? *Hurry James.*

......*

        James got up and ran out of the room, making his way down the stairs, first floor hallway, opening the door at the end of the hall, and rushing down the stairs. He scanned the room and found what he was looking for. She was right. There were four oxygen tanks and two sterile tubes for the nostrils. He grabbed one of each and rushed back up the stairs. Being in medicine he knows how to attach everything. He placed the tubing in her nostrils and tucked them around her ears. And turned on the oxygen at the lowest setting.

The sudden pressure in Michelle's nose made her cough. But after a few minutes it seemed to be working well. James had a terrible feeling, things are going to get much worse before they get better. James waited patiently for Michelle to wake. She lay motionless, one would think she's dead. It's truly fortunate that James is there. Otherwise she probably would be. The moon light stretched across the back yard. Kissing the tops of the trees. Every once in a while he would adjust her pillows and make sure she's comfortable. Her cell phone rang, Tim Bryte Came up on the screen. James took a deep breath, "Hello," James answered.

"Hey James it's Tim," Tim whispered.

"Hey," James said softly.

" How's Michelle doing?"

"She's not good. She can't breathe on her own. So we're using oxygen. And now she's not waking up. But I think that's because she needs the rest. But she's a fighter. Just like her sister. I'll message you and keep you posted," James replied softly.

"Thanks buddy, I'd appreciate that. How are *you*?" Tim asked.

"I'm as good as I can be. I'll be better when all this is over," James sighed.

" You and I both. If you need anyone to talk to, I'm here," Tim said quietly.

"You too, man. I'll talk to you later," James said.

"Bye," Tim whispered, and ended the call.

"Bye…" James sighed. *Hopefully she'll wake up soon.*

......*

Tim let out a sigh. He kept his cell phone in his hand. He didn't know how not to tell Kinzie. Michelle is her only family. And if anything happened to her Kinzie would be devastated. He stayed seated on the bed, unable to move yet. He heard a knock on the door, "Come in."

Bron peeked his head in the room and stepped in quietly, " Are you alright Tim?"

"No," He said quietly.

"Is it Her sister?" Bron asked barely audibly.

Tim nodded, whispering, "And Michelle doesn't want her to know."

"Alright. I think that's the best thing to do. She doesn't need that extra concern. I'll help you keep this private. If you ever need to talk, I'm' here," Bron replied.

"Thank you. I hate keeping things from her," Tim put his phone in his backpack.

"I know, But it's for the best. And in this case we need to work quickly," Bron said.

Tim nodded, "You're right. Let's get to work."

Bron smiled and exited the room. Tim followed by shutting the door behind him. They came back to find Kinzie still resting peacefully. Bron turned to Tim and said softly, "I'll go to the friend's house tonight while she's resting. And see if they will come here. I'm afraid to move her," Bron knelt next to the couch and put his hand on her forehead.

"She's getting warm again," A hopeless look crossed his face.

"I'll get a cold bath going. I would imagine it wouldn't take you long to return," Tim replied softly.

"Yeah, Okay. Fair enough. Thanks Tim. I'll be back as soon as I can," Bron Left the house and Tim followed him closely with the buckets. Filling them up with water. It wasn't long before they went their separate ways.

Tim rushed to get as many buckets of water as he could into the bathtub. And at long last lifted Kinzie's heavy body into the bathroom. She was definitely asleep. Tim got her into her bra and underwear before submerging her into the cool liquid.

It wasn't much longer before bron returned. He came into the bathroom to find Time stroking Kinzie's hair, "Welcome back."

"Thank you, Tim, this is Anna. She's a mutual friend if Quinn's. From my understanding, she's already been informed because Quinn stayed with her," Bron said, gesturing his hand toward a woman with red hair.

"Hello Tim," she said softly. Her voice rang with a British accent, which gave him a sense of comfort.

"Hello," he replied, giving a nod.

"May I?" She asked, gesturing her head toward Kinzie.

"Yes, of course," Tim rose and stepped to the side.

"Why don't you and I talk outside Tim?"Bron suggested.

" Alright, let's go," Tim nodded and stepped out of the bathroom. The walk outside seemed longer than it should be.

"I need you to tell me what's going on. You need to get your emotions out so we can focus," Bron said softly.

"I'm worried about Michelle. Kinzie's this bad and I don't know how much longer it's going to be before Michelle is in the same condition as she is. I'm worried Kinzie will never make it out of the state she's in," Tim exhaled a sigh.

"Alright. Fair enough. Now you listen to me very carefully, " Bron's eyes got bright. And firm, locking Tim's eyes to his, "She's not giving up and neither are you. She's been tortured, stabbed, and many other things. She's a fighter. And she's not going to leave this world and her sister behind. Nor you. Nor me probably. Okay? Be strong Tim. Don't let this asshole defeat you before this battle has ended. I know how you feel. I do. That's my sister in there! But we need to be strong and strategic. Do you hear me?"

Tim nodded," Yes."

"I'm not telling you not to be emotional, I'm telling you not to let your emotions affect your strategy. You let that happen. You're giving the bastard power! Now I'm gonna go inside. You stay out here. Smoke a cigarette, do whatever you gotta do. Then come back refreshed. You got me?"

"Yes sir," He gave a nod. No wonder why Kinzie and Bron are so close. They carry themselves with pride. And don't allow anyone to falter. They both give strength in their speeches. And are brutally honest. And don't allow their feelings. To get in their way of the work they're doing at the time. Bron closed the door gently. Tim lit his cigarette, and exhaled heavily.

Bron was right. Now isn't the time to wallow in emotion. This isn't the human world where we go to the hospital and feel helpless and doctors run a million tests and feel the wave of uncertainty crippling your emotions. But here in the country where it is always night. We take control. We find out what's wrong and take action. Tim smoked the last little bit of his Cigarette and went back inside. Putting the remainder in an empty pack.

He peeked back into the bathroom to find Anna quietly talking to Bron, "She's fading slowly, but that gives us more time. We need to find William. And get him back here somehow "

"How much time does she have?" Tim asked.

"She has a week, maybe more. I think I know how he's doing it. There are very dark spells that can manipulate others. But they need something of that person, a lock of hair, or something they touched," Anna said stiffly.

"That bastard!" Bron shouted. Making everyone in the room Jump. Before Bron said another word. Tim knew what it was.

"He's using the handcuffs he bound her with..." Tim's voice was barely audible. He spoke clenching his fists.

"It's important that we have a low stress environment, no shouting, and less anger. I understand you're both angry, but you have *got* to compose yourselves. For her sake," Anna said softly.

"Anna?" Kinzie breathed.

"Kinzie, yes I'm here," she turned toward the tub and knelt down to meet Kinzie's gaze.

"Anna it's so good to see you, I'm sorry you have to see me like this," Kinzie's voice croaked.

"It's good to see you love. And I don't mind at all," She tried to give a reassuring smile.

"Stay with me awhile?" Kinzie croaked.

"Yes, darling I'll stay," Anna replied, stroking her hair.

"Okay," Kinzie smiled and faded back into her sleep. A soft exhale escaped her lips.

"What just happened?" Tim asked.

"I gave her something to get out of whatever is making her sleep so much. This is a good sign. What concerns me is she breathed," Anna said, feeling her forehead.

"Is that a bad thing?" Tim asked, eyes wide.

"It can be. It puts her at a high risk of being more vulnerable, but other than that. I don't think so," Anna replied, stroking her hair, " Alright, let's get her out of the tub. We need to watch her closely."

Bron got a towel, and Anna being closest to the tub drained the water. Tim grabbed the towel, and lifted her out of the tub. And carried her into the bedroom.

Anna followed, "Tim if you'd like I can get her dressed. You look like you could use some rest," Anna said softly.

"Erm. Alright," Tim sighed "I'm sorry, there's just so much going on."

"I understand Tim, all the more reason to rest. No one can care for anyone, if they're not taking care of themselves," Anna replied, drying Kinzie off.

"You sound like I speak from experience, "Tim sat on the bed.

"I do. Where are her clothes and her hairbrush?" Anna Asked.

"It's in the back pack , I can get it," Tim started sitting up.

" No, I see it here. Thank you," she smiled,"Alright darling let's get you into some fresh clothes. And get your hair brushed." Anna grabbed the bag and pulled out an outfit.

Anna took her time. You could tell she's done this before. Does she have a child? Maybe she and a couple of friends went out drinking and she had to do this for them. There was something about her energy that was calming.

"No, I don't have a child, if that's what you're thinking. Part of my job is changing patients in a coma. I talk to them. Because I couldn't imagine hearing machines and trying to sleep. It must be so lonely to be by yourself in your own head," she replied, her voice trailing off.

"Yeah. Must be," Tim replied, eyes growing heavier.

"Rest well Tim," Anna's voice drifted afar.

"I hope Michelle is alright," He thought to himself as his vision went black.

......*

Michelle Lay resting in her bedroom. She appeared far more pale, and they were on the second oxygen tank now. She's going to need more soon. James sat next to her patently. Waiting to see if she'd wake up. A soft knock at the front door brings him out of his daise.

"I'll be back, love," James kissed her head. And lightly jogged down the stairs, "Coming!" He opened the door to Find a familiar face.

"Hello James, I apologize for my delay. I was hoping to be here much earlier, however we had an unexpected surprise that arrived, a-" Quinn stopped and returned the embrace James had given him.

"It's really, I mean *really* good to see you," James said, pulling Quinn tighter.

" Why thank you James. I appreciate that very much, however we should probably go inside. I need an update on everything that's happened since Kinzie has gone," Quinn replied, letting go of his embrace.

"Alright, first we need to go upstairs," James nodded and pulled away. Stepping aside, Quinn entered the foyer quickly.

"Michelle is upstairs in her bedroom. I'll be right behind you," James said, closing the door.

Quinn started walking up the stairs and James followed not too far behind. Quinn froze once he reached the door. Quinns heart sank into his chest.

"How did this happen?" Quinn whispered, unable to talk at any other volume.

"We believe Kinzie and Michelle are bound in the spirit. Since they both survived the attack of their family. So whatever happens to Kinzie will happen to Michelle," James sighed.

"How did you come to discover that?"

"My father told me in a dream," James replied, rubbing the back of his neck.

"That does make sense. I apologize this is a lot of information to retain all at once. We need to get the proper supplies to keep her alive. Poor dear looks so pale," Quinn at last walked into the room.

James just lingered in the doorway. Trying to comprehend why and how this was happening. In a way he felt defeated. But deep down this was dark magic. And even the best of healers would have the same issue. Why is it always so? Something goes well. It has to go bad right after? Or so it seems. James took a deep breath and put aside his emotions. *"She needs more oxygen, a feeding tube, and a heart monitor. For now. We don't know when she'll wake up,"* James thought to himself.

"James?"

"Yes, Quinn?"

"Are you Alright?"

"No, but I will be. I was just making a mental note on what supplies we're going to need for Michelle while Kinzie is away," Jame spoke softly while rubbing his eyes.

"And what have you come up with?" Quinn asked, taking Michelle's hand.

"We're going to need more oxygen, a feeding tube, and that machine that monitors her sinus rhythm and blood pressure. I can't remember what it's called," James yawned.

"Ah yes, I'm assuming you're referring to a patient Monitor, I need to find Kinzie's bank card and phone book. I think I know who to call," Quinn replied heading towards the bedroom door, " I suggest you get some sleep James. This is going to be a long and very trying time."

"But what if som-"

"Nothing is going to happen. And plus you'd be lying right next to her. I'm sure she would want you to rest," Quinn said firmly. Giving off the 'no excuses' tone. He let go of her hand.

All James could do at that point is nod in agreement and force himself into the mattress. Laying next to her. He doesn't want to hurt her in her already delicate state. But it was nice being closer to her. He heard Quinn going downstairs.

"Hey shell. Can I pull you close to me," he looked over and waited patiently for her response.

All Michelle's body would allow was a slight nod. But James was grateful. That's much better than nothing. Carefully he tucked his arm under her head and reached to her mid back and pulled her closer. Putting her head to his chest. Michelle's last moment was putting her arm across his chest.

"Thank y-" She breathed.

"Always my love. Let's get some rest," James replied. He felt his eyes getting heavy and at last he allowed himself to enter a state of sleep.

......*

Quinn sat in Kinzie's office rummaging through her phone book. And found the credit card and at least a few hundred thousand in cash in case of any emergency. At last when He found the number and dialed as fast as his fingers would allow. He heard the phone ring once, twice, then a voice came on the other line.

"Hello?" A man answered.

"Hello, is this Daniel?" Quinn asked.

"It is? I assume this is Mr. Roberts?" He replied, his voice trailing off.

"It is," Quinn replied.

"How can I help you today sir?" Daniel asked.

"Do you happen to have any oxygen tanks, a paetnet monitor and feeding tube supplies handy?"

"Yes sir as a matter of fact I do. But It's going to cost extra since this is the last of my supplies."

"That's not a problem at all. How much is that going to cost me in total?"

"One hundred and fifty thousand," Daniel replied.

"And how much would it cost for delivery tonight?"

"I'm going to have to charge an additional fifty thousand, is everything alright?," Daniel asked.

"Yes, sir. I'll explain further when you arrive. And I'd also like to add more oxygen tanks to the order please. I'm aware you don't have any more in stock so I would like to place a personal order, and have that for delivery also," Quinn replied, kneeling under the desk, and opening a small compartment built in. A small hole appeared in the space with more cash.

"Yes, Mr. Roberts, That is going to be a total of three hundred and seventy five thousand dollars," Daniel replied happily. Quinn could hear him smiling.

"Thank you Daniel, I will see you tonight," Quinn replied, removing the additional cash from the small compartment.

"You're welcome sir. See you tonight," Daniel spoke quickly, ending the call.

Quinn too ended the call. Daniel was the one who delivered Tim's medical supplies to the McCoy house last time. He's not one to ask many questions. But this is the first time he's ordered this many oxygen tanks in one order. Which is probably why he inquired if everything was well. Deep down Quinn was holding on to the thin hope that somehow Kinzie and Tim will detain William. And everything goes back to the way it once was. His mind drifted off to the day he discovered Michelle and Kinzie's parents and brothers were dead.

<>...<>...<>

"Quinn!" A woman's voice rang loudly from the outside.

He jumped and ran outside to find Michelle's laying on the back of the family's horse, Caesar. Her burns are fresh and peeling off. She must have passed out from the pain, "Oh my..." He breathed, "Bring her inside and clean those burns immediately! I need to go to the McCoy house!"

"Yes sir!" A said.

"Also find the healing man James! Send her there if i'm not here," Quinn's eyes filled with tears.

"Yes sir! John, come help me get her inside!" The woman replied.

In this town everyone knew Quinn. He was the main middle man. Quinn hopped on Caesar and went back to McCoy house. Thankfully it wasn't far, but as Quinn approached closer, he saw the McCoy House High in flames. Quinn rushed Caesar to the house so he could have a look inside. He saw his dear friends and their three sons. "Where's Kinzie?" *His voice rang in panic. Echoing. He looked down to find her small footprints.*

"Tell me what happened my friends," he said, referring to the elements around him. He knelt down touching the snow and closed his eyes. He heard Michelle's scream and Kinzie's rescue. And he saw Kinzie out Michelle on Caesar, and told him to find Quinn. Then he saw her get bitten and carried away. They're going east.

"Come Caser! We must go get Kinzie. After this I promise I'll set you free," Quinn's eyes snapped open. The loyal horse came to his call and off they went into the forest. It wasn't long before Quinn was approaching Kinzie's attacker. Kinzie bouncing like a rag doll in his arms. He was hooded so his face remained unknown. But Quinn managed to cut him off, and Drew a sword," if you enjoy your life. You will put her down and run along. "

"Hey out of the way old man, that blade won't cut me," The man growled

"Oh Really?" Quinn swung the weapon into the Vampire's arm, blood started pooling in the snow , " Now I'll say it again, "Put her down and walk on."

The man snarled and placed Kinzie on the ground before running off.

"Caesar, Kneel," Quinn commanded. He did so. Quinn picked Kinzie up and gently wrapped her up. He held her close and made himself comfortable before commanding Caesar to go on.

Quinn arrived at his destination many hours later. Outside of a mansion, Bron stepped outside, and strolled across the front porch.

"Hello Quinn," He Bowed.

"Hello Bron," Quinn gave a single nod.
"I'm sorry to arrive unannounced but I need your help. This is Kinzie. She's just been bitten today. She's lost most of her family. Her sister is going to be in recovery for a while. Could you look after her for me?"

"Oh," Bron paused, "Poor girl. Yes, sir. I would be happy to look after her. I too am sorry that we had to meet under these circumstances," He reached out his arms.

Quinn gently put her in his arms, and a few tears fell, "Goodbye, love. I apologize for this night. I hope to see you again."

Bron took Kinzie into his arms and went back into the house. Quinn cried a little harder but it was silent. He and Caesar rode a little longer. Then the sun started to appear. Knowing exactly where he was he got off Ceaser.

"Alright Friend. This is where our journey ends. Thank you for all of your assistance," he said, taking off his saddle, and the reins. Any other equipment. He cried a little before walking away. He heard the horse neigh in thanks and gallop away. Quinn took this time to take in all that happened before. He sat with nature on his own that morning. And allowed himself to mourn McCoy's fate.

Chapter Eleven

Quinn rose to a knock on the front door. He rubbed his eyes and looked at the nearest clock. Right on time. He rose rubbing his eyes. And made haste to answer the door. There stood Daniel, slicked back hair and mustache and goatee, "You're delivery Mr. Roberts," He said, stepping to the side. Revealing his order.

"Oh I'm sorry. I left the money in Kinzie's office. Do come in. Would you like some coffee, or another beverage perhaps?" Quinn Turned around and headed back inside.

" Erm, sure I'll take some coffee," Daniel followed, bringing in the supplies into the foyer, and then following behind him into the office.

"Alright, I think I'll have a cup too," Quinn sighed, retrieving the money from the desk and handing it to Daniel.

"Sir, forgive me for asking. But Is everything alright? I don't recall you ever drinking coffee. And your order is larger than last time. I'm sorry if this is too personal," Daniel replied, taking the money.

"Well Michelle isn't well. And there's nothing any doctors can do. We have a healer here, and he suggested the equipment. So, I wanted to get extra in case her recovery doesn't go as planned,"Quinnn shrugged.

"Alright, I'm sorry to hear that. Let me get everything set up for you," Daniel nodded, while putting the money in his back pocket.

"Alright, I'm going to Tell James you're here with the equipment," Quinn remained emotionally drained. Both exited the office and Quinn went straight upstairs, to Michelle's room. He gently knocked on the door. And heard James give permission to enter. He lies on the bed next to Michelle stroking her hair. Quinn gave word that Daniel arrived with the medical equipment and is going to be bringing it up stairs to set it up. James nodded in understanding and continued to provide Michelle comfort. Daniel came in not too much longer. And started hooking up the machines. And telling Quinn how everything works. James was listening and occasionally asking questions. Daniel answered them. Once all the machines were hooked up, the last thing to do was put electrical adhesive stickers in the right locations so the patient monitor could work. Daniel explained where to put the stickers and apologized again for having to deliver in these types of circumstances. James nodded in thanks and Quinn escorted him down stairs, and made some fresh coffee, before bidding him goodbye. Daniel said he'll call and let Quinn know when the oxygen tanks get delivered, before he got into his truck and drove away.

......*

James put on the medical monitors Where Daniel told him, and double checked on a diagram given to them through the company who provided the equipment. He did so. Being a medical man for as long as he has he'll know when, Something is wrong. He's learned about blood pressure since he was young. Some of the methods changed but he kept himself up to date. But this will definitely give him peace of mind. Now it's just a matter of time. Why does everything have to feel so heavy? He continued to pace, and tried to think of a potion that could fix this. He didn't have the heart to connect the feeding tube down her throat.

"James?" Michelle whispered. James froze in shock and relief.

He turned to see Michelle laying weakly in bed but with her eyes open. This made his heart sink. "Yes?"

"Come lay with me. Please," She asked, her eyes were glossed over.

"Of course my love," He replied, walking over and getting into bed gently.
He lay next to her face to face, "How are you feeling?"

"Happy. I'm Awake, so I can see your face, " She smiled.

James tried to smile back, " I'm glad love."

"Hey, I'll be alright. I'm not as bad as you think. I'm just weak. And I'm drained. I promise," Michelle reached for Jame's face and stroked his cheek with her thumb.

"Alright. Thank you for the reassurance," James Kissed her head, "Are you in any pain?"

"No, I'm okay. Just weak, and a little light headed," Michelle shook her head.

"Can I make you something to eat?" James asked.

"No, I think a protein shake should do it. I'd like to see Quinn as well, please." Michelle's breath became a little shaky.

"Alright, should I Paige him?"

Michelle nodded.

There was a setting on the home phone that allowed someone to be paiged. Quinn agreed to get the protein shake. And sounded more than enthused Michelle was awake. It wasn't long before they heard a knock at the door.

"Come in," James called

Quinn Entered protein shake in hand.

"Papa, it's good to see you," Michelle breathed wearily.

"Good to see you too my dear," Quinn smiled entering the room. He heard the beeps from her sinus rhythm as he approached, " I'm glad to see everything is working so well."

"Indeed, I don't know how long I'm going to be awake. So let's make this quick," Michelle replied sitting further up.

Quinn handed the drink to James. And James pulled Michelle up to his chest, " Alright you ready?"

Michelle nodded, and James brought the drink to her lips. Slowly and steadily she drank. Thankfully she had oxygen so her breathing could be steady. Once she finished she let out a sigh, "Thank you."

"Always, love," he replied softly, and lay further back, while Michelle still rested on his chest.

"Are you alright, Shell?" Quinn asked.

"Yes, for the most part. As I told James I mostly feel weak and light headed. But I do feel a bit better after drinking that protein drink," Michelle shook her head.

"I'm glad to hear you're feeling slightly better. I'll leave you two be then," Quinn smiled, reaching for the cup in James' hand. James handed it to him.

"Thank you, Papa. I love you," Michelle whispered.

" I love you too, Shelly. Rest now dear girl," Quinn bowed and left the room, shutting the door quietly behind him.

"I hope this ends soon, love. I hate to see you like this," James replied, putting his hand to her cheek.

"It will end eventually. But I'll be alright, as long as I have you here. You give me strength James," She breathed, her voice sounded drained.

"I'm glad. For now I think you should rest," James kissed her forehead.

Michelle just nodded and curled into him closer. It wasn't long before she fell asleep again. James felt touched, she trusted him so easily. It's understandable as to why. He was there through her pain, helping to encourage her to keep moving forward. And reminded her that despite the scars she wears, she's beautiful. He was lucky to have her because in a strange way she saved him too. Despite his appearance, he wasn't as strong as he looked. He's seen the deepest of horrors one would be damned for. That's why he tries his hardest to spread Kindness. However he's been used, and mistreated. But something in Michelle's vert presence silences the negative thoughts within. How can one woman make the demonic voices go away? She's stronger than she realizes. If Quinn hadn't sent her to James when he did through that woman, she wouldn't be in his arms now. He was happy he could save her. She deserves it. She's spent almost her entire life helping people. There's such a light in her. Even in the dark. James tried to tune out the beeping of the machines and fell asleep with her close.

......*

Tim woke to a woman's voice humming a lullaby. It's been a while since he's slept so soundly. He stretched a little and the humming continued. Anna was sitting in the window knitting what looked to be a scarf. The moonlight lit her red hair.

Tim sat up, "Good morning Anna."

"Good morning Tim," She replied, turning toward him.

"You have a beautiful humming voice," He replied with a smile.

"Thank you. You should hear Kinzie sing. She usually doesn't but once I caught her," She smiled.

"Really? I didn't know she could sing," Tim smiled and looked down at Kinzie who was sleeping soundly. Her hair was well brushed and clothing was dry. He looked up next to her to find a couple of steel mugs, "How long was I out for?"

"A day and a half," Anna stopped knitting and set it down.

"What?" Tim gasped.

"Yes. Your body needed rest, and you haven't been eating like you're supposed to," Anna adjusted the chair so it would be facing Tim.

"How do you know that?" Tim asked.

"Your stomach was growling like a leopard," She smiled and chuckled softly.

"I brought food, I Just haven't thought about eating. I've been so focused on Kinzie," Tim sighed.

"I can understand that. It also doesn't help that the time is different here," Anna's voice drifted deep in thought.

"What do you mean?"

"A day here could be three days or even four in some other places," She replied, still knitting.

"So I haven't eaten in almost two weeks, and I've been out for almost a week?" Tim's eyes widened.

"Exactly. I know Kinzie didn't have a chance to tell you, poor thing has been through so much already," Anna's eyes drew to Kinzie.

"If you don't mind my asking who exactly are you?" Tim asked as he got up to get some food from the back pack and sat back down. His head started to spin.

"I'll answer that question after you eat," Anna smiled.

"Fair," Tim nodded. And opened one of the two granola bars, and took a bite, and another. Before one could blink they were both gone. Tim lay back down.

"I'm a private investigator for the council. I keep things in order. I am Witch. I don't dabble too much in spells. However, potions

and healing I find that I'm excellent in," Anna said softly.
Careful not to wake Kinzie.

"How long have you been practicing for?" Tim asked.

"Many many years. I'm older than I look, you know. How about
you? How long have you been practicing for?" Anna asked,
crossing one leg over the other.

"I don't know what you mean," Tim tried to keep his voice
steady.

"Yes you do Tim. I'm not a fool. And I see your Aura. It's not
like anyone else's," Anna replied, giving a look. A look that says
lie to me again and I'll tell you what you're lying about.

Tim Sighed, "Since I was eight. No one knows. Quinn doesn't
know. James, Michelle, Kinzie or Bron. They don't know. Or
maybe they do and they haven't said anything.I haven't told
anyone. Not since my father died. I was very close to him. And he
passed books down to me, and a lot of herbs that hardly exist
anymore. And recently my mom died. So I haven't been able to
talk to anyone about my craft or ask any Questions. And Then
what happened to Kinzie. I'm just buried with burdens I can't
even begin to comprehend. And I have the knowledge and books.
I just don't know how to tell anyone else. I'm sorry," Tim felt
tears fall down his cheeks.

"It's alright Tim. I'd be happy to keep your secret and teach you what I know. I'm sorry to hear about your family. And if you need anyone to talk to I'm here and so is Bron," Anna replied gently.

"Thank you," Tim replied, wiping the tears from his eyes.

"You're welcome darling. I know it's not easy. And being a Witch is not to be advertised. It can be extremely dangerous. So I do have to give you some kudos for that," Anna paused, "Come in Bron."

Bron opened the door, "Is everything alright?"

"Yes, Tim and I were just talking. He's still a little weak from not eating in so long," Anna nodded with a smile.

"Are you sure, I thought I heard someone crying, and there was a lot of pain," Bron replied looking at Kinzie.

"Everything is fine, I promise," Anna replied, firming her face.

"Alright alright. I just don't want anyone feeling alone in my house. I'll leave you to it then," Bron turned to shut the door.

"Actually Bron. I'd like to go out for a smoke, and talk to you if that's alright," Tim chimed in.

"Alright, well come on then. I'm not gonna let you fall," Bron replied, stepping away from the door.

Tim got up, still slightly light headed but not as bad as before. Took a few steps steadily. And Managed to meet a pace where he wouldn't fall. Bron then walked with him outside. The cool air felt refreshing on his skin. Tim pulled out the pack of cigarettes from his shirt only to find one left. Sighing, he lit the cigarette and paused for a moment, "You wanted to know something about me. I'm a former marine. And I lost both of my parents. My dad died when I was young. And my mother died just a couple of years ago. It seems like yesterday."

"How long were you in the Marine Corps?" Bron asked.

" Three years," Tim replied, inhaling his favorite poison.

" I'm sorry, I underestimated you Tim," Bron eyes filled with sincerity.

"Thank you. I accept your apology. I don't really talk about My past because it's not one that I can remember without something coming back," Tim sat on the floor.

"After your Cigarette I have something I'd really like to show you," Bron smiled.

"I'm assuming it's a good thing?" Tim chuckled.

"Yes, I think you might enjoy them," Brons eyes turned bright with the reply.

"Wait, them? Did Kinzie send you a ton of letters or something?" Tim asked, smiling even more.

"I guess you'll just have to finish your cigarette and find out," Bron smirked.

Tim puffed a few more hits and knocked the cherry off of the bud, "Alright then," he said standing.

"You know Tim, I do own a few trash cans," Bron teased.

"Oh now you tell me," Tim laughed.

Bron led him to the kitchen and pointed out the trash can. Tim threw away the pack with a laugh. And went back to the bedroom. Bron entered a few moments after handing him a stack of letters. Tim smiled and thanked him. Bron smiled and exited the room.

"I'll watch her next," Tim offered.

Anna looked up, "Very well dear, I'll be in the next room. And please, make sure you eat." She stood up with a stretch and yawned.

"Yes ma'am. Good night," Tim got up to sit in the chair.

"Night," She replied, shutting the door behind her.

Tim grabbed the backpack before making himself comfortable. He opened the first letter.

> *Dear Bron,*
> *All is well with Michelle and I. Work is going well. I do miss you and the City Of Night very much. However I feel like something needs to be done here. I don't know how else to say it. I hope you're doing well. I look forward to your next letter.*
>
>
> *-Kid*

"Well that one was short," He said softly, folding the paper and setting it aside, "Lets see what you say." Tim whispered as he opened the second one.

> *Dear Bron,*
> *I find myself stuck between a rock and a hard place. My new partner is in our office. And I can't help but find myself looking at him. It's almost as if I have no control over my eyes. He's so attractive for a human. I don't understand why. There's something about him that makes me want to just linger in his presence. He's smart, and has a quick eye for detail. And he*

seems to care a lot about me and the squad. And I admit, I ran a background check on him. I know what you're going to say. That's a no no. But with all that's going on lately I didn't think it would hurt. He served in wars too. He knows the pain of the past. He's been through so much but picks a profession that helps people. He's such a big heart. And I hate to admit it, but I think I'm falling in love with him. I'll write back again soon.

-Kid

Tim felt his heart pounding against his ribs. And without any hesitation he folded that letter and opened the next. Before reading, Tim notices teardrops on some of the letters.

Dear Bron,
My heart remains heavy. The partner I told you about was severely injured, and now he's staying with Michelle and I while he recovers. He's been having nightmares. And all I do is sit with him, lingering in the dark. This is the kind of dream you never want to go back to. The cries make my unbeating heart bleed. I feel so sorry for him. Admittedly I cried too. As the scream of horrors escaped his lips. I lay next to him. And he would cling to me. Like a child holding onto it's favorite toy. Now I know how you felt when you saw me in this state. His fever is spiking to a dangerous degree. And Michelle Keeps saying she wants to take

him back to the hospital. His wound is almost healed. It's not physical. It's mental.

I'm doing what I can to comfort him. But I wish I could do more. For a split second he woke and thanked me. Why did that move me so? After that I cried. For him. He's a man simply seeking comfort and he got it. He's so special, Bron. I hope one day you can meet him and see how amazing he is. Such a remarkable man who's been through hell. He'll never be the same again, after his wound is healed. I think I'm going to have him stay here for the recovery. I want to make sure He's alright. I never thought I would be this emotional over a human. But he's growing on me.

-Kid

P.S. I've found that stroking his hair helps take those nightmares away. I'm still going to have him stay longer though.

Tim's heart swelled. He didn't remember what happened most of the time before physical therapy. But maybe that's for the best. He folded the letter neatly and pulled out something to eat. While doing so he couldn't help but Notice Kinzie's body Curled into a fetal position. Her long hair gently draped over her shoulder. Tim smiled. *"I'm glad she loved me too."* Once he finished eating, he picked up the next letter.

Dear Bron,

I don't want to worry you but there have been recent complications. I haven't been feeling well. I don't know what it is. I think I can figure it out. Perhaps it's a change in my stress. But I'm not sure. I'll update you further. And my partner has fully recovered. I haven't seen Quinn in a while and I'm beginning to wonder how he's been. Admittedly I'd like to see you, however I can't come to you, I would love it if you could come see me.

-Kid

Tim took a deep breath, and closed the last letter. She told Bron what was happening, but she didn't tell him. But he didn't know she was a vampire. Deep down he was glad to know that she trusts him enough to tell him. There were a few more letters. Tim decided to open one more.

Dear Bron,
I'm getting worse. I've decided to put myself on call, and take some time off work in the meantime. Why is this happening to me? I've been weaker than usual. And I've lost my appetite. And I'm unsure what to do next. I know Michelle is worried. But unfortunately there's not much she can do. I hope all is well. And as always I'll keep you posted.

-Kid

Then he held the last letter in his hands, hesitant, but then decided to read it.

Dear Bron,
I've officially found myself in sin. Lust. And a thirst for one man who is my partner, but he's a beautiful person. In one of our undercover operations, we went to a club to spy on an assassin. Who loves to drink and dance with pretty ladies. We went in a number of days, and Bron. He and I danced. At that moment I craved him to touch my skin. Our Hips rocked from side to side and we acted like a couple. A newly married couple on our honeymoon. Dancing at one of the most expensive clubs in the city. I've caught myself wondering what life would be like with him. And I don't want anything else. Thank you for listening to my story. I miss you brother. Come see me, please.

-Kid

After reading that letter, he immediately started remembering everything about that operation.

◇...◇...◇

Kinzie wore a silver sparkly dress with black high heels. And black jeweled earrings. And had her hair down. She was wearing an irresistible perfume. Her make up was light but it was perfect.

"Are you ready?" Kinzie asked.

He whistled and replied, "Ms. McCoy I was born ready."

He was wearing a white shirt, and black slacks, and black shiny dress shoes. His shirt was open revealing his chest.

"Alright then, let's go," Kinzie replied, with a smile.

"Yes, let's." Tim walked over to the door, and opened it.

Kinzie blushed a little and exited the room. That was when he found out she was allergic to gold jewellery...

They made it to the club, and there was dance music. With lots of low bass. Kinzie started dancing and drew Tim onto the dance floor. She turned to face him and swung her hips back and forth. Tim followed her lead, Kinzie dropped down when the bass dropped. That was when Tim knew he fell deeper in love with her.

<>...<>...<>

Tim heard a soft knock on the door and gentle creek. It was Bron. He had something in his hand.

"You read them, I see," Bron replied, coming around to where Kinzie lies.

"Yes, I'm actually quite flattered," Tim let out a soft chuckle.

" You should be. She didn't mention your name. So I didn't know it was you. But I should have guessed considering what happened to your arm, " Bron replied, kneeling down, "Kinzie, you need to eat hon. Can you eat?"

Tin stood up, and quietly approached closer. Enough to see kinzie nod.

"Alright, that's a girl," Bron helped her sit up. She leaned up against the wall.

"Where's Tim?" She asked with a soft murmur. Her voice was still husky.

"I'm right here," he replied in a whisper.

She patted the spot next to her weakly. Tim quickly came around and seated himself next to her. She Leaned against him. Bron brought the drink to her lips. Slowly she drank, and it was long before she was finished. Bron wiped her face, "Alright Kid, back to sleep you go," he said while standing back up. Quickly he cleaned up all the cups and left the room.

Kinzie rolled over into Tim's neck. He lay back further so she'd be laying down completely on his chest. He couldn't help but smile. He was more than happy she trusted him with ease. He wondered what made him so trustworthy. But eventually he stopped asking. With Kinzie trust doesn't exactly come too easily with anyone else. Tim's thoughts paused for a moment once he noticed Kinzie tapping his heartbeat on his chest. It was soft and gentle. Tim pulled her closer and drifted off to sleep.

......*

Anna woke to find the house quiet. When she left the guest bedroom she found Bron asleep in the living room chair and kinzie and Tim cuddling. She took on a sigh and went back to the living room. This was a perfect time to find a way to lure William to where they are. The books she brought with her we're still sitting on the couch. Very powerful spells and luring potions. They aren't light spells or potions. Some looked to be days to complete, others looked to be longer. Also they'd have to consider how to get him into the City of Night. When he was banished there also was a spell forbidding him from entering from any portal. Maybe this is what he wanted. So there must be traps set wherever he comes. But where? Plus it can't be just anyone to confront him. It has to be Kinzie.

"Anna," Bron said softly.

Anna's heart jumped into her chest, she gasped for a second, "Yes, Bron?"

"Are you alright? I didn't mean to startle you," His voice was calm and reassuring.

She took a deep breath, "No, it wasn't your fault. I'm just very focused. You remember when William was banished, there was a spell placed for him so he couldn't enter?"

"Yes, I remember," Bron seated himself in the chair across from the couch.
"Well if we need to summon him here. We need to reverse the spell," Anna sighed, "I'm scared for Kinzie Bron."

"I am too, but we're here to protect her," Bron locked eyes with Anna.

She knew that look well. That's the battle look he gives when he's ready to lay his life down for his family. Or someone he loves, "I'm not saying you're unable to protect her. I'm saying we should be careful and take as much extra caution necessary to take William down. You know he's a dangerous Vampire," her voice ringing with reassurance.

" I Know, Anna. You're right. What do you suggest?" As much as Bron wanted to care for kinzie himself.

"I'm not sure yet,"Anna sighed.

"Alright, well I'm sure I figured it out," Bron replied, pinching the bridge of his nose.

"Are you alright?" Anna asked, standing, and walking towards him.

"No, my heart is breaking. And I just want her to get better. Poor thing has been through so much already," Bron's voice, filled with pain and despair.

Anna bent down and pulled him into an embrace, "I know darling I know. It's unfair. But that's why we're here. To help bring her comfort, and figure this out. Have you tried connecting with her mind?"

Bron shook his head.

"Well then maybe that's the best way of speaking with her about these things," Anna played with his hair. Her motherly affection made his heart melt.

"You're right. It's worth a try," Bron nodded in agreement.

"Who knew such a muscular vampire would be such a big baby?" Anna thought to herself. She chuckled softly.

"What?" Bron asked, pulling away.

"You're so childlike sometimes. Admittedly it's adorable," Anna replied pulling back. She turned to continue looking at the spellbooks. Then she felt a cold hand pulling her back. She turned to find Bron Crying. His begging honey gold eyes called her back, " Oh, Bron. I'm so sorry." Anna stood in front of him, speechless. She didn't mean to hurt anyone's feelings. He had no words. He buried his face in her chest and cried. Anna being the motherly person she is, ran her fingers running through his hair. She hushed him gently and allowed him to cry as long as he needed. It took a few more moments for bron to compose himself.

"I wonder if she too has nightmares," Bron thought to himself.

Chapter Twelve

Brons house still remained silent. Anna's sitting on the couch reading the spell book. Bron sat at the dining room table trying to remember what spell they cast on the day the council banished William. They couldn't ask because no one has seen or heard from them.

"Hey Anna, how do you feel about possibly going up to see the council?" Bron asked.

"I wouldn't be too comfortable with the idea, however that might be our only option at this time. Perhaps I can find a potion to help the council members. And maybe then we can get some answers. Or maybe I can find that spell and we can work backwards from there," Her voice trailed off.

Bron rubbed his temples, "Damn. He's doing a fine job at making this complicated."

"Well we live in a complex world darling. Even in magic there are rules and balance," She replied stroking a page. *"This potion can reverse dark magic brought upon the minds of the vampire. The time taken to complete this potion is two weeks in the city of night.* " Anna exhaled a sigh, "Well I found the potion we need. But there are a lot of ingredients. And it'll take two weeks to complete."

"Alright that's good news, I suppose," Bron replied, feeling slightly optimistic.

"We still need to come up with a plan when William gets here," Anna thought aloud.

The bedroom door swung open, Tim's voice called both of them in. The two exchanged a concerned look before rushing in. Anna exhaled a sigh of relief.

"That is uncool dude! Uncool! You don't want to piss off a vampire in a fragile state like this!" Bron pointed a finger.

Kinzie was sitting straight up, " Don't get mad at him, I encouraged it."

"It's good to see you're doing better," Anna smiled.

"Thank you, I've been listening to your conversation. And I think I have a way we can do this," Kinzie paused, "There's a pond of healing here in the City of Night. It can heal vampires and restore everything, and it's close to the council. If we can get William here we-"

"Wait, wait," Bron chimed in.

"Bron I'm sorry. It won't be long before I feel sick again so please let me say this," Kinzie gave him her apologetic eyes, "Anna will go to the council and give them the potion, and find the spell. The spell is written in a banishment book in the library. In case someone is able to reverse it. I also believe there is a reversal spell on the back of that page. Bron and Tim, you'll stay here and keep me safe, and healthy as much as possible. Once everything is done Anna will meet us at the Pond of healing. And that's where I will battle it out with Will. Bron you'll have to get my sword. But stay up in the trees. And if we have gold handcuffs that'll be even better."

"Well that's a damn good and very well thought out plan, but who's going to protect Anna?" Bron asked.

"Hades will," Kinzie smiled.

"Oh, yep. She's good," Bron threw his hands in the air.

"Wait, who's Hades?" Tim asked.

"Bron whistle please," Kinzie reached out her hand.

He reached into his pocket and handed her the whistle. She blew into the silver thin object. No sound came out. A loud howl erupted into the forest. Kinzie got up, and insisted everyone go outside. Kinzie waited smiling. The patterned sound of an animal running came closer. And it wasn't long before a figure appeared across from them. Kinzie knelt down to her knees and reached her hand out. As the creature came closer, Tim's jaw dropped. Coming towards them was a tall wolf. Looked to be almost eight feet tall. All black. And he had three heads. And his bright red eyes met all of them. He lay across from Kinzie's hand and touched it with his nose.

"Hello, My old friend," Kinze said softly, stroking his nose with her thumb. He let out a soft whine, "I need your help. I'm not doing well and I need you to take my friend Anna to the council. Guard her and when she's done you bring her back to me?" Hades closed his eyes and nodded all three of his heads.

"Thank you my old friend. I'll see you again soon," Kinzie replied.

Anna stepped closer, "Hello Hades, My name is Anna." She bowed.

Hades bowed back, his eyes snapped open and started to growl. He sniffed the air, and his eyes locked on Tim.

"Easy easy boy," Kinzie stood up, "His name is Tim and he's helping me. I'm sorry I brought him here. But I need his help too."

"Tim," Hades growled.

Tim gasped and exhaled, "Yes?

"What brings you to the City of Night?" Hades' voice is deep.

Tim knelt down low, "I come to this beautiful city to assist the care of Kinzie. She's been ill for a long time now. And I'd like to protect her. I'm sorry for trespassing. I seek nothing else. I just want Kinzie to be well. I love her. I want to find the one who's hurt her and bring him to justice."

"Thank you, it brings me peace knowing not all humans seek power and destruction. The city is out of balance and one is looking for power," Hades spoke while meeting Kinzie's eyes.

"Is it William?" Kinzie asked.

" I do not know. I don't recognize his aura if it is him. Be careful of my children. Anna, are you ready to ride?" The night wolf asked.

"Let me grab something, and I'll be right back," Anna replied, running in the house. She came back moments later with a bag strapped around her arm, the bag reached her waist. Hades knelt down to allow Anna on his back.

"Be well Children of night," His deep voice rang in Brons yard and ran into the forest.

After no one could hear his footsteps in the brush Tim turned to Kinzie, "Okay, what the hell? Like honestly. That was the most terrifying thing I've ever experienced in my life. I thought coming to a vampire city was bad enough. But no, no, no this takes the cake. A three headed wolf who could literally eat me, spoke to me. I thought I'd seen it all."

"Tim, why don't you smoke a cigarette and I'll explain," Bron suggested.

"Yeah, okay," Tim lit a cigarette, and started to pace back and forth.

"Alright Hades is the manager of this world so to speak. You can call on him whenever you need. But it must be dire. If one enters this world intending to do harm. He raises hell, hence why we call him Hades. His real name is long and incredibly difficult to pronounce," Bron replied waving his hand.

"So the fact that I didn't get eaten by a giant three headed wolf is a good thing?" Tim replied, puffing his cigarette.

"Correct. Notice he said be well Children of Night. That means you too. I need to go lie back down," Kinzie replied slowly walking back into the house.

"So other humans have entered the city, with poor intentions?" Tim asked, puffing the last of his cigarette.

"Yes," Bron replied, leaning on the wall and crossing his arms.

"And they've all been disposed of?" Tim asked using fingered quotations, before putting his cigarette out.

"More or less," Bron shrugged.

"Well that makes me feel so much better," Tim's voice filled with sarcasm, as he entered the front door.

Bron pushed himself forward with his feet, and followed Tim inside. He couldn't blame him for being so anxious. It's not everyday that you find out the woman you love is a vampire, and lives in a different realm. And that realm was a three headed wolf by the name of Greek God from Hell. This is why most of the time Vampires Keep things secret. But They do make an exception. And Tim handled that situation extremely, well considering. Bron was impressed. He may not say it now. But it's not often a mortal enters the city at night and meets Hades. And live to tell about it. They both went to the bedroom and found Kinzie laying in bed with her eyes open. She looked up and smiled. It was nice to be able to talk to her and figure out a plan. It was nice to hear her voice.

......*

The moon light lit up the path to a castle on the top of the hill. The cool breeze hit Anna's face making it. They'd been riding for a while now. Part of her missed the old world. Everything took more time to get to place, to cook, to clean. But now the world is at such a high and fast pace. Some forget the value of hard work and true efforts. Hades began to slow down and eventually come to a stop. All three of his heads, panting.

"If you need to rest, please do," Anna replied gently stroking his fur.

"Thank you Anna," He replied, lowering his front paws. Anna jumped off and looked around. It looked as though they were half way there already. Hades lay himself down on the side of the dirt road. Anna seated herself next to his multiple heads. The crickets sang softy, and there was an owl hooting in the distance. Anna took a deep breath in and grounded herself. Occasionally looking over at hades. He truly is a magnificent beast. The question comes to mind, how many men has he eaten? How long has he been in the City of Night? How long has he known Kinzie? Does he speak to most people? Anna tried to silence her thoughts.

"If you have questions, please don't hesitate to ask," Hades said, looking up at her.

"Alright, how many men have you eaten?" Anna asked, looking directly into his fiery red eyes.

"Ten, But only in the time that the city of night has existed," He replied with a small chuckle.

"How long have you lived here?" She asked, smiling.

"Since this world has been created and I Believe the correct term in your world is melania," He gave a curious look, "You're fascinated by me, aren't you?"

"Yes, I am," Anna chuckled, "How long have you known Kinzie?"

"Since she's arrived here. He was pretty Badly wounded, and most often when new vampires arrive, they stay here a few years. To get adjusted to their new life," Hades Paused and looked ahead deep in thought.

"Do you talk to everyone?" Anna asked, reaching out to him.

"No, this time the circumstances are different. Kinzie McCoy is one of the most valued protectors of this land. And since her life's in jeopardy, my ability to speak is irrelevant," He said quietly. His deep voice is still audible. He sniffed the air and brought his large nose to Anna's hand.

She smiled, and heard a twig snap. She shot up and so did Hades. Not a sound after. They both froze for a little longer, "We should get going," Anna said in haste. Without hesitation Hades bent down and scooped Anna up and ran up the hill. Their hearts are pounding. Why wasn't there a scent in the air? Are they being followed? If so, who is it? How long have they been tracking Anna and Hades? Regardless, there's no turning back now. Kinzie needs Anna to reverse that spell, and wake the council from whatever magic they're under. Hades sped up and the castle on the hill grew closer and closer. Anna looked behind them to find no one following them. No one, maybe it was an animal. Hades wasn't taking a chance. He and Anna continued to ride it.

After several miles they made it to the castle. Anna exhaled a sharp breath. There wasn't a soul in sight. And it was far too quiet. Usually there would be two guards at the gate inquiring why one was there. And the estimated time it would take to see the council. And more people usually walk in the background, running the castle. Maids going various corridors. Anna could feel her heart pounding against her ribs. She was glad to have Hades with her. She has weapons of her own. However, in case someone wants to ambush her, she'll have help. Hades lowered himself so Anna could hop down. As they walked, Hades stayed close, his ears perked.

......*

Bron was the next to stay awake. Tim lay next to Kinzie, knocked out. And Kinzie lay wide awake unable to rest. She was worried about Anna, and Michelle. But provided comfort, by reassuring her they're not alone. And he was proud of her. For allowing herself to be vulnerable. It's never easy asking for help. But Kinzie's gotten much better at it. She's not showing her full discomfort. Probably because she doesn't want anyone to pity her. But that's what Bron loves most about her. She's strong, tiny and temperamental. But also motivated and a natural born leader.

Bron sat smiling and remembering the first night he saw Kinzie break through her timid shell and became a person of strength.

The moonlight lingered in the crisp cold air. Kinzie and Bron patiently waited for someone to return back with a report on the perimeter. It felt like forever, Kinzie's guts churned. Something isn't right. Why is he taking so long? They were about to go into battle; they didn't have long. Thankfully the rest of their army wasn't too far. Waiting on her instructions. Bron looked up. Kinzie followed the direction that no one was there. They waited silently, then heard a strange noise that followed. In the air came an object. A boulder? No, it was too light for that. Kinzie saw it clearly, and felt a rage of fire course through her veins. What landed on the ground as their brother's head. Bron's eyes went bright yellow.

"Archers take positions!" Kinzie yelled.

Behind them, slight movement.

"Swordsman follow me!" Kinzie yelled, again.

And up in the trees they went, silent and swift. Stealth was too important. With one wrong move they would be slaughtered. Bron stayed behind to keep an eye on the archers, and give them the signal to fire. It wasn't long before a blood curling war cry escaped Kinzies throat. Bron felt his skin crawl. He squinted his eyes to see that Kinzie was using her rage as a center of focus and then briefly Kinzie gave the signal to bron to release the arrows. Bron made a bird-like sound and arrows released into the night sky. The silent deaths made the many enemies drop dead to the ground. Kinzie's movements remained minimal. Saving energy is most important in battles such as these.

After the battle was won. Kinzie knelt to the ground and cried again. The fight of nature versus nurture. She never wanted to kill anyone. Bron ran after her.

"Kinzie, Kinzie, Shh," Bron knelt down with her and pulled away. But Bron held her close, "Go ahead and cry. Let it out. Don't hold back Kid," Bron whispered.

Kinzie buried her face into his chest and sobbed. The cruelties of the world had a grip on her mind. But the question is who did she pity? Did she pity the men who died? Or the men who brought harm to their families. Snow started to fall again.

"Kinzie we need to go," Bron said while rubbing her back.

"Why am I so angry, Bron? They're dead," Kinzie barely uttered her words.

"Because you wanted to punish them for what they've done," Bron pulled away and looked her in the eyes, "This is why death isn't the solution. Success is the best victory. You did what you had to, in order to protect your kind. But that can only go so far. Her moon blue eyes glossed over, "Perhaps this is why my father never wanted me to join the war."

"Perhaps, but Kinzie. Please listen to me. You're in this world now. There will be lives lost. It just won't be us. Make the best with what you have. You must learn to feel and let go. This life isn't an easy one. You've got to learn to let go," Bron touched her cheek.

Kinzie nodded, "So learn to feel, but not allow my feelings to cloud my mind."

"Exactly," Bron nodded.

"Thank you my friend. I appreciate that. Bron, why am I bleeding?" Kinzie asked, looking down at her hand.

"Come on. Let's go find out," Bron stood up and held out his hand for Kinzie.

She grabbed it, and stumbled into him.

"You alright?" Bron asked.

Kinzie shook her head, " I'm dizzy."

"I think you might've been cut with a poisonous blade. It's not as bad as you think. You won't die. But we do need to go," Bron replied, picking her up in bridal style. And carried her back to her house. He laid her in the bed.

"I'm sorry, I'm going to need to undress you," Bron replied walking out of the room.

"It's not like you haven't seen me before," Kinzie winced. A sharp throb came from her side. She removed all top layers and rested her arms across her chest.

Bron returned with a bowl and some towels, "Alright then." He rolled her over on her side, "This is going to hurt. A lot. And I'm sorry Kin, bu-"

"Just do it! It hurts already!" Kinzie snapped.

Bron looked at the small scratch that was surrounded by black small markings. He sank his teeth in and sucked all the poison out. Split it into the bowl. The black wasn't completely gone. So he did it again. Who knew a scratch would cause so much damage? Idiots didn't know they were immortal. Good thing too. Otherwise Kinzie would actually be dead. It took a total of five times for bron to get it completely removed.

"Thank you. Far less pain that's for sure," Kinzie chuckled.

"Alright, get some rest," Bron replied, exiting the room.

"Please, don't go. I don't think I can sleep now. And I really don't want to be alone," Kinzie pulled a blanket over her.

"Alright let me put this up," bron replied, putting the tools away. Only moments later returned.

Kinzie lay curling in the fetal position. Wincing every now and again.

"Do you want me to lay next to you?" Bron asked softly. Kinzie nodded. He knew she was in pain. Despite the fact the effects of the poison won't kill her. It does put her in pain. A lot. Bron slid under the covers and stroked her hair, "I'm sorry, Kid. I know it hurts."

"Yeah. It's strange because it comes in waves," She let out a soft groan.

"I've dealt with this once. Someone tried to kill me with a Poison dart. That didn't go too well for them or for me," Bring whispered. Attempting to reassure her.

"Interesting," A soft groan escaped from her lips.

"I know right? It'll be a day or so before you'll be back to normal. But the pain does reduce over time," Bron started running his fingers through her hair.

"Thank you," her voice faded as she replied.

"You're welcome, get some rest now," Bron whispered, giving her a kiss on the head.

Bron stayed smiling even as Kinzie slept. The amount of memories they have together seems unlimited. Their friendship is effortless. And he saw the same effortlessness in Kinzie and Tim's relationship. And that is truly a sight to behold.

Chapter Thirteen

Michelle lay resting, her breathing ragged. James sat close to her. Afraid to leave her alone for even a moment. Quinn has helped greatly. And took shifts to allow James to sleep. And they came to an agreement. James would take the night time. And Quinn would take the day. They helped one another by cleaning up, and having a potion and food ready for the next person. Very much like a hospital. More so since they'd leave one another notes on what happened. I'm the time Kinzie has been gone. Michelle has lost a lot of weight, she's begun to have more frequent epileptic episodes. And occasionally wakes up and talks for a little bit. But those days are very few and far between.

James still talks to her as if she's awake. But mostly he reads and draws. What else is there to do? Kinzie is the only one who can save Michelle. Since they're bound. Not just by blood. But in many other ways. Why else would Michelle still be alive? After so long. James was drawing a meadow, and wooded scenery. The sound of the machines was normal. Sadly, Normal.

But he could tell Michelle was holding on by a thread. A timer went off. And James sighed. This was his least favorite part. Having to feed her through the tube which is uncomfortable placed down her throat, through her nose. Jame's chest sank as he fed the liquid in the tube. A notification sound came from Michelle's phone. He looked and found it was Tim.

Tim:Hey How's she doing?

You: She's not good at all. She's having seizures again,
we've had to give her food through a tube.
All she ever does is sleep.
Sometimes she'll wake up
and talk to me, but that's very seldom.

Tim: I'm So sorry to hear that. But I have good news,
Kinzie bron and I have made a plan.
It's kinda dangerous. But we're confident it'll work.
We just need more time.

You: That's great! Alright, I can do that.
Thank you for the update Tim. I hope it works.

Tim: No problem. I'll keep you posted.
Take care James.
I'm here if you need me.

You:Thank you. Same to you. Stay safe.

Tim: You too.

At last. There's a light at the end of the tunnel. A thread of hope he can cling to. She's suffered so much already, they both have. A wave of relief brought tears to his eyes. Quinn won't be asleep for much longer. James couldn't wait to tell him the good news. *Not much longer now my love. You've been doing well. Please keep holding on.* He thought to himself. The world seemed a little less dark. And it became much easier to breathe. A gentle knock on the door.

"Come in," James said as quietly as his voice would allow.

"Is everything alright James? I sense something's happened," Quinn entered the bedroom.

"Yes, everything is going very well. And I received a text from Tim. According to him, Kinzie, her friend and himself are executing a plan. And the girls will be well soon enough," James' eyes sparkle bright.

Quinn beamed, "Oh James, that's wonderful news! Oh I am so truly relieved by such news from him. I'm confident this will end. At least that's my truest of hopes."

"Lets just hope nothing falters. I'm scared she won't be able to hold on much longer," James exhaled slowly.

"I too fear such a fate for her. But we must be strong James. It's truly unfair that this happened to her. Kinzie unfortunately has always had misunderstandings with many other people. I've always expected her to be under attack. But Michelle, she's always kept a safe distance from any danger. And Kinzie would be sure to keep a distance also. I don't think we should underestimate Michelle either, She's much more capable than most assume," Quinn replied, his eyes glossed over.

"I'll never lose faith. I just wish this whole thing would end," Jame allowed a tear to fall, " I'd like to talk to her again. To hear her laugh again. And I truly can't stand the uncertainty. I want to know she'll be alright. She's the most amazing and incredible woman I've ever met. She smiles every day, she's always so optimistic. And for the longest time I thought she was dead. But when I found out she was alive, I promised myself I wouldn't allow myself to lose her again." Now James was sobbing.

Quinn over and held him closely. He too felt the same way James does. The world would be a much darker place if Michelle did pass on. And it would leave a wound deep in the hearts who knew her. She's been hanging on this long. Hopefully her body can hang on a little longer. Quinn hushed him gently and allowed James to cry as much as he needed. James wouldn't normally cry in front of anyone. But He's known Quinn for long enough. He considers him as close to family as one could get. For any man this moment is secret and private. A man's emotions are usually frowned upon. Oftentimes if a man cries, he's told to get over it without someone asking, why? It's so exhausting to pretend that everything is alright.

Now everything is not alright. Not in the least. He knows Michelle is strong mentally, and physically. But the question remains how long can she stay strong for? It took what seemed to be several minutes later, but James pulled away and thanked Quinn for the support. Quinn simply nodded. In moments like these there isn't much to say at all. They both sat numbly.

Hanging on to the small shred of hope they had left. Before long, James lay next to her and fell into a deep sleep.

......*

The silence in the castle was deafening. Anna still was wandering around the castle to find the answers she craved. Hades behind her. Their stealth is flawless. Maybe the council members were in the holding cells. That would be a place to keep all the guards and well pretty much everyone. She did her best not to exhale a sigh of relief to find the Library up ahead.

" The spell is written in a banishment book in the library. In case someone is able to reverse it. I also believe there is a reversal spell on the back of that page." Kinzie's voice rang in Anna's head. The large cherry wood door creaked lightly and Anna made her way in quickly. Her heart was pounding against her ribs.

"I call upon the moon goddess, help me find the item in which I seek," Anna thought to herself, and thought about the instructions Kinzie gave her. A light became brighter in the corner of the library. She moved slowly, and was ready for anything. And sure enough there sat the book on the shelf.

"Damn, I wish everything was this easy," Anna chuckled under her breath. She took the book and put it in her bag. She heard Hades start to sniff the air. She froze and waited to hear footsteps in the hall. Her heart now in her throat, she tried to stay silent.

There was a female voice, " Who dares enter here?"

Anna wanted to give a smart retort. But she and Hades sat motionless.

A loud sigh of frustration exited the woman's lips and very loud footsteps receding away. She and Hades exchanged looks. *"We need to hurry and find the council,"* Anna thought to herself. He gave a nod in agreement. Carefully they opened the door and hastened down the hallway opposite of where that woman was. Hopefully they'll find some sort of staircase. It's been so long since Anna has been in the castle. She'd forgotten it's large size. Tall dark wooden double doors were a common theme. And the old decor spoke volumes, however they were still beautiful. Perhaps that's why she missed this place so much. At last after walking through several corridors they found a spiral staircase going down. The entrance was wide enough for Hades to enter. And rather tall.

Hades sniffed, barely audible, he said, " There are two guards down below."

Anna sighed, and pulled out a hunter's knife from her bag. And a bow that looked to be folded in thirds. She unfolded it and placed it on her back and lastly pulled out a quiver of arrows.

"Well that's handy," Hades said softly.

"Indeed," Anna whispered with a smile. She held her blade at the ready and quietly entered the prison below. Hades kept his distance.

Anna crouched low and peeked around the bottom of the entrance and saw six guards right off the bat, "I thought you said there were two?" Anna whispered.

"My apologies Anna, I didn't think my nose would fool me either," Hades whispered back. His deep voice sends chills down her spine.

She nodded in understanding and let out a sharp exhale, and removed her bow from her back. And removed her first arrow. This is the person she's long forgotten. She doesn't want to be this person anymore. However for Kinzie and the rest of the Vampire community she'll do it. She released all six arrows, one at a time. And all targets had the same shot in their heart. She looked around once more and stepped forward. Every single cell was filled with castle members. They all were laying down. Were they all asleep? Anna realized she had to go to the kitchen and look for all of the ingredients for the potion, and there were a lot of people who needed a potion.
She looked at Hades, " Could you do one last thing for me?"

"Yes, of course," Hades gave a slight nod.

" I need to go to the kitchen, and make a rather large potion. I need your assistance to guard the door while I do so. If you need to sleep, you're welcome to. It's going to take a while to make this," Anna asked, reaching out her hand.

Hades brought his nose to her hand, "Yes, Ms. Anna. I'd be happy to assist you."

Anna nodded, and gave thanks while running up the stairs. She hastened to the Kitchen, which was conveniently just down the hall. They paused outside the door. Hades sniffed the air.

"Do I want to know how many?" Anna asked.

"Given what happened last time, I'd rather not answer," Hades growled low.

"Alright fair enough," Anna whispered. She took a deep breath and entered the Kitchen. A woman yelped in surprise. She tried to sucurry away. But chains held her to the counter top. Anna approached her slowly, "Who are you?"

"Who am *I*? Better question is, who are *you*?" She breathed heavily looking at hades.

"Please stop staring at him and look at me," Anna said firmly.

The woman snapped her head toward Anna and held her gaze, "You're human."

"Yes I am. I'm also one who's particularly upset. Now tell me. Who. Are. You?" Anna crossed her arms.

"M-My name is Mary. An evil Vampire took me because I can do magic. And spells and stuff. He made me stay in chains so I can make this potion that puts everyone in the council asleep. It has to be given to them daily to maintain its effects. He can't come here though so there's another magical being here that stays here with me. It's just the two of us. She's been trying to figure out how to get him back," Mary's voice shook. She looked up at Hades again.

"He's not going to hurt you unless you hurt me. Now where is this magical woman you speak of," Anna's voice stayed firm.

"Right here," A woman's voice echoed. It was dark, and deeper than expected. It came from the shadows.

"Who are you?" Anna asked.

"Oh you know me very well. Though you refuse to admit it," She let out a dramatic sigh and stepped into the light. Her irises Purple the rest of her eye red. Her long blonde hair curled into spirals. She remained pale with scars all over her face.

"Ashely?" Anna Gasped. Her blood began to boil.

"Hello dear sister. It's nice to see you too," She giggled and stood across from Anna.

" You're not my sister. You turned your back on us the second you chose dark magic," Anna's rage grew.

"Oh come now. Don't be such a sour puss. Come join us," Ashley waved her hand forward.

"Sorry, this isn't a friendly visit," Anna replied through clenched teeth.

"Alright very well then. So be it. I suppose you're here to stop what's happening to Kinzie and Michelle McCoy," Ashly began to pace.

Anna stood silent. She had no words. Just rage, disappointment and hurt.

"I take that as a yes. Very well," Ashley removed gold handcuffs from behind her, " You remember the stories with these? How he tortured her for days and held her prisoner?"

Anna's teeth clenched harder, as her breath grew heavier. He fist clenched around the knife she had hidden behind her back. Ashley was powerful and was excellent in dark magic. But Anna never expected her to try and attempt such a crazy thing. Making sleeping potions daily, so the people that could stop them were disarmed.

"I take that as a yes again," Ashley continued to pace back and forth, "I was going to let William in. But I could never find that Damn book. But you did. I sensed your magic in the library."

"Good for fucking you," Anna spat and threw the hunting knife to her sisters chest. And she heard it sink into her flesh.

Ashley gasped and screamed. Blood exiting her lips, " Anna!"

Anna stood there cold, and calles. It wasn't long before her sister fell dead. There was a poison in the blade. With one small cut could end a life. Let alone a deep flesh wound. Anna walked over and removed the blade from her sister's chest, and sighed, "Mary."

"Yes?" She replied, her voice shaky.

"I need you to tell me everything that's happened here. All the spells, potions, everything and I'll let you go," Anna glanced at her with cold eyes.

"Yes ma'am," Mary bowed.

......*

Michelle gasped and sat up, startling James awake, and Quinn who was seated across from her. She started to cough. Quinn rushed over and removed the tube from her nostrils. She cleared her throat and took a few deep breaths.

"Are you alright my dear?" Quinn asked, removing the last of the tube from her nose.

"Yes, I'm fine. I'm sorry to have startled you both. But I just had a strange vision," Michelle rubbed her temples, " I think the magic has been lifted. On me at least. I'm not so sure about Kinzie."

James gave Quinn a look of surprise and relief, " I'm happy you're alright, but how do you know this?"

"A very strong instinct," Michelle replied. She paused for a moment and looked around the room, "How long have I been out?"

"Almost three months," James replied, feeling his heart ping.

"Well that explains why I'm so hungry," Michelle replied, holding her stomach.

Quinn rose with a smile and exited the room. He was happy to cook something special for her. He remained smiling. Relieved to see she's doing well, and hoping Kinzie will do the same. While Quinn was downstairs, James sent a text message to Tim,

You: Hey, I just wanted to let you know.
Michelle just woke up. She's doing lots better.
Says that the magic has been lifted.
Hope all is well.
      -James

Chapter Fourteen

Tim saw the text message from James and sighed in relief. That meant the plan Kinzie created was working. Anna was able to get to the root cause of the problem. And hopefully soon He, Bron and Kinzie will be heading to the pond of healing. But it's only been a couple of days. Kinzie had shown no sign of improvement which worried both himself and Bron. Somehow she knew that this would come to be. Tim figured her instincts have developed and grown over time. But this isn't an everyday occurrence for humans or vampires. However Tim was looking forward to things going back to normal. If that's even possible. With all the information he knows now, it may never be back to normal. But he's willing to accept it. Maybe they could stay longer and she can show him her house.

"You're wandering off again," Bron observed.

"Sorry, Erm. I got a text from James. Michelle is awake and she says that the magic is lifted," Tim gave air quotes. He sighed and pulled out a pack of cigarettes from his shirt pocket and rose from the couch to step outside.

"That's great news! That means the plan is working," Bron smiled and followed behind him.

They stood silently and listened to the crickets and the owls. Tim sighed in satisfaction. He inhaled the cigarette.

"You like it here don't you?" Bron asked.

"Yes, I do. It's so beautiful," Tim smiled.

"I'm glad. Most humans have never seen this place. And if you and Kinzie decide to go back to earth, please don't mention this to anyone," Bron said softly.

"I won't if anything this was all a strange dream I had the night before," Tim smiled and leaned on the patio fence.

"Fair enough," Bron Nodded.

Tim chuckled, and inhaled his cigarette.

"What?" Bron asked, leaning against the wall.

"I'm just remembering the first time I took Kinzie home," Tim said smiling.

"Oh this should be good. What happened?" Bron laughed.

"Well apparently she was speeding to get to work and punctured both of her tires. So I offered her a ride and I didn't believe her when she said that she lived far away. But this woman gives me one hundred dollars in gas. And it was one of the best drives I've ever taken, It was beautiful. But she made me swear that I wouldn't tell anyone. And of course I said I would," Tim's voice wandered off.

"That's amazing Tim. I'm glad. But as her brother, I need to prepare you. She carries a lot of weight on her shoulders. She holds a lot of dark memories in her mind. With those memories comes a lot of pain. There will be some good times and bad times. And those bad days can be brutal for anyone who doesn't really know her. Are you ready to care for her, and comfort her in all ways?"

Tim thought deeply for a moment, " It's only fair. She's saved my life. Literally. More than once. I know what it's like to carry a heavy weight; it eventually cuts off your airflow. And if you have no one there to talk to, you eventually lose all motivation to move forward. The greatest thing about Kinzie is how selfless she is. She doesn't crave constant attention. But yes, I'm ready to care for her. Why do you think I'm here? I could've stayed back on earth, but no. I want to be here. I want to help her see this through," Tim inhaled the cigarette and sighed, "I understand you're worried about her. And you've been there for her. You're her brother. She's lucky to have you. But I promise you. From man to man. I will care for her in the best way I know how."

Bron nodded, and smiled, " Excellent. I'm glad. I just wanted to give you a heads up. But I'm glad she has someone like you with her. It makes me worry a hell of a lot less."

"Thanks," Tim smiled, "And if I hurt her, I know you'll kill me."

"Yeah, pretty much," Bron replied, not able to decide whether he's impressed or proud, "I'm gonna go check on her."

Tim nodded and Bron stood up and with a few steps made it to the bedroom. Kinzie still lay resting. He wished she'd wake up. But the truth is she needed as much rest as possible. If she's going to fight William. His mind wandered off and began to wonder how Anna was doing. It's only been the second day since she's been gone. But time is of the essence. The good news is Michelle is awake. Perhaps it's because she didn't get sick until later? Or maybe Kinzie was supposed to be the only one affected and Michelle got crossed in the crossfire. Who knows what anymore? When she wakes up, she goes back to earth. Maybe Bron should go with them. Just for a little while. Tim interrupted Bron's thoughts, entering the room with a piece of paper in hand.

......*

Anna stood in the kitchen over the stove top stirring the potion, which was in a massive pot. That young girl Mary told her everything. William hired Ashely to put Kinzie under a spell, she used the handcuffs and a voodoo doll to do so. Mary was apparently Ahsley's servant. And was teaching her how to do magic. She also told Anna all the ingredients in the sleeping potions, and gave Anna the words Ashely used for Kinzie. If they were said aloud it wouldn't have made things any better. Everything has been written down and documented. And since Bron asked him to stay close, Hades lay in the corner of the kitchen asleep. For a large three headed wolf he was quiet when he slept. Perhaps it's out of habit? The amount of work cut out for Anna was crazy, so she had a bird sent to Bron's house. To see if Tim could help her with this. Hopefully he got it. She already knew Bron and Kinzie were coming along. That was no question.

Several hours passed in silence until Anna heard a soft Whoosh. She Turned around to Find just Tim. She beamed and jumped up and down in excitement.

"Tim, it's so good to see you! Oh my Gods, I need your help," She exclaimed.

"Alright, what do you need?" Tim chuckled nervously. He looked around the room.

"All I need you to do is literally stir this, nice and slow. Come, come," She replied using all four fingers to bring forward.

Tim walked over and stood next to her on the stove.

"That's it darling, there we go. Now I can come over here, and look at all these spells and see how to reverse it," Anna said, turning to look at the books.

"Who gave you all of this information?" Tim replied, glancing at all the paper.

"My sister's servant, poor girl. I told her I'd let her go in exchange for all of this," Anna gestured to the middle table used as an island.

"Where is your sister?" Tim asked, stirring the potion slowly.

"Erm, she's dead," Anna's voice shook.

"Anna I'm so sorry," Tim's heart sank. Remembering when he had to bury his family.

"I'm not. I still love her and all, but she was a witch practicing dark magic. And she would've killed Kinzie or me. If she had a chance. So I didn't give her that chance," Anna let out a small cry, and took a deep breath, "I'm sorry, I need to look at these potions."

"No need. Where's her Body? Maybe when Bron comes you can give her a proper burial," Tim asked, turning to Anna. She simply pointed to the corner of the room where Tim didn't look, but he could now see. He saw the woman who was in Kinzie's room that night, "I know her! Well I've seen her once. She was in Kinzie's bedroom making threats and gave me a message."

"Oh bloody hell, Tim. I'm so sorry," Anna let out a sigh.

"No, no, Anna. It's not *your* fault. You are *not* responsible for her actions. You can't be," Tim replied. His voice was firm.

"You're right. I just wish I knew sooner," Anna replied, flipping through the pages.

"Tell you what. I've got the potion, Kinzie and Bron are going to be here soon. And They're gonna need somewhere to lay her down. Do you Want to go find some things he could lay on?" Tim asked.

"Oh no I have something in my bag," Anna replied happily.

If there was one thing Tim was great at. It was a distraction. He's learned the power of keeping the mind busy, and every once in a while passes it on to others. Anna had what looked to be a small cot looking mattress and a sleeping bag. She set it up close to the table. And proudly projected a sigh of satisfaction and went back to the table. She had separate pieces of paper scattered everywhere. Tim was still standing at the stove. Slowly stirring the pot. It was boring as hell. But at least this is something that he could put an effort towards. Anna would occasionally ask Tim if he knew any spells that would reverse this mess. And he told her the small number. But it wasn't anything strong enough to undo the damage. Though she was impressed with the spells he does know. Another whoosh came into the castle. There stood Bron with Kinzie in his arms. Anna Pointed to the bed she made. Bron gently lay Kinzie down, and asked how progress was. After a sharp sigh, he asked to take a look. Being a healer himself he knows of some magic. But by the looks of this, it was some seriously dark magic.

It wasn't long before Anna confessed she needed help with her sister's body, and Bron nodded. He asked how it didn't stink and Anna said she used a spell. She turned to Tim and announced that they would be back. Tim nodded in understanding. Bron carried her into the woods with Anna, and allowed her the spot where her sister would be buried. As they dug, Anna let out a soft cry. And this time allowed the tears to roll down her face. Once Bron was finished he pulled Anna into a tight embrace. No words were needed here. Just reassurance, support and comfort. They didn't leave the burial sight, until Anna's eyes were dry.

When they returned Tim was still stirring the potion, and Kinzie was still sleeping. Tim noticed Anna's slightly red eyes, but said nothing else. Bring asked what was going to happen when they gave everyone the potion. Anna's response was that everyone would wake up but the four of them should be ready for everyone to be in shock, have a fuzzy memory, and maybe even some grogginess. Only four more days until the potion is ready. In the meantime Anna was researching the spells. With magic there's always a way to reverse something. Usually they include a counter spell or a potion. And in some severe cases, both are required. Kinzie's case is severe enough. She started tapping her fingers on the table while writing.

"Tim, what was the message my sister gave you?" Anna's voice trailed off.

"I am the one of a different time. Try to find me in the future or past. The present nay born to last. I thirst for pain. I seek for lady thy Kinzie to join the game," Tim reapearted. The anger he felt for Anna's sister was too painful to bear. Even though she's dead.

"Interesting," Anna whispered, flipping to another page.

"What's interesting?" Bron asked. He seated himself on the floor next to Kinzie.

"He thirsts for pain. I think I've got it. I don't know why that helped as well as it did," Anna smiled, " Bron can you get me the ingredients from the cabinet's please?"

She grabbed a large bowl from the cabinets behind her. And Bron stood up and joined Anna and waited for her to announce what she needed. The potions were neatly placed in a tall cabinet. One by one until most of the table was full. She gave Him thanks and continued her search for answers. Bron seated himself again. Anna muttered to herself while adding the ingredients to the bowl. She was chanting a spell. Tim listened closely as he stirred. He couldn't hear much. But what he did hear he found interesting and beautiful. It sounded like a reversal spell but in a different language. His head was down, but he was smiling. One step closer to the end.

Bron had to draw back into his own mind and meditate. His anger Towards Ashley ran deep. He saw the golden handcuffs on the table. Anna tried to cover them before he saw them. He did appreciate that. Good thing Tim didn't see it. If he did, it would have torn him apart. He pictured himself sitting at the bottom of the waterfall. And the waterfall cleansing his thoughts. He's had to bring Kinzie here a time or two. Though she decided her safe haven was a beach. And explained the sounds of the waves are calming. Water has always been a grounding place for the both of them. If it was dark and it was raining that was the best time for Kinzie. It was as if Mother nature was saying hello. Cleansing the bad, and providing relief for creatures in need of fresh water.

"I think this is it!" Anna exclaimed, making Bron jump a little.

Rubbing his eyes, Bron replied, "I'm glad. Do you need me to tilt her head up?"

"Yes please," She replied, putting the potion in a jar. Tim looked and assumed it would be easier to drink that way.

Bron moved over slightly and Put Kinzie's head on his lap, "Alright, I'm ready when you are."

Anna came sound quick and put the potion to Kinzie's lips. She made a sour face but she kept drinking it. Anna pulled back to give her a second. Then put the potion to her lips again. Once all was said and done they lay Kinzie back down.

"Give it a bit of time. Maybe two days at the most. Then we'll see the results," Anna sighed, and turned to Tim, "Hey why don't you take a break and smoke a cigarette. Maybe have a look around. I'd suggest just staying in the hallway, or having Bron go with you."

"Thanks," Tim replied, stepping away, "I think I'll just stick around the hallway." He was relieved to smoke a cigarette for sure. Only a few more days till he can talk to Kinzie again and bring her world back to normal.

⚹...⚹...⚹

Michelle sat up in bed wide awake next to James. She decided to keep the machines going just in case she felt ill again. But ever since she woke up she's been fine. Still she couldn't explain how she knew the magic was broken. Quinn often asks about it, and James just leaves it be. He was just happy she's awake and almost back to normal. As of this moment they're eating breakfast. And chatting. James asked questions about her experiences while she was in a coma. Michelle said it was being awake, and wanting to open your eyes, but you just can't. You can hear everything, you can feel everything. But you can do nothing. James's eyes glossed over and whispered an apology, which of course she accepted. She didn't blame anyone. Well anyone in the house.

"Do you think Kinzie's woken up?" James asked, taking a bit out of bacon.

"I don't know. Somehow I doubt it. I would imagine it would take a lot for her to wake up. She's been affected much longer than I have," Michelle finished her french toast. Her phone vibrated. She looked and saw that it was Tim, "Tim messaged me."

"What's it say?" James asked.

Tim: We gave Kinzie a potion,
Hopefully she'll wake up soon.
Hope all is well.

"They've given her a potion and hope she'll wake up soon," Michelle replied, sipping her cup of coffee, "God it feels good to have actual food again."

James chuckled softly, "I bet."

"James, can we please go downstairs? Just for a little while? I'd like to get out of bed for a day," She turned to him with big eyes.

"You swear you won't do any cleanin?"

"Yes," Michelle smiled.

"No cooking, no nothing. You will take it easy?" James smiled as he drank his coffee.

"I promise I will take it easy," She replied, holding out her pinky finger. It was on her burned hand.

James smiled and crossed his pinky with hers. And Kissed her hand. The sinus rhythm sped up a little, "Alright, alright. Let's go. You need to work your leg muscles anyway."

He detached the machines and helped her change clothes. She allowed herself to lean on him. And they walked slowly together. It was almost as if her legs forgot how to work. She remembered the first time she could walk after her burns fully healed. After that she learned how to count how many steps go where. Even now James can hear her whispering the number of steps. James just smiled and walked alongside her. Down the stairs and outside on the back porch. Once she was seated she took a deep breath. The warm sun hit her face. And she smiled. James sat across from her and filled his pipe with tobacco.

"Thank you," She sighed.

"You're welcome, my love," James replied as he lit the tobacco.

"I can't believe you're still smoking," Michelle teased.

"It's not like cigarettes where it gives you cancer. It's just tobacco. Why don't you nag Tim anyway?" James laughed.

"Because he's not the man I'm in love with," She replied, facing him. Giving a grin.

"Fair enough," James replied, inhaling the smoke.

They remained outside for a couple of hours. The warmth felt so refreshing. The birds started to sing to her which made her appreciate the world even more. She decided to close her eyes and start meditating. Keeping her feet planted to the ground she pictured herself reaching for the earth with her feet and growing a root. She smiled because it felt like mother earth was reaching back. She pictured a rose garden with butterflies. And she saw Kinzie. Happy and healthy, tending the bushels. Then memories of their childhood flooded to her mind. Walking with their brothers and their parents. Christmas mornings, and early breakfasts. Life as it was before. There were so many memories. Then Kinzie rose and turned to face her.

"Michelle, Anna gave me a potion. And I feel much better. Have hope sister. For I will wake. Soon…" Kinzie's voice trailed off.

The rose garden went black.

Michelle started falling asleep. Smiling James glanced over and scooped her up into his arms, and carried her upstairs. Fortunately she wasn't limp. She put her arms around his neck and held herself up a little. James hurried to the bedroom to reattach the machines. And Michelle went back to sleep. And this time James joined her. Everything was stable. This time he knew she would wake up.

......*

Quinn remained in the office and kept all the updates on the cases neatly organized. He peeked through and found some interesting information. All victims were burnt to a crisp and left in a car. Unidentifiable. The cause of death was inhalation of the smoke. No stab wounds. And of course the ID's were taken from the victims. And the killer was intelligent enough to remove their teeth. And based off of their build and Skeletal structure they were all women. Now there are a total of Twelve women murdered. And no way to identify the victims or the Killer. There wasn't a shred of evidence at the crime scene. So instead Quinn decided to look at the locations of the where the bodies were found and see if that has some sort of direction in which he can take this case.

       Quinn exhaled a sigh and rubbed his temples. He missed Kinzie being behind the desk and walking in her office hearing her mutter under her breath. His Instincts told him she'd be staying in the City Of Night for a little while longer, so it took it upon himself to make sure she still gets a paycheck. He's done it a time or two before when she had to go to the Vampire realm to handle council business. And Michelle would take messages for Kinzie and Quinn would respond in email. Ans since she's so famous for solving multiple cases no one questions her. She's good at what she does because she's got an eye for detail. Later on she did go to school for law and keeps all of her knowledge up to date. Any new laws that were established she'd update it. As a matter of fact most of the books in her office are law books. Boring to most people, but fascinating to her. More often than not she'd forget to feed. And Michelle would be sure to bring her some nutrition before she went off to bed. Sometimes She, Quinn, and Tim would throw idea's back and forth. And because of that.

Quinn knows how Tim's mind works. And Kinzie is like a daughter to him. And with all that he had the tools he needed to finish this case.

Chapter Fifteen

Michelle's eyes flickered open and the sound of the machines drew her focus in. She could hear Jame's voice but it was fuzzy. She took a deep breath and focused on James's voice. At last she heard his voice loud and clear.

"Michelle?" James breathed.

"Yes, I'm here," She replied, rubbing her eyes.

"Are you alright?" James asked, letting out a sigh of relief.

"I am now. What happened?"Michelle reached for his hand

"You had another seizure. And You fell asleep outside. I'm just scared for you," James replied, taking her hand and pulling it closer to his face.

"I know love. I'm sorry. While we were outside I was meditating and Kinzie reached out to me. She said someone named Anna has given her a potion and she'll wake soon, and not to worry. Then I fell Asleep. Maybe that's why I had a seizure. I just need to take it easy," Michelle sighed. She hated being in bed and resting often.

She felt bored and useless. However she was grateful she wasn't alone in this.

"Ah, that actually makes plenty of sense," James smiled. Relieved knowing she's getting better.

Michelle Curled up into his chest. She liked hearing his heart beat. For the moment, time stood still. And James embraced her affection with the truest of joy. And with a kiss on her forehead, she went back to sleep.

......*

Tim was back in the kitchen with Kinzie and the others. This time he was the one sitting next to her While Bron Paced. Two more days and the potion for the council will be ready. The tension in the air was high. Anna found the reverse spell to have William arrive in the city of night.They continued giving Kinzie the potion. Now it's just a matter of time before she opens her eyes. Bron felt a large lump of anxiety in his throat. Tim felt a flutter of anticipation. And Anna continued her high level of patience. Then the silence was broken by the sound of a familiar voice.

"Tim," Kinzie said softly.

Tim looked down to find Kinzie's eyes slightly open. They were the moon blue he'd been so desperate to look at again. He beamed, "Kinzie?"

"Hey," She said with a smile, "How's everything coming along?"

"Anna's done with the potion, we have to wait a bit longer. They're both here," Tim said softly. It was as though he was trying not to shatter the air with a loud voice.

"Where's Hades?" Kinzie said softly.

"I'm here, I'm in the corner," Hades's deep voice rang out.

"Excellent, Bron?" Kinzie smiled.

"Present," Bron replied sarcastically. He approached her side.

"Very good. Thank you Anna by the way for that potion, and healing my sister," Kinzie smiled.

"No problem darling, I've found that page you told me about. The reverse spell for William's banishment," Anna replied, coming around and kneeling next to her.

"I'm glad. By the way, Erm. I'm sorry about your sister," Kinzie locked eyes with her.

Tears filled her eyes, "Thank you." She paused, "I'm glad to see you're awake."

"Kid, how did you know about Michelle? Or Anna's sister?" Bron asked, hardening his eyebrows.

"I wasn't asleep. When all those things were happening. I was as close to sleep paralysis or a coma as one can get, so I heard everything," She replied slowly sitting up. Tim reached out in case she needed assistance. She closed her eyes and readied herself to stand up, "Tim."

"Yes, love?" He replied.

"Could you help me stand up. Bron Get behind me in case I fall back," Kinzie replied, eyes still closed. Tim knew exactly what was happening. She was grounding, which is what one does when you need to be balanced. She waited until bron was standing behind her before she stood up. Tim pulled gently and she came forward. Was at first a bit wobbly, but she stayed standing.

"Kin, you just woke up. You shouldn't be pushing yourself," Bron's deep voice.

"There's work to be done, brother. I can't lay helpless when the world is in danger. If I am to die. It'll be for our kind, and the human kind. Nothing else. I have laid helplessly in bed waiting for some hero to help me. I hate that feeling. However it has taught me a valuable lesson. There's no shame in asking for help. It just sucks to feel that way. I've been weak for far too long. And that bastard tried to take my *sister* from me. So you're damn right I'm standing! Because He's already taken so much from me! And I'm not going to *stop* until that bastard is dead! Do you Understand!" Kinzie growled and walked off. Tim was about to walk after her. Bron grabbed his arm.

"Let her go. She needs to cool off and get her head in the right place. She had every right to be upset," Bron replied, rubbing the back of his neck.

"You did that on purpose?" Tim's eyes widened.

"Yes, I wanted to make sure she was actually okay. She's good at hiding a lot of things. But she's back to her old self. Firey and protective of others. I know where she's gonna go, We'll check on her in a bit," Bron replied, patting his arm.

Tim nodded, "He was the one Who killed her family?"

"We think so. William has been jealous of Kid since she arrived. She's a natural born leader. The headmaster of our training camp talked to the council and suggested that they put her in a higher rank. And they took their suggestion. William was upset because He'd been there *longer* and worked *so hard*. So instead of congratulating her. He grew more envious. Which leads us to believe that he killed her family and turned her into a vampire to break her. But she never did. Even when she was tortured. She didn't…" Bron's voice trailed off.

"Bron?" Anna asked, giving a concerned look.

"It's just hard to see someone you're close to, so injured. She's been through so much hell, but she is still standing. I had to beg to treat her because they were going to assign someone else. I wanted to be there. William has tried to Kill her multiple times. The last time, the council was merciful. Allowed him to walk away. I knew the bastard should have died. But the council did everything they could. But somehow he still got to Kinzie. And she just woke up and is ready to go at it again," Bron let out a soft chuckle of disbelief.

"I'm sorry," Tim breathed.

"It's nothing to be sorry for. She's just an incredible person, and sometimes an incredible pain in the ass because of her stubbornness. But you learn to love her," Bron smiled and shook his head, "Alright, Lets go. Hades, would you like to join us?"

"It would certainly be a pleasure to get out of this dreadful corner," A deep voice replied.

"I'll stay here and mind the potions," Anna smiled.

And the three of them headed off behind the castle. And wandered down the path into the darkness. They continued to walk through the trees. Bron kept looking up, and around. Tim was captured by the sounds. And Hades stretched happly, and went roaming elsewhere. Probably close to the castle. Tim wanted to ask him how Kinzie was when she first turned.

"Look if you want to ask me something man. Please ask. I'm not fond of being stared at," Bron replied, continuing down a large hill.

"I didn't even realize, but how was Kinzie when she first got here?" Tim asked, keeping an eye out for rocks.

"Hopefully she wasn't in any pain, but she probably was. She slept for days and it took her almost two weeks to get her to drink blood. Quinn brought her to a house I was assigned to at the time. And since she just got bitten she became first priority. So I teleported us and shouted to open the gates. We were outside of the castle at the time. All newcomers stay in the castle to be monitored for the first month or so. And they stay here for longer. To get adjusted to the night life. But she adapted quickly and had basic skills in fighting. She was respectful and strong. Feisty as hell, but she has a big heart. She wants to keep things in balance between humans and vampires. So if they don't know we exist, they won't be horrified of us," Bron paused.

"What is it?" Tim whispered.

"I think I hear her crying… Stay close to me," Bron tensed up and kept moving forward.

They exited the bush into a seating area. And past the seating area were tombstones. And Kinzie was indeed crying. Bron turned to look at him, *"Give me second to calm her down. And wait here. Listen if you can."* His voice rang in Tim's mind. Bron exited the bushes. And crouched in front of her. Which made them equal height.

"Hey kid," Bron said, taking his thumb to her cheek to wipe the tears away.

"I'm sorry I yelled at you… I'm just so angry at him," Kinzie sniffled.

"I know, you have every right to be," Bron just sat there and listened.

"There's something I haven't told you or Tim or Quinn or anyone...He…" Kinzie heasited.

Bron's eyes got dark, "Please tell me Kinzie."

"When I was being tortured, erm… He raped me," Kinzie sobbed.

Tim saw Bron's arms stiffen up but instead he pulled her close, she buried her face in his chest. "Come here. I'm so sorry. Shhh. Shhh it's okay. You're safe. Tim's here. Do you want Tim to come hug you?"

Kinzie nodded. And with that, Tim came running out of the bushes and knelt down to the ground. Kinzie threw herself into his arms and kept apologising. Bron sat back with fury. His eyes were now completely black. Tim felt the same way. He too was furious. But he had no idea how to defeat a vampire, let alone fight one. Kinzie's tears on his chest broke his heart. Which made him more angry. Bron gave him a look. A look any man knows well. The "He's dead," look. However they both knew if they got angry now, it wouldn't help kinzie. So they had to suffer in silent seething rage. Waiting for the right time to strike. Eventually, Kinzie's tears were spent. And she ended up falling asleep.

Bron's eyes went back to his normal light honey color when he spoke, "I've got her."

Tim Just nodded. There wasn't much else to say. He was glad she trusted the two of them with her secret. But the cost is heavy heart. He doesn't think Quinn could handle such news. It would literally break his heart. Bron picked Kinzie up and pulled her head to his chest. It was a long walk back to the castle. Hades was sitting outside in the castle courtyard. It was nice having him on their side. Just in case they had unexpected visitors. Instead of taking them back to the Kitchen Bron carried Kinzie into the medical hall. With large dark double doors. And Four rows of metal beds that went for what seemed like ever. Bron lay Kinzie down on the one closest to the door. Tim sighed.

"You should get some rest," Bron patted his back.

"I'm not sure I can sleep with what I just heard," Tim replied, rubbing the bridge of his nose.

"I know, but it doesn't hurt to try, I'm gonna have Anna come in and get some rest also. We all need to be ready for what's to come," Bron replied.

"How are you dealing with this? You know her better than anyone And you just fou-"

"You just answered your own question. I know her. And as much as it pains me to hear what that *bastard* did to her. This is her battle. She knows I have her back if she needs me. And she will do the same for you. You're in her world now. When she calls your name, go running. She can carry her own. But to answer your question, I know she can beat him. That's why I'm carrying this so well. So clear your mind and get some sleep. I'll have Anna bring something if you can't. Good night, Tim. Sleep well," Bron replied, turning on his heel and shutting the large double doors.

Tim exhaled a sigh. And looked around the room. This place is massive and incredible. The kitchen was just down the hall and it would take one ten minutes just to get there. The beds were rather small so Tim decided to lay in the bed next to her. As much as Bron was right, Tim still felt the weight in his chest. But he hadn't ever seen her fight before. He inhaled deeply and exhaled slowly. And allowed his troubled mind to clear. He was a little more tired than he thought. It wasn't long before his eyes grew heavy, and sleep overcame him.

Anna came into the room to find Kinzie and Tim asleep. Facing one another. She couldn't help but take a picture in her mind. That's probably going to be something she paints later. She too went to sleep Quickly. Bron stayed in the kitchen stirring the potion. Remembering the first time Kinzie called out to him. She had just finished her training and she was fighting a rather large vampire. He got on top of her and almost stabbed her then she screamed his name. And an arrow ended up in his chest. From that day forward she was grateful for him. It took a while to build trust. But once his trust had been earned, they became friends for a lifetime. Despite her hard core approach to things. She is gentle and emotional. By the time everyone wakes up. The potion will be ready.Anna and Bron hoped it will wake the council sooner rather than later. And the potion they made for Kinzie was only temporary, since it was made so quickly. Which is why they're going to the pond of healing. Bron closed his eyes trying his best to clear his mind. He needed to remain focused. And ready. In the worst possible way he hoped William would come to the City of Night. And he hoped that if Kinzie couldn't defeat him for whatever reason, she would allow him the honor and drive a knife through his heart. Or beating him till he was no more. Bron let out a growl of anger. Which woke Kinzie. Her eyes snapped open and her body jerked up. She looked around to find Tim in a bed next to her. And Anna in a bed behind him. She quietly got up and ran to the Kitchen.

"I'm sorry I woke you," Bron said through gritted teeth.

"It's alright. I know you're upset," Kinzie came over slowly.

"Kinzie, please promise me you'll let me Kill him," Bron growled.

"I can't make that promise. But what I can do is try," Kinzie put a hand on his shoulder.

"Please try," Bron looked at her, his eyes were black.

"This isn't the Brondan I know. It will be alright. If we don't kill him out into the forest. Where the pond is. I'll see if the council will allow you to execute him. You know I could never do that. I can't kill someone in revenge," Kinzie's eyes teared up.

"Thank you," Bron nodded with gratitude, "Love you Kid."

"Love you too, I'm gonna go back to bed. Are you going to be alright?" Kin asked.

"Yeah, I feel much better. Thank you," Bron forced a light smile.

"I'm glad, goodnight," Kinzie smiled, and exited the room. She lay back down in the bed that she was in, and looked over at Tim. He and Anna both remain sound asleep. She rolled on her back and closed her eyes. In a few days she'd face her enemy. The vampire that tried to take her sister's life, as well as her own. Who knows how much stronger he's become. It's highly likely that She's going to need Bron and Tim's help getting him. They gave crossbows in the armory that Tim can use. As long as it's got a gold tip to it. It's not like herself to want a man to die. But after all the torment he's put everyone through his time has come to leave this world. Deep down Kinzie wished the forgiveness was enough. But sadly that's why she's I'll and Michelle was under attack. A tear ran down her cheek.

"Kin, are you alright?" Tim asked.

She looked over to see his eyes wide open. She didn't realize how loud she was snifflining until he drew her attention back in. She shook her head. And he patted the bed and moved as close as he could to the edge. Kinzie's more than glad to embrace him. She cried into his chest. Tim stroked her hair and gave her gentle Kisses on her face. She needs this. If she doesn't get it out now she's going to be very emotional later on. And this is a fight

Kinzie can't afford to lose. She just felt sorry it took this long for her to realize the punishment he had deserved in the first place. The remainder of the evening was quiet. Hopefully this pain will ease over time.

After a long evening of little sleep the three of them woke up and wandered to the kitchen. They found bron still in the kitchen stirring the potion. Anna came over to the stove, while Kinzie and Tim went over the island looking over the spell book.

"It's ready!" Anna said happily, " Now remembember, They're probably going to be in a bit of shock and It's going to take some time to get their full memory back. So that being said, wait until their full memory is intact before we tell them about William. It's best that we don't bring any weapons."

"Alright, that's fair. They're going to be hungry and irritable. So Tim I would stay in the Kitchen," Kinzie replied.

"Actually, I wouldn't recommend that, only because they might come into the kitchen to find blood,"Bron chimed in..
"Alright what do you propose so I won't become a four course meal?" Tim asked.

"I'm going to add some blood to the potion then. It shouldn't reverse any effects. If anything it might taste better," Anna replied, rummaging through the cabinets.

"It's better than someone tasting me," Tim muttered under his breath.

"You do realize all of us can hear you right?" Bron asked.

"Yes, I'm aware. But forgive me if I want to live another day. I think I've been doing rather well this whole thing," Tim replied, crossing his arms.

"Please stop! If you start arguing William will get more powerful. And Kinzie will go back to being weak," Anna spoke sternly.

"Alright, alright," Bron raised his hand.

"How about this, Bron and I will go feed everyone in the. And Kinzie and Tim you go check on Hades. We haven't seen him in a while," Anna suggested.

"Sounds good, I could use a walk," Kinzie replied smiling.

Tim nodded, " Fair enough."

"Alright then, we'll see each other in a little while. And Tim, please eat something. I don't want you to have to struggle again," Anna gave a mothering look.

"Yes ma'am. Come on baby. Maybe you can show me around," Tim picked up the back pack, and reached for Kinzie's hand.

Kinzie took it, and led the way out of the Kitchen. She was smiling and she looked almost back to normal. It was nice to have her awake and talking to him again. She realized that he called her baby, and it made her happy. In her mind her heart fluttered. Though she was concerned with what Anna had said to him. She waited till they were away from earshot.

"What was Anna talking about?" Kinzie asked.

"Oh, well, I didn't eat for a while, cause I was so worried about you. Then she explained to me that A days time here is three days back on earth. And I didn't eat anything for the first two days, maybe two and half days. I didn't eat anything," Tim laughed nervously.

" Oh okay. Well I'm glad she told you. I suppose that's partially my fault. I should've told you ahead of time. It didn't cross my mind though," Kinzie replied.

"Hey, it's okay. We needed to find a way to make you better. And now we have. It's so good to see you like this Kinzie. I've," He sighed, "I've really missed you."

"I've missed you too, Tim," She whispered, and looked up to him. Her eyes were glossy.

"What's wrong?" He whispered.

"I didn't think I was going to make it. But you helped me through. It was the thought of you that Kept me moving forward. And I just want to thank you. Thank you for doing all this for me," She smiled and tears rolled gently down her cheek.

It was at that moment Tim touched her face and pulled her into a deep Kiss. Kinzie heard his heart pound. It's pounding as hers would. Kinzie pulled herself up to his shoulders and wrapped her legs around his waist. And held on tight. He gasped for air as his lips parted from hers. Kinzie pulled away gently.

"Come on, love. We need to go check on Hades," She smiled. Deep down she didn't want to stop. But she let herself back down off of his waist.

"Alright," He breathed.

She just smiled and took his hand leading him to the front of the doors. And outside they found hades. He was seated outside in front of the gate. The cool breeze brushed through their hair. She ran over to hades.

"Hades!" She laughed.

He laughed also. The deep rumble carried through the courtyard.

"It's good to see you well again my dear. I was worried," He knelt low to allow an embrace.

She hugged the head in the middle, " I was too. But I have a strange feeling about all of this. As if it's not over yet. Perhaps he has something up his sleeve."

"If he does. We'll handle it accordingly," Hades replied.

"You're right. I was thinking about heading to my old house here. Would you like to join us?"

"You should probably rest," Hades advised.

"Yes, I probably should," Kinzie smiled, "How about we sit out here with you?"

"That would be lovely," Hades gave a deep chuckle.

Kinzie walked over to some benches nearby and seated herself. She patted the seat next to her. Tim walked over slowly. The moon light came from behind a cloud and shined down on the two of them. She imagined him with black angel wings. Her angel. He's been so supportive of all of this. She thought he would run away once she found out she was a vampire. But instead, he stayed. And that is something to be thankful for.

<u>Chapter Sixteen</u>

Anna and Bron finished giving everyone the potions. Now it's only a matter of time. They both knew everyone there. Bron seemed slightly annoyed. Anna asked what's wrong. Bron told her that he's ready for things to get back to normal again. She nodded in agreement. The most Important people in this room are, William, Adrian, Bethany, Arron, Matthew and Tyerr. The council members. She's worked with all of them prior. Everyone started stirring in the cells all at once. Vampires begin sitting up and stretching. A familiar voice rang from the back.

"Anna?" It was Bethany.

"Good to see you finally awake," She replied smiling.

"Thank you. What happened?" She asked.

"I'll let you know what happened in just a moment. I'm going to let everyone rise first," She smiled.

Bethany nodded. Groans and yawns filled the room. Anna waited patently. She had her arms to her side to show she was unarmed. She stood tall and confident. Her red hair wandered in waves down her back. Bron remained next to her in case something went wrong.

"Seeing that everyone is awake, It is my responsibility to tell you what's happened. Do you all remember William?"Anna paused.

"My son?" William senior spoke up.

Anna Nodded, " Yes, Councilman your son. He has attacked Kinzie McCoy in the comfort of her own home. But not in person. By magic. He had my sister remain here along with her maid to see that you remain asleep. And Kinzie, Bron, and myself are here now. To see to it that you rise and we punish William at the fullest extent of the Vampire law. Which is death," Anna's voice carried.

"Very well, What is your plan Shadow Anna?" William asked.

"Kinzie's plan is to reverse the banishment spell to allow William here. Bron, and myself will be there to make sure no harm comes to her. She will remain in the pond of healing until he arrives. And the two will battle. And lure him here," Anna gestured her arms to the castle upstairs.

"Alright, that seems the most effective seeing that's what he wants," William nodded, " Very well. Let's get to work."

......*

Kinzie and Tim were talking and heard a loud echo in the courtyard. Hades's ears perked up. And Kinzie looked up with a smile. Tim smiled back at her. Hades ran over to them and kelt down so they could climb on. Kinzie climbed on first and Tim climbed on after. He hurried into the castle bolting through the double doors. Even on his back it took Tim and Kinzie a while to arrive in the council hall.

Kinzie Knocked on the door. Tim's heart started to pound.

"Calm down Tim. It'll be alright," Kinzie whispered.

He did his best. A male voice replied "Enter!" Kinzie Paused. And shoved the large deep wooden double doors open. Kinzie entered and paused. She was waiting for Tim. He slowly entered the dimly lit room. There were candles all along the walls and a large wooden table that was in a circumference. He looked up to see there Were six thrones to the right along the back wall.

"Kinzie, who's this gentlemen?" Arian asked.

"This is Timothy Bright. He's helped us in so many ways,"
Kinzie stood patiently.

"Come, take a seat. There's much we need to discuss, William
Gestured his hand. His Strong jaw and bright green eyes made
him look more angry than he actually was.

Kinzie bowed and Tim followed her gesture. And pulled out a
chair, once they were seated.

"Now Timothy, or do you Prefer Tim?" William asked.

"Yes sir, I prefer Tim," Tim replied, locking eye contact.

" Welcome Tim. We just had a few questions. Then we will
Kinzie the same. She is not permitted to answer for you. And we
Will Know if you're lying. So please be honest. Do you
understand," William replied.

"Yes sir, I understand," Tim replied confidently.

"How did you meet Kinzie?" William asked.

" We met at our office," Tim replied.

" Did she tell you she was a vampire?" William asked.

"Not then, but recently yes," Tim's eyes were still locked in Williams.

"How long has she been sick?" William asked.

"I'm not sure, in the time that I've seen months. I don't know how long specifically," Tim replied.

"Were you aware of this realm, when you and Kinzie first met?" William asked.

"No," Tim replied.

William nodded, "Very well."

They went through the same questions as promised with Kinzie and her answers were also short.
William nodded. It seemed like they were praying, but Kinzie seemed to be picking it up first.

"What is this about?" Kinzie asked.

"We're not accustomed to having humans pass through the portal without some sort of consequence. And we're wondering if you have any special abilities?" William asked,

"Yes, I suppose so. I've been practicing magic since I was a young boy. My father, who was also my teacher in magic, passed away. Since he's passed I've been teaching myself," Tim replied with a sharp exhale.

"Tim, if you need to smoke, Please feel free. I understand this is a sensitive topic. But there's no need to be nervous. We're just trying to understand some things," William reapplied, his voice filled with reassurance.

"Thank you very much," Tim replied with a sigh of relief.

"No thank you, You've done a great deal of service to us. And to Kinzie. It's comforting to know that she's in such good hands," William smiled.

Tim lit his cigarette and exhaled.

"Kinzie, Are you alright?" William asked.

"No, I'm still pretty weak and frankly very hungry," Kinzie replied in short.

"I understand that, but I mean psychologically, It's my understanding that my son hurt you. And well… Ra-" William replied. There was a pain in his eyes.

"Yes," Kinzie' felt a lump in her throat. And There it was like someone opened the floodgate to her tears.

"Kinzie, Why didn't you tell us?" Adrian's voice was filled with concern.

"Because I didn't want to Hurt Councilman William. And it was too painful to speak of," Kinzie replied as best as she could through the tears.

"You listen to me Kinzie. William Is not my son. You however are like my daughter. Anytime something happens like this. Please tell us. For the love of the moon," William replied.

" Yes, I will," Kinzie sank deeper into her chair. And it didn't take long before all six council members were at her side. Tim kept smoking, that was the only thing to keep him in check.

The ladies took her out of the room to calm her down and go over details. And the men sat and spoke with Tim. He let out a yell. And inhaled the cigarette some more. Matthew asked him if he loved her. And of course he said yes. Everyone was apologetic and so accepting. He literally had nothing to worry about. Tim remained worried so he lit another one. He didn't like seeing her cry. Though Tyerr, Matthew, and William reassured her that she'll be fine. This is not an unfamiliar situation. Tim asked if they too were angry. William knelt down close to him and replied "Very." His eyes are a brighter green than before. Bron's eyes got darker, when he got angry. But he wasn't familiar with anyone else's. But the point is, when a vampire's eyes change it means fury. He wondered what Kinzie's eye color was.

"There's only one time I saw Kinzie's eye color change," Tyerr said softly. His voice wasn't too deep, "It wasn't too pretty."

"Wait, can you read my mind?" Tim asked.

"Yes," Tyerr nodded.

"Oh okay. That's how you would know if I were lying or not. Interesting," Tim replied deep in thought.

"No, Kinzie changing eye color is not something you want to see. We call it 'Seeing white.' Because we're in the dark all the time. So seeing black or seeing red wouldn't be deemed appropriate," Tyerr started to pace impatiently.

"Seeing red," Matthew replied with a loud laugh that rang after.

"Come Matthew this is no time for jokes," William replied, annoyed while rubbing his temples.

"Ya'll are just a fun lot aren't ya?" Tim replied sarcastically.

Matthew broke out into a strong laughter that carried through the room. William rolled his eyes, "Tim, I think you broke my councilman." And that remark made Matthew laugh harder.

Kinzie peeked her head in, "Is everything alright?"

"No, your boyfriend broke my councilman," William squinted his eyes and looked at Matthew.

"I'm glad to see all of you gentlemen get along so well," Kinzie Chuckled.

"Kinzie can you shut him off please?" William groaned, rubbing his eyes.

"COUNCILMAN MATTHEW!" Her voice carried loudly. Causing Tim to jump out of his chair. For someone so small her voice projected rather loudly. He stopped and jerked up to his feet.

"Be seated," William said and nodded a thank you to Kinzie.

Kinzie nodded back and seated herself. Reviewed the plan once more. And notified them that the others have already done the spell to reverse the banishment. Now it's only a matter of time before they expect his arrival. The gentleman nodded in agreement. Kiznie's anxiety kicked in. Everyone looked around the room nervously.

"What's going on?" Tim asked.

"Tim, there's a very good chance if she goes to the healing pond, it won't completely reverse Kinzie's effects. Which is why Anna and Bron will be going with her. However we will have a bed ready and medical staff on board for Kinzie when she returns. And we will have a cell ready for William Junior," William looked more overwhelmed than before.

"Oh," Tim gave a sharp exhale.

"Look, Tim. Everyone is going to do their best to protect me," Kinzie reached for his hand.

Tim took it numbly, "I don't want anything to happen to you."

"I can't promise that. But what I can promise is that I won't go down without a fight. We have to try this Tim. And it's not for us, it's for *everyone*. He is a danger to all worlds. Not just ours. Please understand that."

"I understand," Tim replied with a sigh, " Is there anything I can do to help?"

"You could be a distraction while Kinzie recovers," Tyrr chimed in.

Kinzie's eyes widened, "No! That's a terrible idea! He could Easily kill Tim!"

"Not if Bron and Anna are there also," William replied.

"Alright, I'll do it," Tim sighed.

"Seriously?" Kinzie asked, taken aback.

"Kin, you risk your well being all the time. Please allow me to help you," Tim said softly.

Kinzie gave a sad look, " Alright. He'll be coming soon.The sooner I can get to the pond the better off we are. Let's go find Bron and Anna. I think it's best that Bron carry me down there. I'm starting to feel lightheaded and very weak," Kinzie replied softly.

William nodded, "Alright then, "We'll see you two when you return."

Kinzie stood up and bowed, "Thank you councilmen. See you in a short while."

        Tim did the same, and they both left the room. Kinzie continued hastily to the kitchen. And found Bron and Anna.

"Time to go," Kinzie said shortly. Bron and Anna followed her in an instant. They knew the tone she used. Tim was in awe of her authority. He also knew that she wasn't happy with his choice in helping to distract William. But she's setting all of her emotions aside. And Tim respected that. Whatever danger he was putting himself in he was prepared to receive. Outside the castle, Bron picked Kinzie up and carried her. The plan for Tim is to act as if he didn't know where he was. A lost man in an unknown world vulnerable to anything. William would love it. It wasn't long before they departed and Bron showed Tim where to go with hand signs. Tim nodded in understanding and waited. The signal was a bird call. His heart pounded hard. Not in fear for himself but in fear for Kinzie. Which helped with the added effects. Bron placed her in the pond not more than a mile away and he and Anna climbed a tree close by. Hoping Tim's scent would cover thiers.

Kinzie lies in the pond focused and ready. Immediately she felt different. The pond was small. There were a couple trees on either side and bushes all around except for a small path that led directly into it. Kinzie heard Tim's heart beating. But there was another presence. A dark one. The familiar scent of someone she wished so desperately to forget. William had arrived. She felt him sitting on the edge of the pond. Kinzie lies still as can be. Her body slowly grew stronger. The sound of an owl exit Bron's mouth and Tim's heartbeat increased as he ran. And he stopped in front of William. Cold black eyes, white skin and long string-like hair tucked behind his ears.

"Pl-please can you help me?" Tim stammered.

"What's wrong Sir?" William asked. Kinzie heard him stand up and turn to Tim.

"I- I don't know where I am. I just woke u-up and ended here," Tim stammered his heart pounding into his ribs.

"Do you see that castle there?" William pointed.

Tim Turned around, "Wh-where?"

"It's in front of you at the top of the hill," WIlliam replied.

"N-no," Tim stammered.

In that moment Kinzie shot out of the water and ran behind William who laughed and stepped aside.

"Oh what a nice surprise, Kinzie McCoy has risen again," William smiled.

Bron threw a sword down from the trees, which Kinzie got to. But just barely, "Yes, I have William." Kinzie replied through her teeth, "Run Tim."

"Oh, so you know this morsel, eh? Did she drag you in here to help save her? How pathetic. You're Supposed to be a great general. Well did you hear her boy? *Run,*" William growled.

Tim turned and ran Towards the castle. William then faced Kinzie. They locked eyes. Kinzie Stood ready for anything. William lunged for her and Kinzie blocked it and threw him to her left. Which had broken a few yards of trees. He came running back with a golden sword, with a silver handle. The swords clanged loudly. And William dodged left and right. Then took advantage of an opening. And Lunged the golden blade right into Kinzie's gut. Kinzie let out a cry of pain and Kicked William in the chest. And gave Bron the signal to shoot. A golden arrow shot from the trees hitting William in his chest. He let out a laugh. The pain was too much for Kinzie to bear. Her knees buckled, ending up on the ground. It's as if in an instant, William appeared before her   and punched her in the face causing her to be thrown further than she threw him. She heard a loud crack. Anna shouted a few words and shot an arrow from above. Which hit William in his back. He was brought down to his knees. His sword dropped from out of his hand.

"What? What magic is this?" William asked.

Anna climbed down from the tree, and landed gently on her feet, "Paralysis magic. You like it?" Anna asked, grabbing his weapon. And tying a rope around his ankles and hands. And Dragged him by his feet.

"Why does it burn?" William asked.

"Golden inlay asshole. Now shut up before I put it in your mouth," Anna replied through gritted Teeth.

Bron then dropped down from the tree, "Kinzie!" He ran towards where she would be. He found her laying limply on the ground. Bleeding from the sword, and lifted her shirt. Her ribs were broken and so was her leg. And her one eye black from when William punched her, " Oh god. Kinzie…" Bron replied feeling his heart ping. He picked her up gently avoiding her broken ribs. Her head turned into his chest, "You did so well Kid. I'm so proud of you," Bron felt tears come to his eyes. And carried her to the castle. Straight to the medical wing. Tim was waiting outside of the medical wing. And gasped, "Kinzie."

"Stay here," Bron replied, kicking the door to the medical wing open.

Tim's heart dropped. In that moment he realized the damage that could've been done to him. How many times Bron had seen her like that. Later Anna appeared with William heading to the council Hall. She took a turn down another corridor before Tim could say anything. Now he completely understood how Bron had been feeling all this time. After seeing her like this as many times as he has. Too bad he couldn't do anything. He sank down onto the floor. His heart even further into his stomach.

It felt like Forever before Bron opened the door again, his hands were bloody. He told Tim he could come in now. Tim jerked up and walked in trying to prepare himself for what he's about to see. Once again she was in the first bed closest to the bed. Her one eye is still black. There was a bowl of bloody water and some clothes on the floor. She was tucked under a blanket. She looked so peaceful. Tim let a few tears fall from his face.

"She'll be alright. She *needs* to rest. She took a decent beating. This isn't the worst I've seen though," Bron replied sitting on the bed across from hers.

"What happened out there?" Tim breathed.

"William stabbed her with a golden sword. He punched her, and I'm guessing he knocked her out. And she broke three ribs and her leg," Bron's knuckles cracked as his fists clenched, " I need to go speak With the council. Can you keep a close eye on her please?"

"Of course," Tim nodded.

"Alright. There's a very good chance you're going to need to give her your blood. Are you willing to do that?" Bron asked, standing up.

"Yes, as much as she needs," Tim replied in a low whisper.

"Good, I'll be back in a while," Bron replied, opening the door. And walked right down to the council hall. He didn't even bother knocking. And walked in.

"Bron! What's happened? You have blood on your hands?" William Senior asked.

William junior was still on the ground in front of the thrones, "That son of a bitch!" Bron pointed.

"Who's blood is on your hands?" Tyerr asked.

"It's Kinzie's. I had to give her *ten* stitches, reset her leg! I'm done. Please let me kill him!" Bron begged.

"We were just discussing that," Adrian chimed in.

"And we've all agreed to it. You may Kill him," William senior replied.

"How did you come to that conclusion?" William junior replied sarcastically.

"He's had to bind her wounds! Take him to the dungeon. Torture him if you must. But he must be dead by morning," William senior replied coldly.

"It would be my pleasure, Councilman," Bron smiled and grabbed the rope and dragged him roughly away.

"Come we need to check on Kinzie," William and the others exited the room and went to the medical room. They found Tim sitting numbly. His eyes wide open. He looked up and then back down again. He wished it were him. Was he a masochist? Or was he a human longing to trade with the one he loves. Though one thing is certain. If he took a hit like that, he'd probably be dead. The raw truth. He's a human. He's strong. But not as strong as Kinzie. Part of him wished he would change. But the other part of him wanted to live his life fully. Now he understands why Kinzie was upset. She wanted to save him. And once again she did. Hopefully one day He can save her.

The night was long. Everyone stayed in the medical hall with Kinzie. It was odd for Tim not seeing her breathe. But he knew she was still alive. Anna came in later and gave Tim some much needed coffee, and a granola bar from her bag. She gave a concerned look. And cleaned up the bowl and tools Bron used to stitch Kinzie. And all the towels. Will Senior, Tyerr and Matthew were called to other council needs. While Adrian, Bethany and Arron stayed. They too seated themselves close by. No one said a word. Who knew silence would be so deafening?

Chapter Seventeen

Kinzie at last opened her eyes. Almost a week later. Her ribs were sore and her leg hurt like hell. Her head was pounding. She looked around the room and found Tim sleeping in the bed next to her. And Bron standing on the other side. She asked how long she had been out for. And he told her several days later. He asked if she wanted to wake Tim. To which she shook her head. He deserves to rest. He's probably been worried sick. More so than before. Though she was glad it was her and not Tim. She'd heal a lot faster than he would. It didn't take long before her thirst got to her. Bron noticed instantly. He rushed over to Tim and woke him up gently.

"Hey Tim. Kinzie's awake," Bron said in a whisper.

Tom shot up and looked over with a smile as a sigh of relief escaped his lips, " It's good to see you're awake. Do you need blood?"

Kinzie nodded.

"Alright" Tim got up and put his wrist to her lips.

Kinzie shook her head.

"You need it, Kin. Please. I'll be alright," Tim replied with a gentle smile. His voice pleaded more than he intended.

Kinzie closed her eyes. So it's come to this. Needing Tim's blood to heal. So he did need to make some sort of sacrifice. Her fangs grew out against her will, and sank into Tim's skin. Tim winced a little and inhaled sharply. It was a few moments Before Kinzie let go. Tim felt slightly lightheaded so he seated himself on the bed behind him.

"Alright. I'll be back. I'm going to get a couple blood bags. I'll be back," Bron turned around and exited the room.

Once Bron left, Kinzie Started to cry. She'd never bitten a human for blood before, "I'm sorry, Tim."

"For what?" Tim asked, hardening his eyebrows.

"For bringing you here, and having to bite you," Kinzie sobbed.

Tim brought himself to his knees and leaned in closely, "Never be sorry for that. I'm happy to be here. Do you hear me? I'm not ashamed of any of this. I'm so proud of you Kinzie. And I *love* you. Stop being so hard on yourself. You're incredible, brilliant, strong, and a leader. You are a warrior Kinzie McCoy. And you're not alone. You have Bron, Anna, Quinn, Michelle, and this amazing council that loves you. And I'm here now. I will do whatever it takes to help you," Tim was face to face with her.

As he said all of these words. She sobbed even harder. Overwhelmed, at the thought of the support she has. It's almost as if her mind has been in a fog and the fog has finally been lifted. William had tortured her with all the lies and manipulation and abuse. And at last she felt safe. Tim couldn't allow her to cry alone so she gently pulled her into an embrace.

"Shhh, I've got you. I'm right here," Tim whispered.

Bron came back in quietly and saw Tim stroking her hair, and comforting her. It warmed his heart to know that she was being so well taken care of by a mortal.

"I've got the blood bags," He said gently.

"Thank you, Bron," Kinzie sniffled.

"You're welcome. Tim, what blood type are you?" Bron asked.

"I'm O negative," Tim replied, confused.

"Alright, you're probably going to need a blood transfusion and some saline. I'll see if Anna will go back to earth and get all the supplies," Bron replied, handing Kinzie the blood bags.

"The best bet is to go to my house. There's a doctor that I get equipment from. That's how I got all of your equipment after your accident Tim," Kinzie replied, laying back on her pillow.

"Alright, get some rest, Kin. You too Tim," Bron replied leaving the room.

Kinzie finished one of the blood bags. And decided to leave the other for later. Bron did as he said he would and asked Anna if she would go and she replied with a "Of course." And added that she would get some food for Tim and herself.

......*

Anna broke one of the Vials in front of the mirrors in the castle hallway and entered through. She found Quinn in Kinzie's office asleep on one of the couches. She passed the desk and spoke in a whisper, "Quinn."

He sat straight up, "Anna?"

"I need to get some medical Supplies from you. Kinzie said that this would be the best place to go," Anna said smiling. She knelt down next to him.

"Kinzie, how is she?" Quinn asked urgently.

"She's alright for the most part. She and William fought. And she was pretty badly wounded. He used a gold sword," Anna replied with a gentle sigh.

"Alright, well let me get that supply for you then. And I also am going to get Michelle. She's going to want to know how Kinzie is doing also," Quinn rubbed his eyes.

"I understand," Anna stood up and waited patiently.

Quinn at last came to life, and rose. Anna follows closely out of the room. She was jealous of how beautiful the McCoy house is. She found her way to the living room, and seated herself on the couch. It wasn't long before she heard footsteps slowly come down the stairs. A young woman appeared, alongside a gentleman. She was short and a little taller than Five feet, and had red hair along with scars that covered most of the left side of her face, neck and almost to the wrist. She was wearing a black tank top and checkered pajama bottoms. And the man was tall. He looked to be about six foot five, Narrow, but somewhat muscular build, tan, and longer black hair. He was wearing a black t-shirt and grey sweatpants.

"Hello, I'm Anna. I'm sorry to intrude. But Kinzie told me to come here for supplies. And Quinn tells me you would want to know of her well being," Anna replied.

"Hello, I'm Michelle, and this is my boyfriend James," The woman gestured to him,

"Hello," The man replied.

"Nice to meet the both of you. I will say your sister is recovering from a few injuries. However she is alive and well," Anna tried to smile.

"She's strong, she'll make it through. Would you like some coffee?" Michelle asked.

"Yes, that would be so great thank you," Anna smiled.

Michelle smiled and disappeared around the corner. James seated himself on the chair closest to the couch. Michelle returned a few moments later, with a tray of steaming hot coffee, and some cream and sugar on the side, " I don't know how you take your coffee so, I figured I'd bring it just in case."

"Thank you so very much. I do appreciate that," Anna smiled, relieved to have something to wake her up.

"You're welcome," Michelle chuckled.

"What happened to William?" James piped up.

"He died a rather painful death," Anna replied, pouring sugar and creamer into the coffee cup.

"Good he's earned it," Michelle said firmly.

"Oh, I meant to ask you if you have any food for Tim and myself," Anna replied, sipping her coffee.

"Oh yes, we do. We have a few extra things I can pack. Does he and Kiznie have fresh clothes?" Michelle asked.

"Erm I don't think so," Anna replied.

"Alright, I'll pack them a bag. I'll try not to make it too heavy," Michelle said, drinking her own coffee.

Quinn came into the living room, " Anna what exactly do you need?"

"Erm, Bron said to bring back supplies for a blood transfusion and saline. It's for Tim," she replied.

"What happened to Tim?" Michelle's eyes widen,

"Kinzie drank some of his blood," Anna replied looking down in her mug.

"Alright, I'll let our contact know what equipment you need. What blood type is he by chance?" Quinn asked.

"O negative," Anna sipped her coffee.

"Right, well. I'd better go make that call," Quinn turned around and shuffled into the kitchen and dialed the numbers, "Hello, yes. Erm, I'm inquiring about blood transfusion supplies and erm saline. Yes, the IV? Oh, It's O negative. Can you deliver it tonight? Oh, Yes. Thank you. What's my amount to? Alright. Yes it is for delivery. Thank you. You too. Good bye," Quinn hung up the receiver, and came back into the living room, "Anna he will be here in a few hours. You're more than welcome to rest while," Quinn said, rubbing his eyes.

"Thank you. I appreciate your hospitality. I will definitely accept your invitation to rest," And replied stretching. Michelle grabbed a blanket from a nearby hall closet. And handed them to Anna. She pulled the blanket over herself and curled up. She fell asleep faster than she even expected.

"Poor thing," Michelle whispered.

"Yes. She's exhausted her powers. But there's something else, a look in her eye," Quinn's voice wandered off.

"Let's go into the office so we don't wake her," Michelle whispered.

The gentleman nodded. And tiptoed quietly to the office. Once the door shut, everyone let out a sigh. Everyone felt a mutual feeling of relief, In the knowledge that Kinzie is alright. Quinn considered going back with Anna, to speak with the council. Michelle understood completely, and agreed. James simply nodded. He and Michelle have been brought closer throughout all of this. She's almost completely healthy. Still occasional weakness, and feeling dizzy. But overall she's made improvements. James still insists on Michelle resting and taking it easy, and when she makes any attempt to overwork herself. James stepped in and insisted she sit down. James helped her pack some clothes and food for Anna and Tim, then returned to the office. Quinn sat in Kinzie's office chair waiting patiently for the medical equipment to arrive. While James and Michelle sat on one of the couches and went over different theories of what happened to Kinzie. In the meantime, Anna was having a strange dream.

Anna finds herself in a dark misty place. She senses a dark presence that is more than familiar. It wasn't long before she saw her dead sister standing before her.

"Hello Anna," Ashley smiled.

" I don't understand," Anna whispered.

"Come now, don't be rude," she crossed her arms.

A sharp pain tore through Anna's skull, " How are you still alive?" asked, barely able to speak. She wasn't trying to show pain but it was no use. It felt like a sharp dagger going through her ear.

"Well the person who killed me didn't put a binding spell on the object she killed me with, so now I'm just a life with no body. But I know the perfect one I can take over," she smiled and batted her eyelashes.

"No, no, no. You mean?" The pain grew sharper which brought Anna to her knees.

"Yes, I mean Kinzie McCoy. Tell me sister. What happens to a vampire when it's denied food for a long time?" She asked, letting out a treacherous laugh. Ashleley walked closer.

Anna's eyes widened, "You cannot be serious!"

"Oh, well. I am. Have a nice evening sister. We'll see each other once again," Ashely laughed, And knelt down to her sister's level, " I'm going to make her pay!" Ashley growled and vanished. Leaving only the feeling of her skull cracking open.

A scream came from the living room hours later. Everyone jumped and looked at eachother. Quinn got up first, and rushed to her aid. Michelle and James are two steps behind him. Anna's eyes were closed, she was tossing and turning. Quinn turned to them and confirmed she was having a night terror. He assured them everything will be alright and requested that they leave them alone for a moment. Anna wouldn't reveal what the dream was about if they were there. Michelle nodded quietly in understanding and took James's hand, leading him upstairs. Once they were out of sight and everything was quiet. Quinn woke Anna. It took a few attempts but at last she sat up. It took a moment for her to gain her surroundings. She tried to smile at Quinn but she cried instead. Quinn pulled her into a warm embrace. He whispered reassurances into her ear. Atlast it was at that moment that she told him about Ashley. Quinn's eyes grew wide and glossy and held Anna even closer. He assured her that none of this was her fault. Ashley was a good girl. Then she grew older and got bitter. No one really knows why but that can contribute to dark magic. Quinn was drying her eyes when there was a soft knock in the door. Quinn gave her one last tight squeeze before answering the door. And letting Daniel in.

"I'm sorry I had to come back so soon, Quinn," He said, bringing in the supplies.

"Me too. However I am happy that we have someone who can assist us in times such as these. I also enjoy assisting you with the income," Quinn smiled.

"So should I just leave it in the foyer Mr. Roberts?" Daniel asked.

"Yes please, and I added a bonus for coming out so late," Quinn replied, handing him a thick envelope.

"Thank you so Much Mr. Roberts!" Daniel beamed.

"You are most welcome. Hope I don't have to call you again," Quinn smiled.

"I will have a good night, take care," Daniel replied, letting himself out.

Michelle and James came down the stairs, " Was that Daniel?"

Quinn simply nodded. He was exhausted. Anna waited patiently until they returned to the living room. Quinn seated himself next to her while Michelle seated herself in the chair near the couch and James remained standing up.

"I've decided I want to join you in the return to the City of Night," Quinn said looking at Anna.

"Alright, When would you like to leave?" Anna asked.

"After you've eaten, bathed and washed some of your clothing. I will do the same, and we will return together," Quinn smiled,

"Very well, sounds good. I'd like the shower first," Anna replied, grabbing her bag and digging through it.

"You're a lady after all," Quinn replied happily.

"We'll be in the kitchen making some food for the both of you," Michelle replied smiling and made an attempt to stand up.

"No, *I'll* be in the kitchen cooking for all of you. You need to rest. You've done more than enough," James knelt down and kissed her.

Blushing Michelle nodded, and sat back. Anna pulled out some necessities for a shower, and asked where the washer and dryer was. Michelle told her it was upstairs, but she can take a shower first downstairs. Quinn waited and talked with Michelle about the visit. She wished he could take pictures. But she understood why it was forbidden, for multiple reasons. To protect the vampire realm and anyone else from knowing. The thought crossed her mind that she should probably text Tim.

Me: Hey Tim, Anna arrived safely and
will be leaving soon.
I hope you're okay.
How's kinzie doing?

Her phone chimed.

Tim: I'm alright,
better than she was,
She's been beaten
up pretty bad.
I'm just drained cause I
let her drink my blood.
It's supposed to help
vampires heal faster.

Me: I'm glad you're both Alright.
Send her my love for me please.

He phone chimed,again.

Tim: I will.
Thanks for checking in.
I love you Sis

Me: Love you too, bro.

She was relieved that Tim and Kinzie were okay. Hopefully Kinzie will recover soon.

......*

Kinzie lay flat on her back, while her broken leg stayed elevated. Tim stayed sitting up on his phone. He didn't want to lay down, yet. Since he felt so drained. After he sent that last text, he asked Kinzie if she was alright.

"I'm as good as I can be. Unfortunately I've been through worse. The question is are *you* alright?" She replied, turning her head.

"Yeah, I just need to get hydrated. I'll be fine.

Kinzie tried to adjust herself and a sharp stabbing pain radiated from the place she was stabbed, she winced, "Get bron please." Kinzie closed her eyes.

"What happened," Tim replied, standing up slowly.

"I think I just tore my stitches. Shit," Kinzie's voice trailed off.

"Oh okay, you got it. I'll be back, okay?" Tim rushed out the door.

Kinzie's sharp pain slowly started getting worse. It felt like it was tearing. Why does it hurt so bad? A groan escaped her lips. Tears filled her eyes. She saw a faded figure over the bed. It was a black aura. She didn't see a face. But whatever or whoever it was, wanted to hurt her.

"Tim!" She yelled. Nothing.

"TIM, BRON!" She screamed. The pain was too much to bear, her vision started to fade.

Then she heard two sets of footsteps running down the hall. The door burst open and Bron and Tim stood witness and the black figure faded away.

"What happened?" Bron aske loudly.

"I thought I tore my stitches but then, that thing, or whatever it is came in here! I think it was trying to open my wound," Kinzie groaned in pain.

"Alright, let me take a look," Bron replied, lifting her shirt. His eyes grew wide, "Tim."

Tim looked over and gasped.

"What?" Kinzie asked, panicked.

"You're not going to like it," Bron replied,

"I didn't ask if I liked it! I asked what it was," Kinzie replied sharply. The pain grew sharper and more intolerable.

"Kin, they didn't just tear your stitches. They drew a.." Tim sighed, "An inverted pentacle on you. Now, you're going to be a much easier target for dark magic users."

"What?" Kinzie's voice was barely audible.

"We need to get the council in here," Tim replied.

"I've already got a voice linked with Tyre and they're on their way," Bron replied sadly.

It was too easy. All of this was too easy. How did this happen? William *died*. And Anna was there to make sure that he didn't perform any magic, maybe he has darker entities working for him than they thought about. The council entered the room.

"Let us see," Tyrre said, approaching first.

Everyone else gathered around. No one knew what to do.

"Maybe we should try cutting it off," Kinzie said out loud, her voice fading.

"No, you can't," Anna's voice came in from behind them. Everyone turned to her. Her hair was wet and Quinn right behind her. His hair too was wet.

"What do we do Anna? I'm getting weaker," Kinzie's eyes started rolling in the back of her head.

"We need to detach whatever spirit thingy that was, and then remove it," Anna replied, walking over Tim's bed. She gestured for him to sit down.

Quinn walked over to see what was on Kinzie's side, "It is dark indeed. We need to be wary of our surroundings. And stay alert. I'm so sorry my dear," Quinn replied sadly.

"Papa, I don't know if I can do this," Kinzie cried.

Tim and Bron both looked at her with concern. That wasn't Kinzie at all. She's always certain and stubborn.

"You aren't yourself, Kinzie. Reveal to me who you truly are," Tim said.

"Well hello, Mister Bright," Kinzie turned to Tim. Revealing her red eyes.

"Ashley?" Anna gasped.

"Yes dear sister. I hope you can save your dear friend before I kill her from the inside out," Kinzie's voice replied with a smile. Then moments later she fell limp. Anna cried out in shock. And everyone looked around in awe. Fear filled the room. It was at this moment they realized they needed to Keep Kinzie there. As far away from society as possible and they must be careful with their words otherwise Ashely would hear.

Characters:

Kinzie McCoy:

Often people consider her selfless. Despite the fact that she is a vampire. Her favorite color is gray. She enjoys medical shows, and she also enjoys detective shows. Despite the fact that they come off as false Her heart can be considered too big at times. But She would rather put her own life at risk than to jeopardise many others. She started off at the police academy, and worked her way up to a detective that is private and travels the world.

Michelle McCoy:

A busy bee despite her blindness. Her favorite color is black. She often finds herself outside listening to birds. Or music. Before going almost blind. She studied some basic Medical techniques. In case someone's life depended on it. She doesn't work, however she does make certain investments and puts her money in stocks. In addition to having savings.

Quinn Roberts:

Quinn finds himself to be the problem solver. He has gained many contacts over the years. No one knows how old he actually is. The estimated age is well over five hundred years. HE enjoys traveling and seeing old friends. His favorite color is light green. Most of his contacts consist of other vampires, witches, warlocks, and many many other types of beings. You'll find that he has many secrets.

Timothy Bryte:

His preferred name is Tim. He lost most of his family. The only two still alive he doesn't talk to. His favorite color is red. He went through the police academy to get where he is today. One of his favorite things to do is to go for a drive and listen to music, before the injury to his arm, he played the guitar. You'll often find him outside admiring the trees and mother nature while smoking a cigarette. That's how he grounds himself, and keeps himself calm. One part of practicing magic.

Anna:

Her last name is yet to be known. Her favorite hobby is baking. She too is a problem solver in a different kind of way. She uses magic to practice healing, and helps with removing curses. His strengths are binding spells, healing spells, and potions. She always comes prepared and often finds herself in other realms. Her favorite color is purple. No one really knows how old she is, but since she looks so young no one really asks.

Bron (Brondan):

His name in the vampire world is very complex. But in english translates to Brondan. He's loyal and a leader. He helped Kinzie lead armies plentiful amounts of times. He often finds himself helping the council and assisting with their needs in the vampire realm. He and Kinzie have been best friends for many, many years.His favorite hobby is crafting weapons and making new tools. His preferred color is black.

Hades:

Since he's the balancer of the City of Night I decided to call Him hades. Since Hades himself is God of the Underworld. Which in it of itself is a dark concept. And the three heads come from the concept of his dog, Cerberus. However I decided to make him a three headed wolf that stands taller than the average human. His eyes red for intimidation, and his voice deep so he can be heard clearly. Despite his harsh appearance Hades is a very sweet and helpful animal. As far as the vampires know he is the only one of his Kind. His favorite hobby is scaring away any animals from his property, and his favorite color is orange.

Councilman William

He is the oldest of the council, his wisdom is the most valued most of the time. He assesses each situation carefully. And can sometimes take too long doing so. However the end result sometimes is the most important one, when it comes to saving lives. His hobbies are painting, and reading.

Councilman Matthew:

He is one of the highest ranking Vampires in the realm. He finds himself laughing at certain situations. Which can occasionally have inappropriate timing. It's not really a disorder. It's more so his humor. His strengths include: Battle training, different techniques in battle, and battle strategy. He's seen a lot of it over the years, and his hobby is recording different historical strategies. He likes finding new ways to improve fighting styles and skills.

Councilman Tyrr:

Though he looks tough on the outside, he really is gentle on the inside. He can Read Minds which comes in great handy. When an enemy is neat by, and they're strategically planning.He is a calm cool collected individual. And is great at interrogation, since he's a mind reader. His hobbies are jogging and working out.

Councilwoman Bethany:

Not only does she have valuable medical Knowledge, she knows a lot more than Bron Does. Even though they're vampires, they do need time to heal. Just not as much as the average human. However Bethany is good with herbs to make things heal slightly faster. Her hobbies are gardening and sitting in the graveyard.

Councilwoman Arron:

She can get glimpses of the future. The reason we didn't get to see her power is because she was asleep and under a heavy potion. Her ability to see the future allows certain predictions and sometimes they come true and sometimes they don't. It's a strong ability. Her favorite hobby is baking, sewing and knitting.

__Councilwoman Adrian:__

She is a balancer and a kind hearted person. Though she doesn't have any abilities, she is sympathetic and understands more than most would. She keeps things calm, and makes sure to remind anyone of realistic expectations. Her favorite hobbies are going for walks, and listening to the owls.

Made in the USA
Middletown, DE
06 June 2022